THE REVELATION

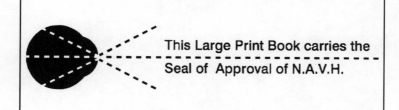

This Large Print Book carries the
Seal of Approval of N.A.V.H.

THE REVELATION

BEVERLY LEWIS

THORNDIKE PRESS

An imprint of Thomson Gale, a part of The Thomson Corporation

Detroit • New York • San Francisco • New Haven, Conn. • Waterville, Maine • London • Munich

THOMSON
—*—
GALE

LIBRARY OF CONGRESS CATALOGING-IN-PUBLICATION DATA

Lewis, Beverly, 1949–
　　The revelation / by Beverly Lewis.
　　　　p. cm. — (Thorndike Press large print Christian romance)
　　　ISBN 0-7862-8913-9 (lg. print : alk. paper) 1. Amish — Fiction. 2. Sisters —
　　Fiction. 3. Lancaster County (Pa.) — Fiction. 4. Large type books. I. Title. II.
　　Series: Thorndike Press large print Christian romance series.
　　PS3562.E9383R48 2006
　　813'.54—dc22　　　　　　　　　　　　　　　　　　　　　　　　2006016775

Published in 2006 by arrangement with Bethany House Publishers.

Printed in the United States of America on permanent paper
10 9 8 7 6 5 4 3 2 1

For
Mary Jo and Helen Jones,
two *wunderbaar* aunties.

PROLOGUE

October 24, 1963

Six endless days have come and gone since that wonderful-good crimson-and-gold-speckled day when Jonas returned to Lancaster County to declare his fondest affection for me. Yet I've had no word since — not even following his important visit with the bishop. And as each day passes I am mindful not to give in to fretting, losing myself in needless worry. I must simply bide my time till I know precisely what my beloved is up against. That decision will be made following Preaching service tomorrow, though I don't dread this meeting as much as I did my sister Sadie's kneeling confession, because Jonas did not commit a sin of the flesh, as Sadie did. His only transgression was to disobey Bishop Bontrager's rigid position on never leaving the church of one's baptism, a sin as defined by our *Ordnung.*

The winds of autumn bluster over Dat's frayed fields and Smitty's silver pond, and the sound reminds me of the work remaining to be done before winter sets in fully. Often I feel as if I'm chasing after the daylight, hoping to complete every last chore on my mental list. All the while the mules eagerly dismantle one bale of hay after another, growing thicker coats for the coming cold.

Sadie and I have talked frankly about Jonas's return — I simply had to share my heart lest it burst apart. She is the only one who knows he saw me before he went to visit Bishop Bontrager, as he should have done straightaway. Honestly there are times when I am nearly giddy with anticipation, knowing Jonas is only thirty minutes away, living once again in the orchard farmhouse on Grasshopper Level. The sky seems nearly like a blue jewel on clear days, and I have never been so awestruck by the color and texture of grazing land, windswept dew ponds, or even the shy silhouettes of clouds. What I thought had long since died in me has sprung to vibrant life, surprising me all to pieces.

Truly, it is a rare night when Jonas is not present in my dreams, and he is my cherished first thought at daybreak. I carry within my heart the hope of one day being reunited with my darling beau, if God should see fit.

Still, I must be ever so careful not to let this renewed passion for Jonas distract me from mothering Lydiann and Abe. The dear Lord knows there are enough issues to provide conflict under one roof, including Lydiann's *rumschpringe,* which, despite an unexpected twist, has thus far been innocent compared to Sadie's running-around time long ago.

We have heard by way of Jake Mast's letters to Lydiann that he's chomping at the bit to get home and right the wrong he feels was done to him by his father — not to mention rekindle the flame with Lyddie — even though I am sure Peter Mast will continue to put the nix on things. My heart quivers at the thought of Jake's potential return — a prickly prospect, to be sure. Although he remains in Ohio at the moment, Sadie and I agonize over what will befall us if his identity should ever be revealed. Truth be told, if the Masts were aware their youngest son is in fact Sadie's, there would be no question in *anyone's* mind that the two youngsters must never marry.

Thinking again of Jonas, I have no way of knowing if he'll be expected to abandon his woodworking. The bishop, in particular, has scorned any livelihood but those related to the soil — sowing and reaping — and black-smithing or other necessary tasks. For Jonas to be forced to farm would be heartache, what with his keen interest and skill in the area of crafting fine furniture. Just how long his Proving will last is hard to know . . . if the bishop will require one, considering the lesser sin he's committed against the church.

Secretly, though, I fear something will yet keep us apart. I pray not, but alas, ever since first seeing swarms of ladybugs a few weeks back, heralding the advent of winter with its dearth of light, I have been aware of a sense of foreboding. Soon snow as thick as lamb's wool will fall, and if I lose myself in the flurry, the road seems to become a looming tunnel . . . and as I imagine riding horse and buggy through its shadowy center, the eyes of my heart become painfully aware of the confinement. Try though I might, will I ever truly find my way out to the other side?

■ ■ ■ ■

PART ONE

■ ■ ■ ■

Our joys as winged dreams do fly;
Why then should sorrow last?
Since grief but aggravates thy loss,
Grieve not for what is past.

Thomas Percy

CHAPTER ONE

A chill had settled into the rustic planks of the old farmhouse overnight, and Jonas worked quickly to remedy the situation. He crouched near the wood stove and watched the kindling seize hold of dry logs in a burst of flame. Temperatures had unexpectedly dropped to the midthirties in the wee hours, and the wind had crept up, too. His aging mother and his youngest sister, Mandie, Jake's twin, would especially mind the cold.

Jonas had roused himself while it was still dark, enjoying the stillness and a renewed sense of duty since his permanent return from Apple Creek, Ohio. He had taken a mere two days to say good-bye to his long-time church friends and to pack his belongings — passing along his unfulfilled orders for several pieces of fine and fancy furniture to a good friend and seasoned woodworker. Here in Grasshopper Level, his father had given him permission to live at home, working alongside him, till such time as Jonas hoped to marry.

His father had made it mighty plain where *he* stood on the tetchy topic of marrying an Ebersol, but there was nothing he could do now that Jonas was thirty-six years old. Jonas pondered just how difficult Dat might make things, especially for Leah as his daughter-in-law. Would he exclude them from family get-togethers? And what of Jonas and Leah's children, if God so willed it; would they ever know their Mast grandparents?

Hard as it was to envision his and Leah's living with such a situation, Jonas was determined to get on with the business of marriage and having a family of his own. When he was most discouraged with his father's disapproval, he had only to think again how the Lord had kept dearest Leah for him all these years!

But, for the time being, he must convince the bishop by his compliant attitude and willingness to come under the People's scrutiny that he was ready indeed to begin courting Leah immediately following his confession at Preaching today. He suspected Bishop Bontrager of wanting to keep him at arm's length. "There's no need to be thinking 'bout doing much of anything 'cept farmin' now," the revered elderly man had pointedly admonished him at their initial meeting. "If you're not so keen on that, then there's not much for ya to do round these parts." Such was not the case in Ohio, where a good number of Amishmen made their living making and selling furniture. Jonas guessed the reason Bishop Bontrager was so set against his woodworking was because he'd been creating fancy, fine furniture for Englishers, using turned lathe pieces and scrollwork. The bishop likely had in mind to get the hankering for such things out of Jonas's system — even though the Ohio brethren had permitted them.

But Lancaster County was the original settlement of their Amish ancestors and remained by far the most traditional. Still, even if it meant Jonas could not sell them, he hoped to someday make at least the necessary pieces of furniture for his own house.

Hurrying out to the woodshed, Jonas was glad to be of help at the start of this Lord's Day. He would do whatever it took to change the bishop's mind about allowing furniture making to be his primary source of income, but only once the Proving was past. He was a woodworker through and through, but if required, he would attempt to make a living as a farmer and dairyman, or even perform odd jobs around the community till such time as he was reinstated with the People.

Opening the shed door, he spotted a fat mouse dart across and then under the dry stack of wood. He made note of the critter's fleshiness as he reached down for an armful of logs. *Winter's round the bend. . . .*

He'd also observed patchy clusters of milkweed out in the cow pasture, their thick-walled pods cracked open to reveal hundreds of downy seeds, each attached to its own glossy parachute. A sure sign wedding season was coming up right quick.

Jonas recalled his childhood as he nimbly covered the very ground he'd walked as a lad. He and his younger brothers, especially Eli and Isaac, had often stopped to count the spidery seeds as they floated far and wide, dotting the skies high overhead. The two-story barn and farmhouse and surrounding apple orchard all looked the same to him, except for the trees having grown much taller. At a glance, it might have seemed as if nothing had changed at all . . . when everything had.

So much catching up to do.

He wanted to get reacquainted with his seven married brothers and sisters — meet

16

their spouses and children, too — as well as keep in touch with Jake, who was in Ohio working with an older apprentice, an arrangement made by the same man who'd taken over Jonas's outstanding orders for fine furniture.

Having enjoyed his all too brief encounter with Jake, Jonas was glad there was still one sibling living at home, though fun-loving Mandie was already courting age. And here she came just this minute, her golden locks hanging loose to her waist, looking *schtruwwlich,* not having bothered to brush her long hair before heading out for milking. Jonas had never witnessed any Amishwoman in such a state, and he found himself wondering how Leah's beautiful thick hair — such a rich brunette it was — looked undone, long and freed from her tight bun. He shook away the inappropriate thought, deciding he must wait to contemplate his soon-to-be-bride's lovely tresses until after he'd married her . . . and not a single moment before.

His arms loaded down with plenty of wood for the cookstove, Jonas called over his shoulder, " 'Mornin', Mandie! Forget somethin'?"

She returned his teasing with a silent smirk and a toss of her tousled hair behind her head.

Somewhat amused at the sight of her, he made his way toward the back porch, quite aware of Dat's dog nipping at his heels. "Ya want a hullo, too? Is that what you're askin' for?"

He rushed to stack some wood inside the screened-in porch, mindful of the dog still waiting. When the chore was done, he went and sat on the back stoop, rubbing the golden retriever's neck and beneath his sides. "How's that, ol' boy?" he said before turning his attention to the important Preaching service to be held at smithy Peachey's place, next farm over from Abram Ebersol's. These days Smitty's son-in-law and daughter, Joseph and Dorcas Zook, and their boys occupied the main house, where they evidently had been living for a number of years, tending to most of the farming and looking after Smitty and Miriam in their twilight years.

Jonas smiled at the thought of comical Joe Zook hitching up with Smitty's serious younger daughter. He well recalled Joe's making fast work of ripe tomatoes at barn raisings and corn huskings as a youngster, eating them whole before the women folk could get to slicing them, the red juice dribbling down his neck. While growing up Joe had helped his own father raise truckloads of tomatoes, no doubt the reason for his nickname, Tomato Joe, as the bishop had referred to him when speaking of the location where Preaching was to be held today. Jonas had been reminded once again of how awful long he'd been gone from home — and from Leah.

His thoughts drifted back to his years in Ohio, recalling different nicknames for the young men coming up in the church, Gravy Dan being his favorite. The name brought Jonas back to the present with thoughts of the big Sunday morning breakfast his mother was sure to cook up, and he gave the dog a final pat on the belly and headed inside.

But when the time came for all of them to sit down to the delicious food Mamma had carried to the table, Jonas suddenly felt he ought to skip eating. He was strongly impressed to pray during the breakfast hour, just as he had observed the traditional fast day prior to the fall communion service that had taken place here a week ago. Recognizing the significance of *this* day, Jonas headed to his room, where he knelt to pray at his chair.

Create in me a clean heart, O God, and renew a right spirit within me. . . .

■ ■ ■ ■

Leah got herself settled on the same back-less wooden bench where Sadie, Lydiann, and Aunt Lizzie sat in an attitude of prayer, waiting for the house-church meeting to begin. Her bare feet scuffed softly against the wood floor, and she briefly wondered when the first snow might fly, making it necessary to don shoes again.

Today several hymns from the *Ausbund* would be sung, including the *Lob Lied,* always the second hymn. The introductory sermon would come next, followed by the silent kneeling prayers of the People. The main sermon, which would undoubtedly address obedience to the baptism vow, the Bible, and the honor due to parents, was most likely to be given by Bishop Bontrager. Even now the ministers were upstairs, deciding who should give the sermons.

What will the bishop require of Jonas follow-ing his confession?

She had awakened in the night to nerve-racking dreams, and now, as Leah sat sur-rounded by her family and church friends, she wondered how Jonas was holding up today.

Her gaze fell on Adah Peachey Ebersol,

20

her best friend and cousin by marriage. Fondly Leah looked away to her younger sister Hannah and her three school-age daughters, Ida Mae, Katie Ann, and Mimi, all of them sitting tall in the row directly in front of Leah. She focused especially on Mimi, whose present delightful disposition bore no trace of the fussy, colicky baby she had been, causing Hannah such emotional trauma at the time. Those days were long past, and Leah anticipated the little one Hannah was expecting next spring, curious as to what sort of temperament he or she might have.

Her thoughts of babies led Leah to note a record number of infants in the house of worship this day. *Will I ever have a baby of my own . . . as Jonas's wife?*

Just then Ol' Jonathan Lapp rose from his seat and announced the first hymn in a feeble voice, and the People joined him in unison, filling the farmhouse with the familiar sound. Glad for the opportunity to raise her voice in song, Leah breathed a prayer for God to be near and dear to Jonas throughout this sacred meeting.

Jonas knew Leah was definitely amongst the crowd in Tomato Joe's front room — all voting church members were required to be in attendance. Besides that, he'd caught a blissful glimpse of her outdoors as she, Lydiann, and Lizzie stood together with the other women before the bishop and the preachers had arrived. Oh, the rapture he felt whenever their eyes met, even briefly. When Leah was near — when she was in the selfsame room — it was as if there was no one else in the world. Just seeing her lovely face, her honest, shining eyes, the bit of hair showing outside her head covering, near the middle part . . .

But no, he must set aside thoughts of Leah, even though she was the singular reason why he was here in this place on this day. It did seem strange not sitting next to his longtime Apple Creek friends at Preaching service, where he'd enjoyed the good fellowship of many other believers while living in Wayne County. Yet this was Leah's place, and so where he belonged. Already it seemed difficult to believe that it was only last week he'd swiftly purchased a train ticket and come home once he knew for certain, via Abram Ebersol's letter to him, that Leah was a *maidel,* having never married. His heart had not allowed room for another love, so here he sat, waiting for the moment when Bishop Bontrager would give the nod and present him to the church membership.

His stomach rumbled unexpectedly during the deacon's reading of the Scripture, yet he was thankful to have skipped breakfast in favor of spending time in prayer. Reverently he had once again committed this meeting, as well as his future — and Leah's — to the guidance of the Almighty.

When Leah's brother-in-law Preacher Gid went to stand before the People, Jonas was particularly interested in observing his manner — this man whom he had been fooled into thinking had been the downfall of his and Leah's affection years ago. The brawny man who'd married bashful Hannah instead of Abram's Leah had an unflinching gaze. How ironic that this relatively young man was now one of the Gobbler's Knob preachers!

Slowly, piece by piece, Jonas was taking in all he'd missed during his lengthy absence. But more essential than fitting together details about people and events would be standing humbly before God and the local church this fine autumn day.

CHAPTER TWO

Seeing Jonas kneeling now before the bishop stirred up something Leah hadn't expected to encounter, and she felt as if she might fail to suppress the lump in her throat. Her beloved looked terribly vulnerable, bending low that way, admitting to a transgression that was scarcely sin. At least, she'd never come across such a thing in the pages of the Bible, although she knew the People viewed keeping the Ordnung agreed upon each year at council meeting as equal to holy submission unto God. She could no longer hold back tears as Jonas confessed in hushed tones to having abandoned the church of his baptism.

Sadie reached over and covered Leah's hand with her own, which made Leah's silent tears fall all the faster. There he was, her dearest love, requesting pardon from the brethren and the membership as a whole, having returned here for *her*, in answer to the love he'd carried in his heart for these many years . . . in the hopes of taking her as his bride someday. For sure and for certain, that undying love was the one and only reason behind the genuine penitence that seemed to flow from Jonas's very soul.

Abram had been altogether curious to observe how this aspect of the membership meeting might turn out, but he had not expected the bishop to insist on a six-month Proving before Jonas could be considered a voting member again. Unnecessary, far as he could determine. Of course, it was not nearly as long as Sadie's time of testing had ended up being, though that had been her own doing. The way Abram saw it, Jonas Mast's past disobedience had more to do with not following the whim of one man than God's law, and his record in Ohio was mighty good. It was rather obvious why the young Jonas had remained in Ohio when he'd heard and assumed that Leah had married another — any upstanding Amishman might have done as much, but this was not for Abram to argue. He felt his indignation rising up, even though he was partially responsible for what had befallen.

He sighed inwardly, wondering if he was

also to blame for Jonas's Proving. From as far back as Ida's early spiritual questioning, followed by Abram's own coming to faith — and his good friendship with son-in-law Gid — Abram and the bishop hadn't seen eye to eye. Was Bontrager retaliating by punishing the man who had returned to marry Abram's Leah?

The bishop was making a declaration now, and it was clear he was not in any way pleased with Jonas's inclination toward making fancy furniture as a livelihood, "no matter what our brethren are doin' in other places." The man of God placed both hands on Jonas's shoulders and stated, "You must turn your back on that worldly thing."

Abram felt his breath nearly go out of him as he heard with his own ears such narrow-mindedness. During the time of his Proving, Jonas was to earn his living primarily off the land, like the rest of the menfolk present, although he would be allowed to work in the harness or blacksmith shop, as well. The membership had yet to vote on this decision, but Abram felt certain no one would stand in opposition to what they knew Bishop Bontrager wanted.

The bishop continued. "I appoint Preacher Peachey to oversee this important time in your service to God and man." He nodded toward Gid.

What on earth? Surely he must not have thought this one through, Abram thought. But no, the bishop was motioning for the steadfast preacher to come and stand with him, and Gid's unmistakably blushing face distinguished him among the crowd.

A cold shiver ran down Leah's back and she held herself stiffly. The bishop was making a formal pronouncement, saying, "The Lord God heavenly Father of us all is manifest in the nearness to nature, the soil — the good earth — and the best way to stay close to the Maker of heaven and earth is to till and plow the land and harvest its abundance."

There was no doubt now the bishop would not tolerate Jonas's talent and enthusiasm for making desks and other lovely wooden pieces. And with her beau's submissive response came the death of his creative gift; she was helpless to stop what was happening before her eyes. Leah sat straight as a yardstick, willing her breath to come slowly, more evenly. *I can't let Jonas agree to do this for* me . . . *this horrid thing.*

At once she wished she might be more outspoken like Lizzie and Mamma and talk

27

up to the church brethren.

This bishop is beyond reason, Sadie decided as she shoved a clothespin down on the shoulder of the dress while hanging out the wash early Monday morning. She thought back to the Preaching service yesterday and to Jonas's having obviously expected the right hand of fellowship from the bishop and not received it. She'd seen the light of anticipation in his eyes — all of them had. And for what? Only to discover that he must submit himself to a Proving and miss out on marrying Leah this wedding season. Truth was, without being reinstated as a church member, Jonas could not marry Leah or anyone.

Hardly seems fair, Sadie thought, but she'd learned not to question this bishop. It was best to do as you were told and nothing less.

She set her mind to the work of hanging out the wet clothing in an orderly fashion — Dat's and Abe's trousers lined up together, followed by their shirts, and then the women of the family's cape dresses and aprons, each item in a grouping all its own, like the coordinated design of the colorful squares she had been carefully cutting so she and her sisters could stitch up another beautiful quilt this winter.

Around midmorning, Aunt Lizzie returned from a trip to Georgetown to stock up on necessary fabric and other sewing notions at Fishers' General Store, her face purple. When Sadie asked about it, Lizzie held up her thumb, which looked as injured as anything Sadie had ever seen. "Goodness, *Aendi,* what'd you do?" asked Sadie, coming to her side.

"Smashed my thumb in a car door gettin' out," she said. "I rode along with Miriam Peachy and her Adah — we hired us a Mennonite driver."

"Aw, let's have a look-see." Sadie led her quickly to the sink, where they gently rinsed the blood off the bruised thumb.

"Abram won't be happy 'bout this." Lizzie was shaking her head. "Drivers are to be used as a last resort."

"Dat won't care you went thataway," Sadie reassured her. "He's hired a driver plenty of times for longer trips."

"I s'pose there's a reason for everything." Lizzie muttered something about getting more behind the hurrier she went. She stared at her thumb and tried to move it but winced at the pain. "I daresay it's broken."

"Best soak it in cold water," Sadie replied. "I'll go 'n' get Dat."

"No, don't be botherin' your father. I'll be just fine."

"But, Aunt Lizzie —"

"Now, ya heard me. I'll just wrap it with a cold cloth and take myself off to rest a bit."

Sadie tried again to persuade her aunt to let her fetch Dat, but Lizzie was adamant. With a determined glance she hurried toward the stairs, still fretting about riding in a fancy car. "*Ach,* and goin' much too fast."

Heading slowly to the staircase herself, Sadie listened, taking care to determine her aunt had made it safely upstairs. She'd known some folk to pass out from the pain of a broken bone, and women folk were more prone to such fainting spells.

Once she heard the bed creak with the weight of weary Lizzie, Sadie went to the front room and began dusting, glad Leah had gone up to the log house to help Hannah do some fall housecleaning. A right good thing to get Leah's mind off the lack of Jonas's reinstatement.

She could only imagine how Leah must be feeling. Though Sadie knew it to be so, most everyone suspected the reason why Jonas had come back was to marry his childhood sweetheart at long last. That was one secret not to be kept, for the light of love was evident on both of their faces. Sadly, their marriage would not take place *this* year. Jonas wouldn't be recognized as a member till next spring, once his Proving was past . . . and then only if the bishop chose to extend the hand of fellowship at that time.

Stepping out the front door to shake out her dustcloth, Sadie was quite relieved *her* days of close scrutiny were over. Because, just this past week, Leah had begun talking about the thirty-eight-year-old who had come along from Ohio with the other traded men. The redheaded man with the sturdy frame was called Eli Yoder, and Leah seemed rather convinced he might be someone for Sadie, though Sadie couldn't help wondering who would want her for a wife, since she had been unable to give birth to a living, breathing baby — except, of course, for Jake.

Never once had she allowed her eyes to meet Eli's gentle blue ones, even though she *had* observed him furtively. Now and then, while she worked around the house, cooking, hanging out wash, canning, and mending, she did find herself thinking about the possibility of getting to know him, considering Leah's gentle urging.

Since arriving, Eli had been renting a small farmhouse a mile or so away, making his living off the fruit of the land and assisting other farmers and doing odd jobs, as were several of the fine young Ohio men who'd also helped with the harvest and silo filling around Gobbler's Knob and the surrounding areas. The newcomers already appeared well settled into their respective homes — families assigned to them for the time being.

Even after only a few weeks following last summer's trade, Sadie had begun to hear inklings from several of the women at work frolics that Eli was a right nice choice for a "perty girl like Ella Jane Peachey." One of Smitty's nieces, Ella was still an unclaimed treasure at thirty-five. Hearing such "whispers down the lane" through the Amish grapevine made Sadie bristle — this was not at all the way such matters were typically approached during youth's blush of courtship. Yet Sadie knew that if ever the Lord should will her to marry again, she would be ever so grateful, scarcely minding others' gossip. She would be as good and faithful as she had been when she was dear Harvey's wife.

Of course, she did not want to enter into

another marital union for the mere purpose of numbing her grief over her husband's death, a grief that ached deeply even still. It simply wouldn't be right, and for that reason alone she must be cautious, protecting her heart.

Sadie sighed. Her tentative curiosity about Eli was nothing akin to what Leah must be feeling now that her Jonas was home. Sadie felt sure that if she were in Leah's shoes, she would have told Jonas she still loved him. But then, she was not nearly as patient as her sister, and she had no desire to get in the middle again. She was, in fact, so nervous about botching things she purposely busied herself these days with additional household chores.

Ready for some fresh air, Sadie wandered out through the stable area to the barnyard, noticing that the animals had worn a narrow path through the paddock. Then and there she hoped to goodness her life living in the *Dawdi Haus* wasn't in any way a parallel to that dreadful rut.

She was undeniably certain she was meant for more than her present existence. And though she thought she would like to help things along, even beseech the Good Lord for a fine husband, she knew she had no choice but to practice the virtue of patience

— truly, her biggest area of failing.

Her impulsive tendencies were further reflected in her desire to get to know her son. She found herself wishing to see Jake again, even though she knew there was little hope of that. And even if there was, it would come at the cost of certain jeopardy for Lydiann, who apparently remained besotted with Jake and seemingly lived from one letter to the next.

Locating the butterfly handkerchief in her pocket, her sole connection to Jake, Sadie looked at it fondly. Always she carried it with her, now that this treasure was back in her possession — thanks to Leah.

She thought again of Jake. If he had any idea how closely connected he and Lydiann were blood-wise, wouldn't he be absolutely repulsed at the thought of their courtship?

Their relationship was doomed from the start, Sadie thought sorrowfully, feeling terribly responsible.

Chapter Three

"Well, I would urge you not to consider such a thing," Aunt Lizzie told Leah on the Wednesday following Jonas's confession.

Leah was leaning against the icebox in the kitchen, waiting for her midnight chocolate cake to finish baking. She wasn't surprised at Lizzie's forthright response. "I'm not sayin' I want to raise a stink," Leah said, defending her wish to speak with Bishop Bontrager and his wife about Jonas. "I just feel like my head might burst if I don't do something 'bout how I feel. It's so unfair to Jonas."

Lizzie shook her head and reached out a hand. "You should know by now our bishop is an exception to the rule. He won't budge. Not one smidgen."

"Still . . . wouldn't *you* speak up if the tables were turned?"

"Ain't any of your concern what Jonas agreed to do during his Proving. He gave up makin' furniture and whatnot for you. Don't ya see? This is a man who's in love, really and truly. Be grateful he's willin' to return to farmin'."

Jonas a farmer.

Leah had difficulty contemplating the idea. As a boy, Jonas had never complained about helping with the milking or tending to his father's apple orchard, at least not that she'd ever known. But he wasn't nearly as called to the soil as even she had been as a youngster. He *was* strong and able — hardworking, too — no question about that, but he'd had a gift that had lain dormant all those years before he received his training in Ohio from David Mellinger.

Just yesterday she had received a letter from Jonas asking if he might pick her up at the end of the lane this Saturday night, *at dusk . . . like when we were courting age . . . if you're willing.*

Willing? Smiling, she'd quickly found a pen and a page of stationery and written her answer, placing her note to him in the mail today. By tomorrow he would know she was very happy to see him again, though she had been a bit guarded about signing off *with love,* as he had to her and she had to him in times past. Truly, she wanted to say those important words to his face on this glorious occasion. In many ways, they were starting their courtship all over again.

Aunt Lizzie was regarding her with a gentle expression. "You're daydreamin' again."

"Jah, s'pose I am. But somebody oughta talk up to the bishop."

"Maybe so, but it oughtn't be you, dear one."

Can't accomplish anything if you don't try, Mamma had always said. Even though fourteen years had passed since Mamma had gone to heaven, Leah wondered what her mother might advise her to do. For all she knew, Mamma might admit she had learned a hard lesson about speaking out of turn. *It nearly got her shunned,* thought Leah, remembering what Lizzie had shared privately some years back.

"I just feel it's necessary to voice my opinion," Leah murmured.

"Your mamma got herself in hot water with the bishop. Best you not do the same. Don't take up this topic with such an unyielding man." Lizzie returned to the dirty dishes. "I'm hopin' you'll listen to me . . . 'cause, for sure and for certain, your mamma would be sayin' the same thing."

"I'll think on it." Leah headed to the wood stove and opened the oven door to check on the cake baking inside. She would wait till she saw Jonas on Saturday evening to discuss the subject further — let him determine what she ought to do about visiting the bishop.

Hannah was at the back door to greet her before Leah was even halfway up the walkway. "Awful nice to see ya again."

"Feelin' some better?" Leah noted how pale her sister's face was and how frail she looked overall.

"Come sit with me." Hannah waved her into the kitchen and pulled a chair out from the table. "Would ya like some tea?"

"No, you should be the one to sit," Leah insisted. "*I'll* pour the tea or whatever sounds *gut* to you."

"But —"

"I won't be treated as a guest in my sister's house, for pity's sake." She went to the cookstove and picked up the teakettle. "You never said how you're doin', Hannah."

"Oh, I'm all right."

Leah eyed her. "Ain't a wise thing for a preacher's wife to fib."

Hannah sniffled and dabbed at her eyes. "I've been strugglin' something awful . . . can't sleep much at night, not with so much pain."

"Then you best be seein' a medical doctor."

"Aunt Lizzie says the same," Hannah said, coughing.

"Maybe you've got a touch of autumn flu. It's going round, I hear. Abe says plenty of pupils are missin' from school."

Hannah touched her stomach lightly. "I hope it's not something the matter with this baby."

Leah listened but felt she could do no more than continue to entrust Hannah to the hand of the Lord and to His mercy.

"Even Gid suggested I pay a visit to Dr. Schwartz." Hannah looked awful serious. "But only one person can help me," she added, "and *she's* dead."

"Who's that?"

"Old Lady Henner," Hannah said. "I don't care to admit it, knowin' you and I disagree on powwow doctors."

Leah said nothing.

"Our family's seen so much heartache, 'specially when it comes to birthin' babies."

Eager to get off the subject of hex doctors, Leah brought up newborn Ruthie Schwartz, Mary Ruth's baby. From what Leah could tell, Ruthie was thriving under her doting parents' nurturing, which came as no surprise, since, like Leah, Mary Ruth had always displayed an especially gentle way with babies and young children. "She's got a mighty strong set of lungs for such a wee one."

"Jah, I should say. I wouldn't mind hearin' her squeal again real soon. One time wasn't enough to hold baby Ruthie." She stopped abruptly, and Leah assumed, by the faraway look in Hannah's eyes, she was chafing under Gid's long-ago decision to keep her from spending time alone with her twin, Mary Ruth having turned Mennonite years back. Though Mary Ruth was not welcome in the Peachey home, at least Hannah could visit with her sister at Dat's house and elsewhere when others were around.

"When you'd like to, I'll take ya over to see Mary Ruth and the baby again," Leah volunteered. "Whenever you're up to it."

"If ever I am," Hannah muttered.

"Well, of course you'll be."

"That's easy for you to say, ain't so?"

Leah looked hard at her. "You seem put out with me."

"S'posin' I oughta be ashamed of myself. I have no right to talk so to ya. Not after all you've been through yourself." Hannah hung her head.

Leah remained silent as she sipped more tea. It was rather clear something more than a physical ailment was troubling Hannah, and Leah prayed her sister wouldn't fall back into the gloom that had plagued her in earlier years. The idea occurred to her to get her morose sister out of the house, perhaps for a long ride, but what with a sudden crash of thunder, she knew better than to suggest it this minute.

"You should head on down the hill to home," Hannah urged. "Wouldn't do for you to get caught in the storm . . . then again, for some, maybe it mightn't be such a bad thing."

Leah looked at Hannah, surprised. "What on earth are ya saying?"

"Haven't you ever heard how Old Lady Henner got her powers?"

"I don't care to know, really." She set her teacup aside, rose quickly, and pushed in the chair. Glancing out the window, she looked over the stretch of woods beyond Hannah's many flower gardens, the trees swaying to beat the band. "Seems a big storm's a-brewin'," she said, hurrying for the door.

Hannah hollered at her, as if afraid Leah might not hear in the midst of the rising gale and now the pelting rain. "Old Lady Henner got struck by lightning when she was little! It nearly killed her, but her healing gifts came to her thataway."

Hannah must be off in the head, thought Leah, shivering, never having heard such a tale.

The morning after the storm, the sky was as gray as the old ivy-strewn stone wall alongside Gid and Hannah's house, and the atmosphere was heavy with the threat of more rain to come. The girls chattered as they dressed for school, and Hannah had trouble keeping her mind on preparations for bread baking.

"Nearly time for breakfast," she called to them, hoping Gid might soon return from helping with the milking down yonder in the Ebersol barn.

She stewed about her condition, thinking that if the pain grew worse she'd have to say something to Gid. The last thing she wanted was to disappoint her husband, who was bent on this being their first son. Hannah was seized with the knowledge that, though many months yet from birth, their coming child was in jeopardy, and she felt helpless to prevent it.

With more determination than was necessary, she pounded the bread dough hard, wondering if the possibility of rain was sink-ing her more deeply into despair.

After she slipped into a clean work dress and apron, the first thing Leah did that Thursday morning was tiptoe downstairs in her bare feet to look out the kitchen door at the barn. From where she stood, her nose nearly against the windowpane, she could see the lightning rod on the top of the barn roof. *Thank goodness for it,* she thought, having witnessed a most astounding event yesterday, following her unsettling visit to Hannah. Queasy with concern over the words Hannah had hurled at her as she darted into the torrent of rain, Leah had lifted her long black apron over her head as a slight shelter. About the time she passed the outhouse, a white lightning bolt had struck its jagged finger at the barn roof, and she saw flashes of electricity. Stunned, she had run helter-skelter to the house, taking cover on the very spot where she stood now.

Even recalling the unforgettable sight caused her heart to race, so she offered a quick prayer. "Thank you, Lord, for sparing Dat's barn and the animals . . . and for giving my father the wisdom to mount the lightning rod in the first place." After saying, "Amen," she opened her eyes and stared again at the roof, still in awe.

Last evening, when she had shared with the rest of the family what she'd seen, their eyes had lit up, though it was clearly Abe who was most interested in hearing how the sparks shot out like "Englishers' fireworks on Independence Day," as he put it. Naturally, this remark encouraged raised eyebrows from Dat, Aunt Lizzie, and even Sadie, what with Abe's growing curiosity in forbidden things such as fast cars and modern electricity. Neither was to be sought after one iota.

Realizing how busy a day she had ahead of her, Leah decided to put yesterday's excitement behind her, along with Hannah's strange words about Old Lady Henner. Turning back to the house, she went into the kitchen, preparing to make her usual eggs-and-bacon breakfast. *Better for lightning to hit the barn than one of us,* she thought.

As Leah was frying up the eggs, Lydiann wandered into the kitchen, all smiles. "Got me another letter from Ohio," she whispered at the cookstove. "And I couldn't be more pleased."

Fear gripped Leah's heart, but she tried not to let it show on her face.

"Jake says he's savin' up his money, hopin' to come home this year." Lydiann paused a moment before going on. "Besides me, he

44

daresn't tell a soul, though. Promise me you won't, either, Mamma?"

Leah felt her toes curl. "You're not sure just when it might be?"

"He didn't say, but he made it clear he's mighty upset 'bout being sent away. It's got his goat, bein' traded for other men, and he sees no reason to stay in Ohio with Jonas back here. Anyhow, I'm hopin' Jonas might clear the way for Jake's return — with their father, ya know."

Leah struggled to fix her mind on buttering slices of toast for breakfast, all the while shuddering to think what was in store if Jake should happen to come knocking on Lydiann's door.

Time to get Lyddie to Sunday singings again! Gschwind! — *Soon!*

"Why on earth didn't ya tell me you broke your thumb?" Abram scolded Lizzie as they dressed in their room.

"Now, nobody knows that for sure," she countered, hoping he would drop the matter.

Nonetheless, he asked her to unwind the makeshift bandage she'd made on the day of the accident. "I wanna see for myself."

"I'll be fine, Abram. Honest."

He persisted till she had no choice but to

show him her wounded thumb, now as purple and green as springtime wild flowers. He peered at it, pushing his bifocals down farther on his nose. "Hmm, this looks awful bad to me."

"I daresay it'll get better right quick." She wanted to stave off any insistence she go to a doctor.

"You can say all ya want, Lizzie, but, truth is, this here thumb's gonna need to be re-broken and set correctly." He waited while she wrapped it up again. "I'll be takin' ya over to see Dr. Schwartz the minute you're dressed for the day."

"Ach, Abram. That ain't necessary at all." She would stand her ground to get her way if it took that. She was a strong woman, after all, with no need for doctor visits and suchlike. *Mercy's sake!*

"Well, I don't know what's come over you, but I'm takin' you, like it or not."

You'll have to carry me to the buggy, then, she thought, unconsciously locking her knees. "I'll think on it," she mumbled.

With a huff about how "awful stubborn this one is," her husband left the room. Lizzie could hear his needlessly heavy footsteps on the stairs, and she breathed a great sigh of relief.

CHAPTER FOUR

"Why do ya s'pose we don't practice bundling anymore?" Lydiann asked Leah clear out of the blue while they were scrubbing potatoes together outdoors, near the well.

Leah took what she hoped was an inconspicuous breath and willed herself not to reply too hastily to her girl's curiosity. "Where'd you ever hear this?"

"Oh, just one of Jake's letters."

"Well, do you know how bed courtship first got started?"

"I think so." Lydiann went on to explain what she knew — how the early colonists lived in unheated farmhouses, so when a young man came to visit his girl, they simply spent time in her bedroom. "For practical reasons."

Leah nodded. "From what I know of this old custom, the couple would lie down on the made bed, fully clothed, and a bundling board was fixed between them as they talked and sometimes held hands late into the night. Later it became a time for the young lady to display her pretty handmade quilts and pillow coverings, as well. At least, that's how it was amongst *our* ancestors."

"A sort of getting-acquainted time?"

"Jah, with much talkin' expected between the twosome." She didn't say what was *not* supposed to happen. No need at the moment to have another talk about the birds and the bees.

"Jake says there are certain Ohio groups that still practice the custom." Lydiann looked rather embarrassed. "And . . . well, I best not be sayin' *all* that Jake knows."

Leah felt suddenly nervous, if not ill, at the thought of this sort of private talk being initiated by Jake; the possibility of his return made it all the more concerning.

"A friend of Jake's says there are some couples that get downright snug as a bug in a rug." Lydiann seemed unable to leave well enough alone. "They slip under the quilts —"

"Lyddie," Leah interrupted. "I daresay 'tis best to turn our attention to other things now."

Lydiann's head bowed. "Sorry, Mamma."

"You surely know there's a time and a place for all things," Leah was quick to add.

"Jah . . . the wedding night, ain't so?" Lydiann wore a fine, sweet smile now.

Wiping her wet hand on her apron, Leah slipped her arm around Lyddie. "You've got plenty of time for smoochin' and whatnot. All good things come to those who wait."

Lydiann looked up at her. "Will *you* ever marry?"

"That's up to the Lord, dear one." She suspected Lydiann had heard enough about Jonas from Sadie, years ago, that her girl would be curious now, although the recent church members' meeting was never to be discussed with folk not yet baptized. Without knowing what Jonas looked like, Lydiann would not have known Jonas Mast was present with the People last Sunday — except for Jake and the incessant grapevine, of course. Such news was hard to squelch.

"I feel awful sad for you sometimes," whispered Lyddie, still standing near.

"Why's that?"

Lyddie shrugged. "You oughta have a husband to hug and kiss ya good night — to cry on his shoulder when need be and laugh with him, too."

"Well, that would be nice, but *this* is the life the Lord God has given me . . . for the time being anyhow." Leah had no desire to be less than forthcoming with Lyddie, but

49

she was thinking of having nearly fulfilled her dying mother's wishes. And if Jonas could regain his eligibility as a church member, they might end up marrying next year.

Fact was, the likelihood of marriage during this wedding season had completely flown out the window with the bishop's decree. Thinking back once more to Sunday made her worry she might lose her peace and march right out to the barnyard to ask Gid what on earth could be done about the unbearable situation, if anything.

Sighing, she looked into Lydiann's trusting blue eyes. She found herself predicting the pain that would surely reside there when, at last, Lydiann was told why Jake Mast could never be her husband. Leah must move heaven and earth to make sure such a union never happened, though just how she didn't know. But she would think of something, even if it meant telling Lydiann the bitter truth at last.

Lydiann bumped into her brother, who was gathering eggs from the henhouse. "This is *my* chore." She stared at the large wire basket in his hand.

"Well, you weren't out here."

"I am now. Give me the basket!"

"Better be quiet or you'll scare the chickens . . . get them all *ferhoodled,* and your goose'll be cooked."

"Leave me be," she said more softly, struggling to keep her voice down.

Abe gave her a smirk and continued going from one nest to another. "You've done quit attendin' singings, sister."

"Jah, a while back. No need asking 'bout it." She turned on her heels and left, not at all interested in bickering any longer with her obstinate brother. Truth be known, there was no need for her to go to singings when Jake was anxious to see her again — even hoped to marry her the minute she turned eighteen. But she was beginning to wonder if he'd gotten in with a wild bunch out in Berlin. How else would he know so much about bundling and whatnot?

Blushing as she rushed toward the house, Lydiann was surprised to hear Abe calling to her. He'd emerged into the sunshine, his blond hair glinting purest white. "Brothers are s'posed to drive sisters to singings, in case you forgot. So *'tis* my business."

"Puh!"

"Near as I can tell, your beau's comin' home, ain't so? That's why you're not interested in the boys here. I can see right through ya."

51

"Hush up! You know nothin' at all." She sucked in air and then, when she felt she might burst out saying further unkind words, she bit her lip and simply walked away. How could Abe possibly know any such thing about Jake's plans? Her *Dummkopp* brother had committed the sin of eavesdropping, no doubt.

Just wait till Abe's rumschpringe. Then we'll see what happens with him. Already less than three years away from the time, she could easily imagine Abe driving a fast car, seeing lots of different girls, getting himself a modern haircut, and only heaven knew what else — all before he settled down and joined church!

Saturday afternoon Jonas heard his mother calling up the stairs. "Preacher Peachey's here to see ya!"

Hurrying down to greet the ordained man who was overseeing his Proving, Jonas wondered if he'd be able to keep from his brother-in-law-to-be his aim to see Leah tonight, especially since he'd just donned his newest shirt and trousers, wanting to look his very best.

Gid, however, seemed to take no specific interest in Jonas's attire but firmly shook his hand and asked if they could talk privately.

Jonas motioned to the front room and they walked there together, taking seats in hardback chairs on opposite sides of the wide room. "I wouldn't be honest with ya if I didn't say this is the most awkward situation I've found myself in," Gid began. "But the bishop has asked me to see how you're doin'."

It occurred to Jonas yet again that the bishop had *intended* the arrangement to be downright uncomfortable. Why else would he have chosen Gid as his overseer? "You're welcome to drop by anytime," he said. "I'm doin' just fine."

"Is there any way I can help durin' this time?"

Momentarily, Jonas thought of making a bit of a joke. He wondered what Gid might say if asked for some solid suggestions on making a living off the land when the harvest was nearly past. Indeed, the bishop's Proving conditions were rather absurd.

"I've been helping my father with orchard and barn work, living here without payin' board and room, but I certainly won't be able to make enough to marry and support a family doing odd jobs."

Gid tilted his head as if to say, *I hope you're not questioning the bishop's decree.*

"Do you know of *any* Amish who make

fancy furniture round here?" A courageous question on his part, to be sure.

"There's the one fella from Ohio — Eli Yoder — but it's more of a hobby with him, I think." Gid frowned and glanced out the window. "Honestly I don't know of any who make their living thataway, but we do have our carpenters . . . those who help with raisin' barns and all."

Jonas was not interested in carpentry, although if he had to in order to bring in enough money to marry Leah, he might consider it.

"Are you willing to make your way farming?" Gid asked.

Jonas wasn't keen on giving a flippant retort to this kindhearted and considerate preacher-man, especially married as he was to Leah's younger sister. Yet with his father so opposed to his marrying Leah, he would not be expecting any help whatsoever from his parents, once he was married. "I'll simply trust the Lord for His leading." *That, and work mighty hard at whatever my hands find to do. . . .*

Gid made a throaty sound and rose suddenly, putting on his hat. He shook Jonas's hand once more as he took leave. "I'll be checkin' in on you every month or so till the Proving is done. If ever ya need anything, feel free to give a holler."

"Denki" was all Jonas said. He followed Gid through the kitchen and utility room and then stood at the back door as the preacher headed for his horse and carriage. Gid was a good man, but already Jonas was missing his wise Ohio bishop and the many times they had openly conversed about Scripture.

Long after the dinner of pork chops with rice, steamed carrots, and broccoli was devoured and the dishes were redd up Saturday evening, Leah slipped away to her bedroom and removed her head covering. *I want to look as neat as can be for Jonas,* she thought as she pulled the hairpins out and shook down her long hair, looking at herself in the tiny hand mirror. *I'm not as young as I used to be.* She sighed. *So many lost years . . .*

She took to brushing out the snarls and then pulled it all back from the middle part. But even as she prepared for their meeting, she dared not allow herself to dwell too much on seeing Jonas tonight, lest she become all scatterbrained and unable to think straight. That would never do, not with the way she'd always felt when they were together. Ever so giddy she was in his presence, though she was fairly sure she could hide this from Jonas — especially on a night like this, when they were permitted to ride in Peter Mast's enclosed family buggy, being they were past the age of riding in an open courting buggy. Such carriages were for young folk Lydiann's age, who whispered dear words to each other under naught but the canopy of heaven.

Her hair smoothed with a comb and knotted in a bun, Leah placed her *Kapp* on her head and offered a silent prayer. *Thank you, O Father, for bringing my beau back home to me.*

She rose to stand at the bedroom window, looking out over the level grazing land that seemed to inch its way to the very edge of the immense forest, her heart suddenly as cheery and hopeful as if she were sixteen all over again.

CHAPTER FIVE

The air had a distinct chill to it, and Leah smiled when Jonas took advantage of her slight shiver. "Move closer." He reached around her. "I can't have my girl catchin' cold just 'cause I didn't offer a warm lap blanket."

A little laugh escaped, but Leah didn't say what was on her mind. Truth was, she much preferred his warm embrace to a woolen wrap any day. She'd missed him terribly, more than she'd even realized until now, having pushed any romantic feelings under the rug of domestic chores and family responsibilities.

The horse pulled the Mast family carriage down a few of the most deserted roads she ever remembered taking, and it slowly dawned on her what Jonas was doing. "Why, I think you must be takin' me for a ride down memory lane."

He nodded. "I wondered if ya noticed."

When had she ever felt this happy? It was well past dusk, but the stars twinkling high above seemed to brighten the way as their conversation began to melt the hours, and soon the moon lent its light to them. Jonas pointed out the silvery gleam it cast over ponds and pastures, and she felt as if she'd never before taken sufficient time to soak in its lunar beauty . . . or, if she had, she'd forgotten. *I've overlooked so many things. . . .*

Jonas was telling her of close friends he wanted her to meet one day — Preacher Sol and others, including Emma Graber, the kind woman who'd rented a room to him for so long. "After we're married, I'll take you to Ohio for a visit. What would you think of that?"

After we're married . . .

The lovely words stuck in her head, and she couldn't move past the echo of them. She relished his loving talk, his nearness.

"Leah? Are ya gettin' tired, dear?" He looked fondly at her.

She wasn't one bit tired, but he'd taken her by surprise, speaking about something so important in such a relaxed manner. Then again, Jonas really had no need to propose, did he? After all, he'd asked her years ago to be his wife, and she'd whole-heartedly consented. Maybe he simply assumed he didn't have to ask twice.

"Sorry," she said quickly. "I think a trip to your former stompin' grounds would be interesting."

"After we're wed, of course." There it was again.

She turned to look at him and noted the sparkle of mischief in his eyes. No suppressing *this* giggle. "Oh, Jonas," she said. "I'm so glad you're back. You just don't know . . ."

He reached to coax her nearer. "I've wanted to see your smile, hear your contagious laughter . . . ach, I've missed everything about you." He paused. "And you must know I never loved anyone but you, Leah. Not one time did I think I'd be happy with anyone else."

She couldn't say the same due to her brief engagement to Preacher Gid. There was plenty of time to talk about her innocent courtship by Smitty's son, now her dear brother-in-law. For now she could say what was burning in her heart and had been from their reunion on Georgetown Road, not too many days ago. "I *love* you, Jonas," she whispered.

"You don't know how much I've wanted to hear you say that again." The earnest tone of his response startled her a bit. "I've dreamed it, Leah — daydreamed it, too — never once truly believing this night . . . us out ridin' like this, could ever be anything more than my own imagination. Till today all the joy and hope of it existed only in my head." He kissed her on both cheeks and then the very tip of her nose. "We belong together. You know that?"

"Yes, for always." She held back the tears of gladness till she could no longer.

"Don't cry, darling. Such a happy night this is." He cradled her face in his hands.

"Ach, I wish . . ." She couldn't go on.

"What is it?"

She leaned her head on his strong shoulder, trying to gather her wits lest she embarrass him or herself, although she felt nearly as helpless as a child. "I feel just awful . . . terrible, really."

"What troubles you so?"

She searched for the right words. "Oh, Jonas . . . you made your livin' with wood. Such a thing is a true gift from God."

"Well, you mustn't be sad."

She sniffled and nodded her head. "All the same, seems so unnecessary for you to have to give it up for your Proving. I've even thought of sayin' something to the bishop . . . respectfully, of course. I just don't understand."

He straightened suddenly, reaching for her hand. "Leah . . . dearest love, it is not such a hard thing. I gladly do this . . . for *you*. To cherish you as my very own — takin' you as my bride — will be the greatest gift I could have. You must not go to the bishop. Promise me this."

The way he so tenderly stated his affections made tears well up all the more. How she longed for him to be her husband! Jonas cared for her enough to do even this unreasonable thing. "Jah, I promise, but it won't make it any easier keepin' mum," she said.

Her heart was ever so soft toward him, and she was somewhat relieved when he picked up the reins and directed the horse to trot, quickening the pace until they arrived at a turnoff to a narrow dirt road, which led to a small hummock where grazing land sandwiched the way on either side.

Soon Jonas stopped the mare and jumped down out of the buggy. "A mighty nice night for walkin'. All right with you?"

The evening was mild, with only the slightest breeze in the leafless sycamores, oaks, and maples. She breathed in the clean air, feeling like an insignificant dot under the backdrop of heaven's twinkling lights. If only the years could be rolled back and all things done differently, their lives might have been much easier. They'd missed so much time . . . so many experiences had slipped from their grasp. But they had now, *this* most precious time, and she couldn't help wishing everyone might have the chance to feel the way she did — to experience this enduring kind of love.

Jonas helped her down from the carriage, and they strolled to the highest point of the grassy rise as he talked of their future together. When he stopped walking, he turned to take her hands in his. "I hope and pray we'll be able to marry — the minute I finish my Proving, in fact. We aren't youngsters anymore; there'd be no need to wait for the weddin' season next year."

"Even so, we aren't widowed, so who's to know if we'd be permitted to marry earlier than a year from now." She wondered how long Bishop Bontrager would attempt to keep them apart.

Jonas continued. "It would be wonderful, though unlikely, for the bishop to agree to a wedding in late spring, when the older widowed folk get married."

She was ever so glad for the light of the moon and studied his dear face, memorizing every feature. She held her breath as she drank in his presence, almost sure what was coming next.

"I wouldn't ever think of takin' you for granted, Leah — your promise to marry me so long ago, I mean." He paused, lifting her right hand to his lips. "So will ya, Leah? Will you be my bride . . . as soon as we can marry?"

Moved beyond her ability to speak, she silently surrendered to his welcoming arms. Love had truly found her, and she nestled close to his heart.

When at last she had composed herself, she drew back and looked him full in the face. "I will, Jonas. I'll be your wife all the days of my life."

"You'll make me the happiest man ever." He went on to say he would be on the lookout for a small farmhouse for them to rent or purchase.

Joy, oh joy! Setting up housekeeping with Jonas filled her with ideas for things to make or sew during the time being, because her own hope-chest items had already been put to good use all these years, she'd so long ago given up on ever marrying. But now? She could scarcely wait to see the dawn of her wedding day.

They talked of how each had changed since the years when they'd first fallen in love. How strong Jonas thought Leah had been, taking on her much younger siblings as her own children . . . making and keeping such a hard promise to her mother. Leah replied with all the dear things she'd longed to say to his face.

"The years have only served to prove what an upstanding, good man I've always known you to be."

Their chatter slowed some, and it was Jonas who again brought up what Leah knew without a doubt. "As much as I want it, we'll never get the brethren to agree to a springtime wedding since we're first-timers, so to speak. I've never heard of its being done that way, have you?"

"No," she admitted. "Besides, don't we want a full day of festivities like the young folks, with as many of our family attending?"

"You're right, Leah. We've waited this long — why sacrifice such a wonderful-gut day just so we can marry early?"

Still, her heart sank a bit, knowing twelve long months stretched before them. *Yet our love has survived this long,* she thought. *What's another year?*

As they made their way back through the meadow on the slender band of road that led out to the paved highway, she was aware of the gray spread of grassland and the dark outline of trees atop the ridge. Even in the deep of night, Gobbler's Knob had to be the prettiest place on earth, and she told Jonas so. She wondered if he might tell her how beautiful his second home had been in Apple Creek, but he only smiled and kissed her cheek.

On the long ride back to the Ebersol Cottage, Jonas changed the topic. "My brother's thinkin' of returning home once he has enough money to make the trip," he said offhandedly.

Leah's throat turned bone dry. She'd heard this from Lydiann, of course, but hearing it from Jonas made the possibility seem more real. "You must mean Jake."

"Jah, my youngest brother. Truth be known, I'm all for it. No gut reason for him to be clear out there when his family's all here . . . and the girl he loves is, too."

For sure and for certain, she couldn't say what she was thinking. Immediately she wished she could tell him what she knew about Jake's blood tie to Lydiann, but she couldn't bring herself to. She didn't want to spoil the memory of this night, not even for something as important as this.

"What will your father say?" she managed to ask.

"Oh, there'll be plenty of words, but who's to say what he'll actually *do* if Jake does return. And I'll do everything I can to help things to that end. My brother's too young to be gone from home, especially with his heart here. I'm workin' on Dat to let him return, at least for a visit."

She cringed at the thought. *Dear Lord, let Jake stay put in Ohio. Please give us more time!*

Mary Ruth walked the floor with her wee bundle, recalling the delicious meal she'd enjoyed with Robert earlier tonight. His hearty laughter as they had joyfully shared the day together resonated in her memory even now.

At this moment, however, weary Robert was sleeping in their bed, and Mary Ruth was hoping to get Ruthie tucked in once again. By the looks of her dreamy eyes, the infant would yield to slumber soon.

Strolling through the front room, she stopped and looked out one of the east-facing windows at the moon. She was drawn to its light, glad for this moment to reflect on God's goodness in giving darling Ruthie to them. Mary Ruth couldn't stop counting her blessings each day. So many there were!

Looking down into the tiny face, she

cooed, "You sweet baby . . . ever so precious to your daddy and me." She quietly stroked Ruthie's forehead and cheek with a single finger before returning her thoughts to God in deepest gratitude. "Thank you, dear Lord, for giving to Robert and me such a healthy little one. Help us raise her to know and love you all the days of her life. Amen."

Mary Ruth did not move away from the window as she basked in the knowledge of God's kindness to them. She was reluctant to leave the spot where ofttimes she had stood to speak the names of her young students in prayer during the years she'd taught school.

She gazed at the rolling landscape awash in moonlight, and when a lone buggy came into view, she assumed the enclosed carriage held a married couple who had been out unusually late visiting relatives.

Bless them, Father, whoever they are.

How can I possibly be thinking straight? Leah nearly panicked. The more she considered the sticky matter, the more she wondered if she was doing the wrong thing by not sharing with Jonas what she knew about Jake. But her darling had *just* proposed marriage this wonderful-good night! What was she thinking, second-guessing her decision to keep mum?

They rode past a familiar house, and looking more closely, she saw that it was Robert and Mary Ruth's place. She suddenly realized how far — and how long — she had been riding around the countryside with Jonas.

As for revealing to him that his baby brother was not his blood sibling, she must not be either foolish or hasty. But as soon as possible, she would talk to Sadie. Together, they would have to decide what to do with this exceedingly knotty problem once and for all.

CHAPTER SIX

"What can we do?" asked Sadie, ashen faced and still nestled beneath her quilt.

Leah had hurried to the Dawdi Haus and up the steps to sit quietly on the edge of her sister's bed, waiting there only a few minutes before confiding in her, so anxious was she to discuss the dilemma. And this with but a small amount of sleep, because Jonas had cheerfully forgotten they weren't courting age any longer, bringing her home mere hours before daybreak, though she wasn't complaining one bit.

"I've wracked my brain and can't come up with anything, except fessin' up to Lydiann 'bout Jake," admitted Leah.

Sadie sighed, frowning hard. "Awful risky . . . unless ya think she'd honestly keep it to herself." Then, looking a bit sheepish, she said, "I have to confess something to you."

"What is it, sister?"

Sadie drew a long breath and pulled the

covers up to her neck. "I s'pose you'll be unhappy 'bout this, but I sometimes pray for Jake to come home. Maybe something inside me is tuggin' him back here." Sadie's sleepy blue eyes revealed a mingling of emotions that seemed to merge into guilty hope, and Leah knew if she were in the same position, she'd feel the same way.

"I can't blame ya, really," Leah replied. "I just wish Jake wasn't still in love with our Lydiann. It makes everything so complicated."

"Jah, and if only she wasn't head over heels for *him*." Sadie went on to say how she'd run into Lydiann up in the woods not but a day ago. "I found her sitting under a tree, cryin' like all get-out. She had herself a pen and tablet and looked to be writing . . . no doubt to Jake." Sadie stirred and then in one quick motion pushed the covers back and got out of bed. She wandered over to the wooden pegs on the wall and pulled down her bathrobe. Slipping it on, she slowly tied a loop in the cloth belt and stood there, looking as forlorn as can be. "I can't get certain things out of my head."

Leah sat still on the bed, not daring to try to comfort her, although it seemed Sadie was distraught about more than the news regarding her son.

Sadie turned and faced the window, staring out at what, Leah didn't know — maybe the forest, or the snug log house at the edge of it. Sadie's chest was heaving.

"I'm so sorry," whispered Leah, going to her.

"Ain't for you to say." Sadie buried her head in Leah's shoulder. "None of what I'm feelin' is your doing."

"Still, I can't help but bear it, too." She wanted to remind her of all the good things the Lord had brought their way — all the blessings she saw as clearly coming from their heavenly Father's hand — but she thought better of it. *Best to simply let Sadie cry. . . .*

Moments later Sadie pulled a hankie out of the pocket of her bathrobe. "We should've told Lyddie right away," she said through sniffles. "Back when we first knew Jake was seein' her. We wouldn't be in this mess now."

Leah nodded, feeling terribly overwhelmed, even helpless. "What on earth were we thinkin'?"

Sadie shrugged. "We thought Lyddie would've forgotten him by now — found someone new — him being her first beau and all. Guess we were sorely wrong."

Guess so, Leah thought, contemplating the calamity the news of Sadie's "baby" come back from the dead would bring to the entire Plain community. Dat and Peter Mast would be fit to be tied. *Oh, I can just see it.*

Truly, there was no love lost between the Masts and the Ebersols, though if Mamma were still alive, she'd dispute that notion entirely. *Got to keep showing kindness whether they accept our love or not,* she'd often said, which meant you never wanted to sever family ties. With these years of awful silence between them and Grasshopper Level, there was no telling what Mamma might've been willing to do to bring an agreeable end to it.

But with their mother long departed, it was for them to make amends. Of course, with Jonas home and working through his Proving, there was no telling what might come of the Mast-Ebersol standoff, especially with Jonas planning to marry her.

Now is not the time for Peter and Fannie to discover Jake actually belongs to us, Leah thought, cracking a pained smile at the irony. If anyone was to be told, she felt strongly that it should be Lydiann, but only provided she promised to keep the truth absolutely silent.

Leah waited for Hannah to get settled into

the carriage before picking up the reins late morning on Monday. "You'll enjoy another visit with Mary Ruth and little Ruthie," she told her gloomy sister, hoping the outing would do them both some good.

"You must've forgotten I don't so much care to be round strangers," Hannah replied, folding her arms across her chest.

" 'Tis all right to be timid with Mary Ruth's quiltin' ladies. That's just how you are."

"They're all Mennonites, ain't?"

"I hadn't heard that. Just a few neighbors and others who want to learn how to quilt."

Hannah let out a *harrumph,* still acting like a child.

"What's gotten into ya? You seem out of sorts," Leah said, eyeing her sister, who sat all rigid and straight.

"I'll tell ya what's ailin' me," Hannah snapped, surprising Leah. It was as if she was desperate for a chance to give voice to her pent-up frustrations. "I'm tired of bein' looked down on by my family." Not waiting for Leah to answer, she added, "It's all 'bout my interest in folk medicine, I daresay."

Leah was surprised to hear Hannah spout off so. "There's nothin' wrong with using home remedies and whatnot. Aunt Lizzie and I've never felt there was, and Mamma

never did, neither . . . as you surely know."
She paused for a moment and then continued when she saw Hannah was sitting with
arms crossed even higher up on her bosom
than before. "What bothers some of the
People is dabbling in areas that are best left
alone."

"Jah, Gid says the People are split down
the middle on powwowing, some saying it's
straight from the pit of hell — though I
don't see why when it helps those who are
ailin'."

"Mamma always said there was no point
steppin' as close as possible to the wrong
side," Leah reminded her. "So I'd have to
say we ought to stay far away from things
that don't set well in one's spirit."

"Now you sound like Mary Ruth. She was
always reciting Scripture and suchlike all
those years back when Gid told her to stop
comin' over to see me."

"But don't you agree there's something
downright spooky 'bout the hex doctors'
way with chants and buryin' dead chickens
and whatnot?"

Hannah groaned and shook her head. "No
. . . you don't know what you're sayin',
Leah. That's all part of the earthy nature of
things. Take people, for example, who can't
wear a wristwatch because they have a

special type of energy coursing through their bodies."

"I don't know anyone like that."

"Old Lady Henner could never wear a watch."

Leah didn't care one iota to hear more of Hannah's thin reasoning behind her obvious curiosity with the sympathy healers' dark, even evil, secret practices. "Sounds like an old wives' tale to me."

They rode along without saying much more, although Leah made occasional comments about various trees or so-and-so's well-tended landscape. But when they arrived at Mary Ruth's house and Hannah noticed the many Englishers' cars parked outside, she uttered in disdain, "Looks like a bunch of fancy folk to me."

Leah hopped out of the carriage and began tying the horse to the hitching post. "I expect we'll *all* have a wonderful-gut time."

Hannah shrugged her shoulders and stepped out of the buggy on the opposite side, moving as slowly as if she were nigh unto eighty years old, instead of her sprightly thirty.

It was altogether pleasing to Leah seeing the eight ladies sitting around the kitchen table in Mary Ruth's modest kitchen, all chattering about intricate stitching and the creative combination of design and color.

Several looked up from where they sat, scissors in hand, smiles on bright faces, waiting expectantly as Mary Ruth happily introduced both Leah and Hannah as "two of my dear sisters." After that Leah and Hannah sat at the table, as well, cutting squares for the project: a nine-patch quilt.

Leah couldn't help but notice how unusually expressive Mary Ruth's blue eyes were as she spoke with one student after another. Her sister had seemingly discovered a way to channel her gift for teaching right here in her own cozy kitchen. Each lady present — three obviously very English, wearing gold scatter pins on blouse collars, and one with big, round red earrings — seemed to lap up the techniques much as a kitten does fresh milk.

Meanwhile, Ruthie slept snug in her cradle amidst the contented hum of the industrious women, whose busy hands flew to doing piecework and cutting squares for the pretty side border.

When it came time for the noon meal, each woman opened a sack lunch containing an extra sandwich or piece of fruit to share, which was exactly what they did. They broke bread together, with Mary Ruth saying the mealtime blessing before a single morsel was eaten.

Spreading God's love in her own way, thought Leah, touched not only by Mary Ruth's sweetness but by her enthusiasm for holding such classes. Even though there was a small charge for the weekly instruction, it struck Leah as a delightful way for Mary Ruth to have a pleasant and meaningful social outlet after being accustomed to teaching and enjoying the company of children all day long. Goodness, she knew how isolating it could be to tend to a new baby. She couldn't have imagined raising Lydiann and Abe without the emotional support of Aunt Lizzie and, at the time, Hannah. In those days, she had even looked forward to doing housework for Dr. Schwartz and his wife, Lorraine.

Sighing, she caught herself glancing around the long table, once the dinner hour was past, drinking in the sounds and sight of the quilters trimming off the *Schnibbles* from many squares.

It was after the last quilter had thanked Mary Ruth at the back door and headed on her way that Leah and her sisters went and sat in the front room, taking turns holding Ruthie. Hannah couldn't seem to get over how small her niece's fingers were, and how

77

"awful tiny the moons are on her finger-nails." To this Mary Ruth remarked that she had put tiny mitts on Ruthie's hands at night. "So she doesn't scratch her face."

Hannah offered quickly that she'd done the same for Mimi. "She had a way of thrashin' her arms in her sleep . . . but only before a visit to the sympathy healer."

Leah's breath caught in her throat.

"Why on earth did you take your baby daughter to a powwow doctor?" Mary Ruth asked, unable to hide a look of astonishment.

Hannah didn't bother to answer. "I've been thinkin' quite a lot here lately. Ain't it time we had another woman doctor in the area?"

"You mean similar to an Amish midwife?" asked Mary Ruth.

"No, someone to carry on the healing gifts, like Old Lady Henner."

Mary Ruth stood right up and went over to Hannah to take sleeping Ruthie from her arms. "I'd rather you not talk about such things within the hearing of my firstborn." Pacing the floor, Mary Ruth glanced every so often at Hannah, who merely sat in the hickory rocker, a bewildered look on her face.

"Why is it you're so against our doctors,

anyways?" asked Hannah at last.

Though Leah flinched inwardly, she hoped Mary Ruth might speak up and share what she'd learned about the matter. She was secretly pleased when Mary Ruth carried Ruthie to the kitchen and returned with a Bible. "Here's why I believe we must call upon the name of the Lord for healing and not seek out the powers of certain ones in our community."

Before Mary Ruth could thumb through the thin pages of the Scriptures, Hannah spoke up again. "Doesn't the Lord God give good gifts to His children? Just look at water dowsers and folks who can find the depth and flow of a well — and they can locate other things, too — do ya mean to say those things ain't from the hand of God?"

"The sort of healing used by sympathy healers is done mostly by chantings and charms," argued Mary Ruth. "My Robert has been doing some research as an outgrowth of a church debate two years ago, and he's discovered that powwowing uses chants and formulas from a book of spells that traces back to the thirteenth century — some of it comes from even farther back than that."

Hannah frowned. "I've never heard tell of that. Old Lady Henner never needed a book. She knew exactly what to say and do to help a sick person . . . or even an animal."

"But she did things in secret, didn't she?" Mary Ruth pressed, the Bible in her lap.

"I guess she did."

Leah couldn't keep still any longer. "We *know* she did."

Looking as though she had been cornered, Hannah said, "Are ya gonna read the Bible now, Mary Ruth?" She gave Leah an annoyed look.

"Will you heed God's Word on this matter . . . *this* time?"

Hannah nodded her head and sighed. "I'm still here, ain't I?"

"All right, then, I'll read from the eighteenth chapter of Deuteronomy, verses ten through part of twelve. 'There shall not be found among you any one that maketh his son or his daughter to pass through the fire, or that useth divination, or an observer of times, or an enchanter, or a witch, or a charmer, or a consulter with familiar spirits, or a wizard, or a necromancer. For all that do these things are an abomination unto the Lord.' "

Hannah's face dropped and she looked like the air had gone out of her. The sisters endured a long and awkward silence.

Softly, yet confidently, Mary Ruth volunteered something Leah had not heard previously. "Believe it or not," she said, "I've heard some of the diseases are supposedly transferred at the time of the healing." Her shoulders rose and fell, and she went on. "Following such a treatment, the sympathy healer must go and rest to recover from taking on the toxic part from the sick person."

Leah wasted no time in responding. "For pity's sake, that doesn't sound like God's doing, does it?"

Hannah remained silent.

Leah rose and went to check on Mary Ruth's sleeping baby. Kneeling on the kitchen floor, she rocked the cradle and prayed silently that Hannah might ponder the goodness and grace of the Lord and take the Scripture reading to heart instead of yearning for the hex doctors' powers.

Please, Lord, help Mary Ruth finally get through Hannah's thick head on this matter.

On the ride home Leah was heartened by Hannah's rather relaxed demeanor. And because she hoped something good had been accomplished for Hannah today, Leah began to hum softly.

"Must be feelin' happy," her sister commented.

"S'pose I am." She couldn't go so far as

to say just why, but another look at Hannah's serene face left Leah wondering what she was truly thinking.

"Mary Ruth seems quite contented, ain't so? All cozy in her house . . . with her first baby 'n' all."

"Ruthie is so cuddly and dear." *Makes me want one of my own,* she thought.

They rode along, Leah humming all the while, and Hannah leaning back against the front seat as if taking in the countryside, not saying much.

Will she consider the Bible verses Mary Ruth shared? Leah wondered. After all, there had been numerous other times when Hannah's twin had tried to link their concern to God's Holy Word for her sake.

Leaving the matter once again to the Lord, Leah was tempted to give in to aimless musing, but an open *courting* buggy — in broad daylight, of all things — was headed their way.

As the carriage drew closer, she looked over at the young couple, expecting perhaps to wave and greet familiar faces. Instead, she drew in a sharp breath.

Jake?

Hannah sat up quickly. "Wasn't that our Lyddie?"

Leah was speechless.

Jake had surprised all of them, possibly even Lydiann, too, by coming home so soon. Witnessing yet again how smitten Sadie's boy was over Lydiann — his arm draped around her — all of nature seemed at once topsy-turvy. The terrible sight led Leah's imagination to run ahead of her to the hour the day would die away into twilight. And all the while, Jake and Lydiann would be out riding alone.

CHAPTER SEVEN

I must turn this horse and carriage around! Leah panicked and checked to see if anyone was coming from behind. On impulse, she reined the horse hard to the left.

Hannah gasped. "What the world, sister? You're gonna wreck us!"

Hannah was surely right; there was no turning as sharply as Leah had attempted to do. Besides, the poor horse was thoroughly confused, pawing at the ground and neighing something fierce. "Leah? You all right?"

Truth was, she was downright upset and determined to put a stop to Jake's obvious arrogance. What sort of young man simply showed up unannounced? He hadn't even waited till after sundown to come calling on Lyddie, the traditional way.

She could not get the memory of Lydiann's blissful smile out of her head — her girl riding next to her dark-haired beau. It spurred Leah to get on home, but the horse was presently not in a cooperative mood.

"Best be more cautious, Leah." Well she deserved it, but how strange for Hannah to be chiding *her*.

She thought ahead to those things that must be said to Jake. Not so willing to get the entire family involved — although what choice did she have — she rehearsed in her mind a make-believe conversation with Lydiann, followed by another with Gid. Thrown in there somewhere, as well, would be at least a question or two or more from Dat and Aunt Lizzie.

"Ach, such a mess we're in," she said flat out.

"What're you muttering?"

Leah caught herself and explained quietly, "Just talkin' to myself." She hoped Jake Mast hadn't gotten any wild ideas about running off with Lydiann. Because if so, all of Gobbler's Knob would hear her sobbing, and she'd send a group of the People after them, or even go out looking for Jake herself . . . anything to rescue her Lyddie from certain heartache.

"I was up in the woods writing a letter to you this very mornin'," Lydiann told Jake as they rode toward Ninepoints. "There's a

85

beautiful old tree not so deep into the forest, and I like to sit under it and dream of you."

He smiled and touched his forehead to hers. "No need for that anymore. Because of Jonas, I'm here . . . right where I belong. With you."

She liked the sound of this. "I missed you terribly. Saved every single letter you wrote," she whispered, afraid she might cry, so happy she was to be riding in his courting buggy. "I thought my heart might break in two if I didn't lay eyes on ya again."

He reached for her hand. "If Jonas hadn't talked to my father, I'd still be in Ohio. It was a downright dirty trick my father did, sendin' me away. I 'spect he's thinkin' I'm only home for a visit, but I'm never goin' back, not if I don't have to."

"Ya mean, you might?" She fretted at the latter.

"That's not for you to worry your perty head over, Lyddie."

"But you said —"

"I know what I want. That's why I'm here."

She looked down at their entwined fingers. She'd yearned to sit right next to him again this way. All their painful time apart had vanished with the morning mist.

"What is it, love?" He leaned closer.

She hadn't realized she'd spoken anything, but perhaps she had. "I'm thinkin' that maybe I love ya more than I oughta," she told him, brushing tears away.

"*Himmel* . . . that just ain't possible!" He squeezed her tight.

She could hardly wait to become his bride — Jake's Lyddie!

Leah helped Hannah unhitch the carriage and said good-bye as she led the horse up to the stable.

Down at the house, Sadie met Leah, solemn faced, standing in the doorway of the kitchen. "Awful bad news," she whispered. "Jake's back. I saw him come for Lyddie not too long ago."

"I know. Hannah and I saw them out on the road."

"What on earth are they doin' . . . out before dark?" Sadie frowned. "What can it mean?"

"He's flaunting his return, I daresay." Leah hurried past her. "I won't stand here guessin' what your son's got on his mind. I say we go out and find 'em."

Sadie followed Leah into the kitchen. "And if we do — what then? Flat out tell them what's what?"

Leah shook her head. "No, we get Lyddie away from him . . . and tell her privately. That's the only way to handle the pickle we're in."

"But we'll cause a big scene if we do it that way, and Jake will wonder why we're interfering. Is that what ya want?" Sadie went to the sink to pour water into a glass. "Sounds like a terrible plan to me."

Leah knew it wasn't a good idea, but what else could they do? "Then I guess we wait till she comes home," she said slowly.

"What if she doesn't?"

Terror flooded Leah's heart anew. "Do ya think Lydiann would fall for doin' such a dumb thing?"

"She's bent on bein' with him, same as I was with Derry . . . and I knew better, too." Sadie went and sat on the table bench. "Love's powerful, I'd have to say. 'Specially at Lyddie's age, when youthful, fanciful ideas get all mixed up inside and confuse you into thinking wrongs are right."

"Jake would surely think twice 'bout taking her away, wouldn't he?" Feeling nearly overcome with worry, Leah joined Sadie at the table. She turned and looked up at the day clock, high on the wall behind her. "I say we give her till supper. If she isn't home by then . . ." She honestly didn't know what she'd do. "What an awful test of a mother's endurance!" She twisted the hem of her apron till she'd made a wrinkled mess of it. "I can't help but wonder what Mamma might do."

Sadie leaned forward. "Mamma *prayed*," she said, surprising Leah. "Sometimes nearly all night . . . she walked the floors and talked to God 'bout everything on her mind and in her heart. She told me so."

Mamma had done something vital back then, and Leah wanted to do the same. *Ach, but I wish Sadie hadn't prayed for Jake's return.* It looked as if God had answered her sister's heart's cry. She rose and headed for the stairs. "I'll be in my room," she said, glancing back over her shoulder.

Evidently Sadie wanted to follow Mamma's wise example, as well, for she had already folded her hands and bowed her head at their mother's old trestle table.

A sob caught in Leah's throat. *Lord Jesus, please keep Lydiann safe . . . and bring her home right quick!*

CHAPTER EIGHT

In the early evening light, Plain children often stayed outdoors playing until the sound of the supper bell or their mothers' voices called them into the house to wash up. Henry Schwartz took note of quite a number of such youngsters on this day . . . young boys clad in broadfall trousers, Amish-green shirts, and straw hats, as well as barefooted girls chasing after one another in pale blue or lavender dresses, white caps perched on their small heads. They seemed to move in slow motion at times, leaning on the white yard gate, giggling, tossing a ball high over the martin birdhouse, playing ring-around-the-rosy near the springhouse, apparently unaware of autumn's end, nearly in sight.

Henry had been out driving for a time after picking up a few groceries for tomorrow's breakfast, as Lorraine had requested. The sun had been falling fast, but he did not rush his pace, not concerned with getting home promptly at suppertime, although his wife would hope that he might. So relaxed was he that he pulled off the road onto the shoulder when he noticed a broken-down carriage, its hitch undone from the lone horse. An Amish boy and girl — both not more than sixteen or so — were flagging him down.

Getting out of his car, he saw Jake Mast and the youngest Ebersol girl. "Well, hello there, young man." He waved to them, his pulse pounding nearly out of control.

Jake removed his hat and smiled. "Good to see ya, Dr. Schwartz. It's been a while, ain't?"

He nodded, feeling almost breathless as Jake quickly introduced his girlfriend. "This here's Lydiann — Abram Ebersol's daughter."

"Hello, Lydiann. How's your family?" he managed to ask, extending his hand to shake her small one. She, however, was obviously not interested in making a good impression, saying something soft and too low for him to hear before looking away to fasten her eyes on Jake, avoiding Henry's inquisitive gaze.

"Would ya mind givin' us a lift?" Jake asked.

Henry agreed and asked, "Where to?"

Jake hesitated momentarily, glancing at Lydiann, as if unsure. Then quickly, he said, "Take us to Gobbler's Knob, if you would . . . to Abram's place."

Lydiann seemed almost passive, as though expecting Jake to make this decision.

"Denki, doctor." Jake went and tied up the horse before reaching for Lydiann's hand to lead her to the car.

Henry felt as dispirited as the day he had exposed to Leah the truth about Jake's origin and his atrocious mishandling of the situation. How could it be that his flesh-and-blood grandson was seeing his birth mother's own sibling? The idea that this young couple, noticeably taken with each other, was now seated behind him — even whispering under their breath — made him feel like an inexperienced swimmer without a life jacket, rushing headlong down the Susquehanna River.

He gripped the steering wheel and drove as carefully as ever he had in his life, willing himself forward through the dense fog that enveloped him on this evening free of cloud or mist.

"Turn here," he heard Jake say, and Henry did so, mechanically clicking on his turn signal and tapping on the brake.

Sadie called to Leah at the sound of the automobile coming up the lane, and the two of them flew down the stairs. Scarcely ever did anyone drive a car onto their property, though she fleetingly recalled the freak snowstorm and her kind brother-in-law Robert's attempt to spare her frostbite by driving her home. Such distress her actions that day had brought, resulting in yet another Proving period.

She ran to the window and saw Dr. Schwartz, Lydiann, and Jake getting out of the car. To think the missing couple was with the doctor, of all people! "Jake's horse and buggy must've broken down somewhere," she told Leah, who was hovering near. "The minute we can get our hands on Lydiann, we need to take her for a long walk," she added.

"Why not go next door with her," Leah suggested, to which Sadie agreed.

Just as she was about to push open the back door, Sadie heard Jake's voice coming from the yard. She had wished to see her wonderful boy once again, to gaze at him for as long as she dared. Inhaling deeply, she made herself slowly step out the back door and down the stoop, moving toward the automobile.

Dat emerged from the barn and waved at Dr. Schwartz, a strange look settling on his face at the sight of his youngest daughter holding hands with her beau in broad daylight.

Sadie could hear Leah breathing hard behind her, or maybe she was mumbling a quiet prayer. Whichever it was, Sadie knew for certain she and Leah must not let Lydiann out of their sight until they had spoken ever so frankly with their sister. *Dear, poor girl!* As much as Sadie cared for Jake, she was horrified at the way he continued to look so fondly at Lydiann, still keeping her hand in his as he explained to Dat how the two of them had come to be riding with the doctor in his car.

Soon Gid came across the yard, more than likely to see what was going on. Right away he offered to help Jake go back and work on rehitching the carriage to the horse, briefly returning to the barn to retrieve an old, rusted toolbox before climbing with Jake into the doctor's car. *Bless Gid for taking Jake away for now,* Sadie thought, breathing more easily.

She watched in silence as Dr. Schwartz backed up the vehicle repeatedly, making several attempts to turn around in the narrow lane. Gid looked out the back window, his face turning shades of red, while Jake sat up front, smiling and waving like a boy on Christmas morning.

Leah broke the stillness. "Lyddie, why don't you come with Sadie and me to the Dawdi Haus? We best be talkin' some things over."

The pointed way Leah had put it just now brought a sudden frown to Lydiann's pretty face, and Sadie felt awfully tense. Yet she followed her sisters down the walkway, bypassing the back door of the main house to head straightaway to her own kitchen next door.

In the quiet and very private room that was Sadie's bedroom, Leah prayed silently for wisdom. "Please listen, Lydiann," she began. "What I must tell you, I should've said right from the start, when Jake and you first started courtin'."

Sadie stood quietly, her solemn blue eyes blinking a mile a minute. Lydiann, on the other hand, held herself like a child caught snitching a handful of cookies, her arms folded tightly against her slight chest, the way Hannah had done earlier this afternoon when Leah had sided with Mary Ruth against powwow doctors. Leah could see unmistakably in Lydiann's eyes this was not to be the easiest conversation she'd ever set out to have with the girl she viewed as her daughter.

"Ach, I don't see why you are so upset," Lyddie burst out. "Your eyes looked like they might pop out of your head when we drove up, and Jake did nothin' wrong." She was shaking her head. "My beau just arrives home . . . comes over to surprise me ever so nicely, and *this* is what happens." She let out a huff and looked away toward the wall.

Sadie eyed Leah helplessly and then shrugged one petite shoulder. "We wouldn't be talkin' like this to you," she said, "if we didn't think it terribly necessary."

"Talkin' like what? Sayin' *what* to me?" Lydiann's eyes flashed with what appeared to be resentment.

Leah moved closer to her on Sadie's bed, aware of Lydiann's sweet-smelling perfume, an alluring fragrance she hadn't noticed till now.

Sadie stepped nearer the door, as if guarding it against Lydiann's possible attempt to flee midrevelation.

In hushed tones Leah said, "Even though I'm opposed to secret keepin' — I've learned some hard lessons 'bout that — you must never tell anyone what I'm goin' to say. And I mean not a single soul . . . ever."

"If the family Bible were nearby, we'd ask you to put your hand on it and promise," Sadie cut in.

Still staring at them with defiance in her eyes, Lydiann sat quietly, not making an effort to pledge anything at all.

"Oh, my dear girl," Leah said softly, "it would affect you terribly, and most probably any future children, if you and Jake were to marry because of being ignorant of what we know." Leah felt she was stumbling over her words . . . wishing there was a better way than to speak this horrid truth that was going to shatter Lydiann's heart.

Lydiann's shoulders dropped and she appeared to wilt at the mention of Jake's and her marriage — or perhaps she was reacting to the comment about their being ignorant. "I'm listenin'," she said.

"And promising, too?"

"Whatever it is, I won't share with anyone. You have my word."

Tears glistened in Sadie's eyes. "Not Jake, neither."

Lydiann grimaced when she caught sight of her eldest sister's tears. "What on earth?"

"Years ago," Leah began again, "when Sadie gave birth to her son, she thought he had died . . . his comin' too early into the world and all."

Sadie sniffled and moved away from the door, coming to sit beside Lydiann. "My sin resulted in a beautiful dark-haired boy . . . who did not go to heaven that night as I'd thought." She stopped, clearly unable to finish.

Lydiann looked first at Sadie and then at Leah and then back at Sadie, as if to ask, *What are you saying?* She opened her mouth to speak but shook her head instead. Finally she ventured, "Surely, you don't mean . . ."

Sadie's eyes met Lydiann's.

"But Jake is Mandie's twin . . . Peter and Fannie Mast's son!" Lydiann insisted.

Leah, still sitting on the other side of Lydiann, reached for her hand, but Lydiann pulled away, her breath coming in short gasps.

Leah quickly explained how Dr. Schwartz had switched Fannie's stillborn twin son with Sadie's premature babe. "He was just barely alive."

"Dr. Schwartz did this?" Lydiann asked in obvious disbelief.

Leah nodded sadly.

Lydiann's lower lip began to tremble, and she covered her face with both of her hands. "If this is a lie, it's the cruelest scheme in the world to keep us apart."

"We would never think of saying a word 'bout this to you if things were otherwise," Sadie said. "We *love* you."

"Ever so dearly," Leah added. "And we want what's best for you and for Jake."

"For your future children, too." Sadie handed Lydiann a handkerchief.

"But Jake loves me and I care for him. Tellin' me this doesn't change the way I feel," Lydiann sobbed.

Leah waited a moment before going on. "We were terribly unfair to you and Jake. We did you wrong by not sayin' something immediately." She told how she'd first stumbled onto Jake with Lydiann in the kitchen last summer. "Once Jake left for Ohio, we thought your affection for him might fade with time."

"How can I just stop carin' for someone so wonderful?" Lydiann was staring now at Leah. "You . . . you knew this for that long? How could you keep it from me?" She bent her head low. "Honestly I don't believe my *first* mamma would've let something like this happen!" With that she headed straight for the door and flew out.

I can't bear to watch her heart breaking so, thought Leah. *How I wish I could do everything differently . . . for Lyddie's sake most of all.*

Sadie wrapped an arm around her. "I won't let her treat you this way."

"No . . . no, just leave her be. There's nothin' more we can do." Leah rested her head on her sister's shoulder and gave in to anguished tears.

CHAPTER NINE

Lydiann had been only five or six when she first realized that folk looked on her and Abe differently than other children, especially women at Preaching service whose eyes shone with sympathy — and pity. Leah had been a wonderful-good mother to them both, no question, but while Abe obviously considered Leah his mamma, Lydiann had always thought of Leah as both a mother and a sister. And when she'd fallen for the first boy who made eyes at her, she wondered if God was somehow making up for taking her mother to heaven early.

Jake was everything I wanted in a beau . . . in a husband and father for my children, she mourned as she headed away from the house. She wept angry tears, infrequently brushing them away with the back of her hand, letting most fall freely. She felt she was rebelling somehow against nature and the Lord God who'd fashioned her in His own image, with tears and emotions beyond her control. She walked as fast as she could to try to drive away the painful feelings, unable to escape them no matter how swiftly she went. "Jake . . . oh, Jake."

She passed the woods on her right and Dr. Schwartz's clinic on the left as she came up on the crest of the hill where the road fell slowly yet decidedly toward the area known as Grasshopper Level. She slowed her pace somewhat, contemplating just where it was she wanted to go — or if she really wanted to go anywhere at all.

Stopping now, she thought what it would be like to walk all the way to the Masts' orchard house. But what good would that do? Jake would wonder why she was there . . . ask why she looked so disheveled, with swollen eyes and a face streaked with tears. He would press for answers and she might give in, breaking her promise to Mamma Leah and Sadie. Nothing good could possibly come of that . . . could it?

Standing there in the road, she brooded further on the possible consequences of Jake's hearing from her — his own aunt, of all things — that he was not his parents' son at all, but the child of a woman he did not know and had been kept from knowing since Sadie and her family had always been off limits to him. *Out-and-out shunned.*

Things don't add up, she thought sorrowfully. *Why does one family reject another?*

All in, she turned to go back home, hardly able now to make her legs move. If what Sadie and Mamma Leah had shared with her was true — and she knew better than to doubt their word — she had no choice but to break things off with Jake.

She knew she could not do that today, nor tomorrow. Just *when* she would bring herself to turn her back on him, she didn't know. She almost wished his dear face repulsed her, but as she again considered the shocking news that he was indeed Sadie's own son, she was moved to further tears. She also felt an unexpected sorrow for Sadie, who had never been able to know her only living child.

Why, O God, should something this dreadful happen to me? To all of us?

Henry gathered up all the trash from the house and dragged it out to the receptacle in the garage. He shuffled back to the clinic, aware of some movement in the air, more subtle than a breeze, and he wondered if it was a figment of his imagination. *The ghost of Henry past, perhaps.* He deserved any haunting he might encounter, even welcomed the notion of rebuke by an accusing spirit.

Inside his office, he picked up the small waste basket and went from examining rooms to the patients' waiting room, not looking forward to Leah's arrival at work tomorrow. He speculated on what she might have to say about his giving Lydiann and Jake a lift.

The sight of the young Amish couple together on the road earlier today had put him in something of a panic, even though he was convinced he had concealed it well. However, he *had* experienced a sensation of nausea, and the more he became aware of the pair's animated whispering in the backseat behind him, the more discouraged he'd become.

All my doing . . .

It seemed as if he had mentally repeated the logic, or lack thereof, in choosing Peter and Fannie Mast to raise and nurture Sadie and Derek's illegitimate infant thousands of times. Had it been the wrong thing to place Derek's firstborn in the arms of birth-weary Fannie . . . tricking her into thinking she had indeed birthed the gangly and gaunt boy? A counterfeit twin to Amanda, with not a scrap of resemblance to her in build or facial features. Truth be known, Jake was

104

the spitting image of his biological father, Henry's second son.

So Henry had committed the riskiest act he had ever elected to do; one he had concurrently lamented and praised, unknown to anyone but Leah — or so he hoped. Now, as he returned from disposing of the last of the clinic rubbish, he happened to look up and see Lydiann walking alone, appearing somewhat agitated.

Sighing loudly, he strode down the sidewalk toward the house. Whatever was weighing on the Ebersol girl was none of his business.

For as long as Leah remembered, she had been careful to follow the rules, doing as she was told by Mamma, by Dat . . . and, once she'd known to, by God. She'd always looked forward to being considered a faithful church member, and now, these many years away from having made her life covenant, she knew she must continually reach for that mark. Even when no one was looking, she was striving to be all that she ought to be before God and the church. The one thing she had done to disobey the Ordnung, though not blatantly, had been to read the Bible more often than she supposed was necessary, and more passages than were ever preached on of a Sunday.

But today, this miserable day, she would have given anything not to have told Lydiann the appalling truth. She felt nearly as if she'd sinned, and she wished there might have been some reasonable way for her to remain silent, especially after witnessing the pain she'd inflicted upon her darling girl. Yet the strong possibility that a marriage between the two might occur; to the potentially disastrous effect such a thing would have on Jake and Lyddie's babies, should any survive; as well as the shame such devastating knowledge would have eventually brought upon Jake and Lydiann themselves had been enough to push her into speaking so plainly to Lyddie.

It was distressingly apparent how much Lydiann cared for Jake. Her affection for him was all over her face — dwelling in her brooding eyes, pulling down the corners of her mouth even as she was hit with the startling facts.

Yet this heartbreaking dilemma was not Leah's doing, nor her fault. When all was said and done, it was Dr. Schwartz's deception that had brought them to this troublesome place when God, in His sovereignty, allowed Jake to breathe his first breath and live.

If the truth had not been revealed to Lydiann, the door would have remained open for more close contact between Sadie and her son. Yet with Jake unaware of his true roots, how satisfying could such a relationship have been for Sadie? Leah could only contemplate such things after the fact.

In the space of one heart-to-heart talk, the what-ifs had been settled. Today the agonizing truth had been laid open to one more person, and Lydiann's heart was surely breaking.

Sadie wandered aimlessly around the large plot that had been last summer's charity garden, feet pressing into the tilled-up earth as she talked to herself. "What have we done?" she whispered, still caught up in the sorrowful scene that had taken place a few hours ago. "I'll never know my son now."

She spoke to the dirt, but she suddenly raised her head. It was dreadfully quiet here past the side yard, not so far from the woodshed and the outhouse — so much so that she thought she could hear the beating of her own heart.

She stared at the rolling lawn that swept up to the front of the house, the location of countless happy family gatherings over these many years. *Family . . . love . . . unity. Have we ruined that?* She shrugged helplessly. Likely Lydiann was experiencing something similar to the grief she herself had felt when the stunning news of Harvey's death arrived at her door. The surge of sadness, even emptiness that had enveloped her had nearly drowned her as each minute ticked by. At times she had yearned for it to do just that — submerge her into oblivion so she might not have to suffer such pain.

Yet with the dawning of harsh reality came a slow but sorrowful acceptance. Harvey was gone from her, never again to knock the mud off his work boots at the stoop, chuckling as he came into the house at suppertime, eager to wrap her in his big, strong arms with an "Ach, I missed ya so."

In her mind she saw the years ahead for Lydiann, her poor sister possibly feeling queasy every time she thought of her hand being held so tenderly by her own nephew. *Will she be able to put this out of her mind? Perhaps even forgive us for not saying something sooner?* Sadie wondered as she noticed Aunt Lizzie coming toward her.

"Dorcas is having a few of the women folk over for a corn-huskin' bee tomorrow," Lizzie announced. "Would you want to go and help?"

Opening her mouth to answer, Sadie suddenly spotted Lydiann walking toward the house, making her way across the side yard. Anxious as to where she'd gone, Sadie watched her sister, trying to think what she ought to be saying to Lizzie. "She . . . I . . . jah, I don't see why I couldn't help with the huskin'."

"All right, then," Aunt Lizzie replied, eyeing her curiously.

Sadie was terribly aware of the lump in her throat as she noticed Lydiann sit down on the back step, hands covering her face. *Where'd she go?* Sadie wondered. *Did she keep her promise not to tell anyone?*

CHAPTER TEN

Tuesday morning, November 5

Dear Diary,
The children are still fast asleep, as is Gid. I have been walking the floors all night, just as I did when Mimi was a baby, since sleep escapes me — my pain is unbearable at times. I am beginning to feel like I'm bobbing along on a dark sea, my head scarcely above water.

I truly believe I must see a hex doctor — if I could just get some help, I know I'd feel much better. No matter what my family thinks of me, I must do this for myself . . . and for the baby. Nothing else has ever worked for me.

The more I think on it, the more I have a desire to seek out the healing gift myself. Surely that would drive away my sadness, and it would make many others who desire to be touched happy, too.

How I long for this gift to come to me! Would that it could be so.

Respectfully,
Hannah

Peace had come to rest on the countryside around the Ebersol Cottage, and autumn's cyclical touch was unmistakable in every direction as Leah walked with Sadie across the meadow to the corn-husking frolic. "I should've stayed home with Lyddie," Leah said softly. She shivered at the gamut of emotions Lydiann was no doubt experiencing — from sadness and disbelief, to intense grief, even probable disgust at the courting relationship she'd unknowingly shared with her own nephew.

"Well, Aunt Lizzie's there, so if Lydiann needs anything . . ." Sadie stopped short.

"Jah, and that's what I'm worried 'bout. What if Lizzie asks what's botherin' her . . . and Lydiann spills the beans?" Leah wished every last one of the family secrets could be boxed up and the lid closed tightly, never to be troublesome again.

"Should I go back to the house?" asked Sadie. "I'd be more than happy to."

Leah sighed. "No, that might signal something's amiss. Let's just pray that all is well."

"Do ya think she'll ever be tempted to talk 'bout this with anyone — besides us, I mean?"

"For now Lyddie's best left alone to consider all that was at stake for her."

"Not to mention findin' it in her heart to forgive us," Sadie added.

"Our being the ones to give her the sorry news will make that difficult, jah."

"But once it fully dawns on her who Jake is to me . . . and to her, won't she feel relieved that someone stepped in?"

"I can't imagine otherwise." Looking down at her feet, Leah realized she'd worn shoes for one of the first times this fall. This coming Thursday the People would celebrate one of the earliest weddings of the season down at the Kauffmans' farm, where Naomi's youngest cousin was marrying her second cousin, a Zook. Leah wondered how Lydiann would manage the three-hour wedding service, or if she would even go.

"I'm not so sure we're out of the woods with this, to tell ya the truth," Sadie murmured.

Leah nodded. "Well, just give her some time. She'll do the right thing, I'm sure. She won't want to keep being courted by her nephew, for pity's sake."

Sadie put out a hand to stop her. "Frankly I think one of us will end up havin' to tell Jake the truth before all's said and done. If he's anything like me, he won't go away quietly."

"Besides, you're still holdin' out hope to get to know him, ain't so?"

Sadie began walking again, though quite slowly, as if her pace were indicative of her pattern of thought. "I just think we haven't tapped the root of it yet. Jake will want to know why Lydiann doesn't want to see him anymore, and she'll have to give some answer to satisfy him. It's an awful can of worms."

Leah pitied Sadie, because even though she'd ignored her pointed question, she was right in thinking the threads of Jake and Lydiann's predicament were just as entangled as ever before — and each strand twisted back to Sadie.

Lydiann sat down in the chair near the window of her bedroom, her light frame feeling as heavy as she'd ever known it. *Oh, Jake, I already miss you.*

Running her hands over the cane beneath her, she could not get him out of her mind, in spite of the fact their good-bye this time must be permanent and said very soon. Yet if he were truly Sadie's son, why didn't he at least resemble her in some respect? Even his personality was nothing at all like her sister's. Of course, Jake looked and acted nothing like Mandie, either, but fraternal twins often seemed more like regular brother and sister, or even cousins, than twins. Still, she couldn't help but wonder who Jake's real father was. *Could it be Jake looks like* him?

She had not thought quickly enough when Leah and Sadie had sat her down and spoken so confidentially. At least a dozen or more questions had come to mind after the fact, taking a toll on her ravaged brain. In truth, she was plain exhausted, the reason she'd stayed home from today's husking bee. All she could think about was her need for sleep.

She went to her bed and lay down, not bothering to cover herself. She whispered Jake's name again and declared to the air how much she had loved him, till her tears found their way across her nose and onto her pillow.

"I'll never love anyone again. I'll stay a maidel my whole life long if need be." She was convinced of her feelings, as well as her words, and she gave in to sleep, wishing she were a little girl again and might remain so.

Wishing, too, there might be a gentle way to break off her relationship with unsuspecting Jake.

Abram knew full well how much Lizzie enjoyed walking through the meadow and up to the edge of the woods and back, sometimes three times a week, getting her fill of nature. Once winter arrived and hunting season came to an end, she'd be back to wandering through the woods, making him mighty uneasy, even though she knew the forest better than most anyone around.

Maybe too well, he decided, sitting next to her in the family carriage as they headed up the road to Dr. Schwartz's clinic. She'd once again insisted that this visit was unnecessary, putting up an awful fuss, saying it didn't matter to her if her thumb mended crooked or not.

"Well, it matters to me," he'd said at last. Like it or not, Lizzie had climbed into the carriage as he'd stood right behind her, nudging her inside like an obstreperous heifer.

She'd let him have it, too, coming close to blessing him out but good as she repeated that she had no need for a doctor. So strong were her objections that Abram began to wonder if she had some sort of beef with the doctor.

"When's the last time you had yourself a checkup?" He looked at her as she pouted up a storm, and reached around her to try to give her a hug.

She pushed him away playfully. "Ach, Abram, ya just don't listen, do you?"

He chuckled and let her be. "Your thumb will look right fine come Christmas, if ya don't slam it in a car door again."

"I don't plan on gettin' near another automobile."

"If ya hadn't broke it, you'd be over at the Peacheys' place huskin' corn with the rest of the women folk."

"Better I stayed put at home with Lydiann, poor girl. Something awful's happened to her . . . haven't you noticed? 'Tis written all over her sad face."

"Her beau's back home, so she oughta be smilin', ain't?" He was growing too old to keep up with his teenage children and their friends. Fact was, young Abe was in and out of the house so much these days, Abram was beginning to wonder if his boy only cared to show up for supper. Soon to be fourteen, Abe was nearly finished with his education at the one-room Amish school, a right fine building if Abram said so himself.

Led by their two preachers, including Gid, all the men who were able had pitched in a few years back, after the public elementary schools were consolidated, raising the schoolhouse in a day much like a small-scale barn raising.

Just then Lizzie said, "Peter Mast is bound to be irate about Jake's seein' Lyddie, ya know."

"Serves him right, don't it? I mean . . . look at the standoff he's made with his family. All for what?"

"Our Leah got their Jonas shunned."

Abram nodded. "That's how *they* see it."

"So . . . what's keepin' Peter from pulling the rug out from under Jake with Lydiann?"

"Assuming he even *knows* they're seein' each other."

"How could he not know with how those two were carryin' on for all to see?" Lizzie reminded him.

"Reckless and in love," Abram offered. "Remember how we were? Not carin' what anybody thought — holdin' hands in public?"

"Jah, I remember." This woman had a deliciously spunky sweetness to her.

"You ain't mad at me, then?" he asked.

"For marryin' me?"

He snorted, trying to contain his laughter

and not succeeding. "No, for draggin' you off to see Dr. Schwartz today."

Her smile faded quickly, as if she wished he hadn't brought *that* up again. "Just never you mind 'bout my broken thumb . . . Abram Ebersol."

From the look on her face, he was in the doghouse or woodshed, one.

All Dr. Schwartz wanted to talk about when he greeted Abram in the patients' waiting room was the beautiful six-point buck his son Robert had bagged with a bow and arrow. "Right over there in those woods across the road," the doctor said, pointing north.

Abram listened, eager to tell him about Tomato Joe's deer. "The smithy's son-in-law got himself a nice deer yesterday, too. He said he saw four doe and two rack bucks, but he finally got the five-pointer he'd had his eye on." Abram looked at Lizzie. "We're s'posed to be gettin' some canned and cubed meat from Dorcas . . . don't ya forget."

Lizzie nodded and said she'd be expecting it. "Wouldn't surprise me if Leah or Sadie come home with some after the corn-huskin' today," she spoke up.

Abram's mouth watered at the thought of what a fine supper the delicious venison would provide. But his concern for Lizzie renewed as she rose from the chair in the reception area to follow the doctor into one of the examining rooms. Abram was thankful she could be seen today without waiting too long, since there seemed to be only a few patients. "You'll be all right, dear," he said, reassuring her as she glanced over her shoulder. "Dr. Schwartz will take gut care." He winced at the thought of Lizzie enduring the pain of having her thumb rebroken if necessary, but he was mighty glad Dr. Schwartz was the man doing it. He'd been relieved to hear the doctor was still seeing patients till his planned retirement some months away yet.

Reaching for a *Time* magazine, Abram settled back in a chair and looked at the cover, which featured a man and his horse. It seemed this Goldwater fellow hailed from Arizona and was planning to ride east, though just why that was, Abram didn't know. Even so, he was interested enough to flip through the pages to find the article about this man, who was not just a cowboy but also a member of the United States senate.

"Englishers sure must like havin' their pictures taken," he muttered, somewhat taken with the magazine all the same, though more accustomed to the format of his favorite publication, *The Budget.*

He looked up now and then to see if Lizzie was coming out of the patients' room, thinking he should've gone in with her, especially since she'd never been sick enough to come here before today, far as he knew. *We all should be so healthy,* he thought.

Lizzie felt a bit awkward having a man other than her husband probe her hand, even if he was a doctor. The X-rays soon showed exactly what Abram had suspected, but having her thumb straightened and reset was not as painful as she might've thought, although at the moment the throbbing had a strong pulse of its own. Still, she was of good, strong stock and wouldn't let this get the best of her. Goodness, she'd been through much worse in her lifetime. Afflictions of the heart, to her thinking, were more difficult to bear.

When it came time for the sling Dr. Schwartz insisted she must wear, he helped guide her arm through it. "You'll need to rest some while your thumb heals," he urged her.

She thanked him but did not agree to take it easy. Truth was, she wasn't the sort to simply put her feet up and slow down, broken bone or not. As far as she was concerned, it was much better all around to keep busy.

She glanced about the room, noticing how tidy Leah kept the place. *Neat as a pin.* And she wondered what it was like working for this man whose dark brown eyes probed her own. Far as she could tell, Dr. Schwartz was in his midfifties by now, even though he could easily have been mistaken for much older. Worry lines crinkled his brow — the sort of frown that made her wonder if the village doctor ever slept soundly.

Her jaw tightened when he patted her arm. "Come back in six weeks. We'll see how you're doing," he said with a winning smile. "And you might want to consider sticking with horses and buggies."

His uncommonly gracious manner provoked her all of a sudden, and she felt it was wrong of him to speak to her that way. She was not a regular patient of his, nor a child to be admonished. But she *was* anxious to return to the waiting room and be on her way, back to the Ebersol Cottage and the life she cherished with Abram and his family.

CHAPTER ELEVEN

As far as Jonas could tell, he was the only person from Grasshopper Level present at the all-day Kauffman-Zook wedding. He'd wanted to be on hand to celebrate with the People and look ahead to his own wedding one day, but there was an even stronger motivation — to steal glimpses of Leah.

While the women prepared to serve the wedding feast indoors, he enjoyed standing and talking outside with the men. He even hoped to visit some with Abram Ebersol, who, unbeknownst to Jonas at the time, had arranged for Jonas's woodworking apprenticeship in Millersburg, Ohio, years ago. The hidebound man who'd once so opposed Jonas's courting Leah had softened considerably over the years.

He wandered over near the barn, where several men, including Smitty and Tomato Joe, stood chewing the fat. No breeze to speak of, two of the men lit their pipes, puffing the sweet-smelling smoke into the air. He caught a whiff or two as he stood there enjoying the sunshine on this early November day, getting a kick out of watching a whole group of Jesse Ebersol's teenaged grandsons standing in a conspiratorial huddle, some of them with visibly fancy leanings.

Old Jonathan Lapp seemed to notice the boys, too, and remarked about the youngest Ebersol boy. "He's the spittin' image of his grandpa Jesse, ain't?"

This brought a chorus of jahs from the men. "The youngster's just as hardworkin', too," the smithy spoke up. "Why, I heard he worked alongside his Dat in the wheat field from sunup to sundown till the harvest was done. Now, that's a *fleissich* young man!"

Jonas agreed, nodding his head with the others. *I was that sort of diligent lad,* he thought, pleased to be of good help once again at his father's farm and apple orchard. But there was no getting around his hankering to work with wood — he missed the distinct tang of sawdust, the feel of the smooth grain in his callused hands. At times he even awakened from dreams at night that had him back making fine furniture in his shop near Apple Creek. To think he'd initially convinced himself he would *not* chafe under the stern discipline of Bishop Bontrager. In the short time since his return, he had already failed miserably.

Leah foresaw this. How well she knows me. . . .

Leah — as pretty at thirty-three as any of the courting-age young women present here today, he decided. He supposed he might be a smidgen partial because he just so happened to love her with every ounce of his being. Seeing her sitting with Sadie, Hannah, Lizzie, and the other women folk during the wedding ceremony had stirred up even greater affection for his intended, to the extent it had even crossed his mind to ask her to ride with him afterward today in his father's buggy. Though he wanted to in the worst way, he knew better than to break with tradition, especially now when he needed to adhere to the Old Ways of the Gobbler's Knob church more than ever before.

"Jonas — hullo!"

He spied Abram and Gid strolling up.

"Gut to see ya," called Gid.

"And *you*, Preacher," he said, mighty glad to see them both. He wanted to say something about the enthusiastic way Gid had delivered one of the wedding sermons but decided not to embarrass his brother-in-law-to-be. Besides, talking about sermons and such just wasn't done here as it was in Apple Creek. There he'd often stood around with the men after a Preaching service, discussing the sermons and even some of the Scripture references, something he'd enjoyed immensely.

"Awful nice day, ain't?" Abram said to the group of men, giving Jonas a bit of a nod.

First time I've encountered Leah's father since my return. . . .

Gid glanced at the sky. "This sort of weather won't hold out much longer."

Several of the older men stepped closer, and one began to tell a story. Jonas listened and watched with interest as Abram stood frowning quite hard until it was said a man named Noah Fisher had lost his dentures in his outhouse a day ago.

"Well, what'd he do?" Abram asked, laughing and pulling on his long beard.

"The old fella just let 'em be. Said, after looking down the hole, 'I'll be gummin' it the rest of my life,' " the storyteller answered. "And just who's to blame him?"

That got Gid going with a story he'd heard while harvesting corn. "A fella from Ninepoints has a cousin out in Walnut Creek, Ohio, who has twelve children and a hobby of workin' with wood" — here, Gid looked right at Jonas. "But honestly, if he didn't have all four legs put on a new *high chair* before he reckoned what his wife wanted it for!"

"Now, that's a thickheaded fella, ain't?" Abram grinned, making eye contact with Jonas for the third time.

Removing his hat, Jonas ran his fingers through his hair, feeling like he was beginning to fit in somewhat. He opened his mouth and offered his two cents' worth. "I'd say after four or five young'uns, he would've figured that one out."

The men who were smoking removed their pipes to let out a belly laugh, and Abram put his hand on Jonas's shoulder. "That's a right gut one, son," he said.

Son . . . He had not mistaken what he'd heard. Such a bold attempt on Abram's part, and in front of so many other men, too. Jonas had no doubt now: He would approach Leah's father when the Proving time was over, and Abram would receive him — even offer his blessing to Jonas and Leah.

A long time coming. Even in spite of all that had transpired between them, he had every good reason to be obliged to this man. Truth was, Abram had been the one to write a letter of invitation, making the first welcoming gesture to Jonas, sending it to Ohio

126

by means of Jake not so many weeks back.

The fences are mended, he thought, mighty glad to have come here on this bright and clear, wonderful-good wedding day.

Sadie busied herself indoors, helping set the very special corner table — the *Eck* — for the bridal party. There in the most prominent place in the front room, the bride, bridegroom, and their attendants were soon to be seated. As she was placing a folded napkin on the bride's white plate, she happened to glance out one of the west-facing windows and spied Eli Yoder wandering over to a group of men that included Jonas, Gid, and Dat. She was heartened by the warm smile and decidedly firm handshake her father and brother-in-law seemed to be giving the handsome widower just now.

What could Dat be saying to Eli? she wondered, lowering her eyes to the table. She would not be caught gawking. Sadie sighed and willed herself to keep moving down the table, putting out the utensils and napkins as quickly as possible.

Even so, she couldn't help but speculate as to where Eli might end up sitting for the noon feast. If given the opportunity to get acquainted, she must be careful not to reveal how fond she was inclined to be of him.

She found herself daydreaming about what it might be like to talk with him, although she knew from overhearing some of the older women in the kitchen again today that an elderly matchmaker had arranged for a private meeting for Eli with Ella Jane Peachey. This news had saddened Sadie a bit, but she would not let on to a soul.

She hurried now to the kitchen, where she and Leah and several other women had been asked by the bride's mother to serve the roast duck and chicken, mashed potatoes, gravy, and stuffing. She opened the gas-operated refrigerator, a newfangled addition to the community. Surprisingly, the bishop had given his blessing for this convenience, and a few families had replaced their old iceboxes.

"Nice big crowd of folk," Leah said when she saw her.

"Seems everyone's turned out for *this* wedding."

"And there's someone here from elsewhere, too," her sister whispered.

Sadie flushed pink. "Best not be sayin' that now." With Bishop Bontrager in attendance, she felt they should be especially cautious, the way it seemed he'd chosen to point fingers at their family. "Do ya plan to walk home, by any chance?" Sadie asked, changing the subject.

"Hadn't thought of it, really."

"Now, sister . . ."

"Sadie, *please!*" said Leah, an embarrassed smile on her face.

Touching her sister's hand, Sadie let things be for now. She could only hope, even pray a bit, that Jonas might drive his buggy right past Leah as she walked along the road and exchange a few thoughtful words before heading on his way. Even though Sadie pretended to be ignorant of their secret meetings, she was sure Leah and Jonas were seeing each other again, and the thought pleased her to no end.

Sadie felt like a matchmaker in her own right — had so much to make up for, truly.

It wasn't hard to locate Old Lady Henner's grandson Zachariah among the menfolk, although Hannah couldn't just go and approach him out near the tobacco shed, where he stood puffing on a pipe. As a general rule, the women didn't mingle with the men outdoors at weddings or on Sundays. This day, of course, the women — relatives and friends of the bride from her church district — busied themselves with setting out the spread of food, so there was no time for Hannah to peek out the window and wish for a way to relay a message to Zachariah. On second thought, she supposed she could say something to his wife, Mary Ann. *Jah, that might work. . . .*

Fact was, ever since her visit to Mary Ruth on the day of the beginner quilting class, where both Leah and Mary Ruth had talked awful straight against hex doctors, Hannah had grown more determined than ever in her desire to pursue the healing arts. Getting better acquainted with either Mary Ann or the newest Amish doctor in the area, Zachariah himself, seemed the best way to do that. More and more, she honestly coveted having the type of know-how Old Lady Henner had once possessed — an ability to heal with hands and words that the elderly woman had transferred to Zachariah prior to her death.

I'll invite Zachariah and Mary Ann for supper next week. She made up her mind before even thinking of asking Gid, something she knew she would get around to sooner or later. For now, though, she hoped she could sit next to Mary Ann during the meal out here in the Kauffmans' long kitchen.

130

"So, did ya end up on foot *all* the way home today?" Sadie prodded quietly because she and Leah were sitting in the kitchen of Dat's house.

Leah ignored the question and motioned for her to slip back toward the screened-in porch, a frown on her face. "I ought not be sayin' this, prob'ly, but Jonas says Jake's awful put out with our bishop."

"Why's that?"

"Well, for slappin' an unnecessary Proving on Jonas. Evidently Jake threatened to see the bishop 'bout getting it lifted early — one of the reasons, supposedly, he saved up money to come all the way back home."

"For goodness' sake! Jake hasn't any influence on our bishop, does he? He's very young."

Leah put her finger to her lips. "Shh, just listen." She leaned toward the doorway, checking to see if Dat or Aunt Lizzie was anywhere near. When she seemed satisfied they were indeed alone, she continued. "Jonas told me his little brother is up in arms 'bout plenty of things. For one, Jake doesn't understand how young men can be sent off 'to a foreign land,' as he put it. He knows

131

Gid went to see Peter Mast back last summer. Perhaps he expects the bishop's behind that."

"I wonder how word of *that* got out." Sadie felt pressure in her shoulders and at the back of her neck as she contemplated whether Jake might discover she and Leah were behind his being sent to Ohio.

"Jake is also bent on findin' out why Jonas isn't allowed to earn a livin' by making desks and hope chests and other furniture. He says up and down that Jonas was given the go-ahead by the Grasshopper Level bishop to learn the trade back when."

"Jonas said *all* this to you?"

Leah was nodding hard. "Jah, and he's tryin' to talk Jake out of doing such a rash thing. Says it's not his place to approach the bishop . . . 'tis *rilpsich* — rude."

"But since Jake ain't baptized yet and likely won't be joinin' the Gobbler's Knob church after all, there's nothin' to lose, really."

"I hope Jonas wins out on this, since I expect he knows best." Then her face clouded. "I hate to see strife 'tween two brothers who scarcely know each other."

Sadie touched Leah's arm. "You mustn't fret, sister."

Leah stared off into nothingness, as if

pondering it all. "It does seem Lydiann's kept her promise to us, which is a relief."

"Thank goodness for that," Sadie whispered, although secretly wishing there might come a day when Jake could learn the truth about his past without causing a calamity. If they could simply bypass the wretched mess it was bound to create if the Masts found out Jake was not their boy and move right to Sadie's getting to know her son, that would be fine and dandy. Of course, she knew that was completely impossible.

Leah spoke again ever so softly. "Time will tell 'bout Lydiann, but I'm wishin' she might simply send Jake a letter to break off their courtship."

"But how miserable would that be for him? Not hearin' it to his face . . ." Truly, Sadie was thinking like a mother again, caught in the middle as she was.

Leah shook her head. "You can't have things both your way *and* the best way, Sadie."

She knew this well enough. *Ach, what a frustrating state we're in!* Jake would be terribly dejected once he heard the news from Lydiann, and what reason would she give for the sudden and hurtful turn of events? Lydiann had been put in a most difficult, even awkward situation. No wonder she was spending so much time in her room between chores, brooding around the house as if her last friend on earth had upped and died.

Naturally, she feels that way. Sadie sensed misery ahead for both her precious sister and for Jake.

From the present conversation, she knew now that Jonas had indeed invited Leah into his carriage and taken her quite a ways toward home. Sadie couldn't be happier for them, being able to spend time alone today, no matter the subject of conversation.

What Sadie would not reveal to Leah was her momentary disappointment when she'd spotted Eli and Ella Jane sitting across the table from each other at the wedding feast, randomly paired according to age — the oldest men and women being seated and served first. She was too aware of the twinkle in Eli's eyes when he smiled, as if Ella were the prettiest woman in the very crowded room.

CHAPTER TWELVE

More than anything else, Abram enjoyed reading the Bible aloud to his family. This evening was no exception as Lizzie and the others in his household gathered around him in the kitchen, beneath the circle of gaslight. He also planned to pray aloud tonight, having eliminated the former silent prayers of each and every night a good many years ago.

Truth be told, he drew tremendous joy from his regular reading of God's Word. Scarcely could he keep his nose out of his old German Bible — or the English one, as well.

Just this past week he'd spoken again with Gid about some of the wondrous things he was learning, cautiously sharing chapter and verse with his preacher son-in-law, though no longer caring what might happen if Gid reported him to the bishop for "studying" certain books or chapters that had never been referred to or preached on during his lifetime here in Gobbler's Knob. No, he was willing to take the chance of being called in by the church brethren if it came to that. But he had been praying, even beseeching the Lord to help him share openly with Gid from the Holy Scriptures. Gid, after all, had been showing more signs recently of being interested in seeking out spiritual truths, just as Abram delighted in his and Lizzie's holy hunger for the Lord God.

After all, the years were flying away. One quick look at the growing Abe, and Abram could see his son heading too quickly toward rumschpringe. Was Abe ever mindful of God's mercy and love? Would he receive the great sacrifice of God's one and only Son?

All this and much more weighed utterly on Abram, and he ofttimes found himself contemplating the purpose of his own life — even thinking ahead to his days as an old, old man — considering all the years he had been the protector of this family.

What will I leave behind for the sake of Christ? Who among my kinfolk will know the love of the Father because of my courage to speak up?

He had a fervent hankering to pass on his beliefs, so following the Bible reading, he closed the Good Book and asked his family to bow their heads while he prayed to their heavenly Father. He paused. "And if any of you want to join in followin' me, that's just fine, too."

He was conscious of a deep reverence in the room, a sense of peace and somberness. Raising his voice first in thanksgiving, a deep assurance welled up in him and he went on to utter his few petitions, making his requests known to God, as Philippians chapter four, verse six, had taught him to do.

When he lifted his head, he saw that Lydiann's eyes were glistening, and an hour or so later, when everyone had scattered and headed off to bed, she crept back into the kitchen, pulling a chair up near him.

He wondered why Lydiann had come. What had caused the concern on her face and dread in her eyes?

"Will you pray for *me,* Dat?" she asked, eyes intent on the Bible he held on his knee.

His heart went out to her, although he was befuddled as to why she seemed blue, especially with Jake Mast back home. "Jah, I'll pray." He rose to return the Bible to its resting place in the corner cupboard.

"No . . . I mean right now."

Taken aback by her urgency, he realized

she wanted him to take her seriously — here and now. "Are ya feelin' sick?" he asked.

"In my heart, jah. Terribly ill I am."

Is she heartbroken? If that was true, just how was he to go about approaching the Lord with that news? Most daughters drew strength from their mothers or older sisters, and Lydiann was blessed to have Leah, Sadie, and Lizzie near. Why on earth she'd sought him out, he didn't know.

Going back to his rocking chair, Abram nodded and sat down, making his familiar whispered grunt, as he always had prior to a silent prayer. But his young Lydiann had asked specifically, so he breathed in, asking God for divine strength, and began. "Father in heaven, I come before you with my dear daughter Lydiann in mind. She's downright heartsick and in need of your help, and I humbly ask for your presence to come now and fill her with divine peace and joy . . . even understandin'. In the holy name of our Lord Jesus, I ask this. Amen."

He heard Lydiann's sniffles and was hesitant to open his eyes lest he embarrass her. But she surprised him by reaching to touch the back of his hand. "What I must do is the worst and best thing I'll ever do in my life," she whispered. "Keep on prayin' for me, Dat. Every single day. I need it

138

something awful."

Well, now she had his interest but good, and his heart beat double time. "I promise I will continue talking to the Lord God about your sadness, daughter."

"Denki, Dat." She stood and kissed his forehead before hurrying out of the kitchen.

He might've stayed put there, soaking in the sweetness of his youngest daughter in the stillness, but he got himself up and lumbered across the room to the stairs. He meant to help Lizzie take down her long brown hair from its bun again tonight, knowing she would be grateful, given her broken and painful thumb, even though his *dabbich* fingers and the hairpins didn't mix so well.

Making his way to the stairs, Abram offered up another prayer, this one silent, for whatever was ailing Lydiann, dear girl that she was.

Shoe polishing was a regular occurrence every other Saturday night, and Hannah quickly lined up each of her daughters' black Sunday-go-to-meeting shoes alongside her husband's big ones, placing them on waxed paper on the kitchen table. She could hear Ida Mae and Katie Ann and Mimi playing happily together in the front room, where Mimi was saying *she* was the Amish doctor, "for pretend." On any other Saturday Hannah might've stopped to ask her eldest, ten-year-old Ida, for help with the chore, but she wished to be alone with her thoughts, still reeling as she was from Gid's firm no to her request to invite Zachariah and Mary Ann Henner over for supper.

His refusal makes no sense, she thought, wondering why he'd objected to having a nice hot meal with good folk from a neighboring church district. She suspected his response was somehow related to having gotten another earful from Dat not too many days ago, because he was now saying things like they best be looking to the Lord God for their family's healing, as well as other things. " 'Tis time we relied more on the Word of God."

She knew better than to speak out of turn to her husband, being that she was his helper, not his equal. But now that Gid was down working at the barn again with her Bible-reading father, she was stewing plenty. *He's one of the preachers, for pity's sake!*

She must respect the divine ordination of her husband, yet she was eager to get better acquainted with the Henners. Had Gid put his foot down because of studying the Bible? He had even been reciting Scripture here lately, which was considered a serious form of pride. She recalled the bishop stating yet again at Preaching service recently that the Bible was not to be freely read and explored except by those ordained of God: in short, bishops and preachers. *And since Gid is a preacher, it must be all right,* Hannah decided. All the same, she couldn't help but wonder if Dat's influence wasn't steadily spilling over onto him.

Being an obedient woman, she set about shining her husband's church shoes, hoping the rubbing and polishing might keep her mind busy, as well as her hands.

If not supper here with the Henners, then maybe a visit to Mary Ann instead, decided Hannah. She wanted to pay close attention to whatever it was growing mighty strong in her these days. Lest she be consumed with her desire to know the secrets of the healers, she began to hum a song from the Ausbund, suddenly aware that she no longer was experiencing a single pain related to her difficult pregnancy. The realization made her hum all the louder.

The handsome cherry writing desk caught Jonas's attention as he entered the front room of Eli Yoder's house. Eli had kindly latched on to him when Jonas was awaiting the feast at the Kauffman farm, and both men had found great satisfaction in discussing familiar landmarks in Holmes County, even discovering mutual friends in and around Millersburg and Berlin. Here it was a week later and Jonas had already taken Eli up on his offer to "drop by sometime," asking about Eli's woodworking hobby.

"To tell ya the truth," Eli was saying, "cutting and sawing wood, stainin' it and all, well, it's in my blood."

Jonas nodded. *A kindred soul,* he thought, withholding an enthusiastic response.

Eli ran his thick fingers through his red hair. "Seems woodworkin' ain't so accepted here in Lancaster County as it was in Holmes. . . ."

"Well, that decision's left to the bishop and the particular church district" was all Jonas said — all he best be saying, too. This topic was something he would do well to steer clear of, although more and more that was becoming difficult. He was altogether drawn to the only livelihood he'd ever really known.

"That there desk was one of the first pieces I ever made," Eli said, eyes alight with the memory. "I wasn't but twenty-five, I guess, when my father and I laid out the plans for it."

Jonas was all ears. "You must keep in close touch with your family."

Eli's face broke into a wide grin. "My brothers and sisters are itchin' for me to find myself a bride. They think a man my age is too young to give up on ever marryin' again."

"Well, seems to me there's some fine pickin's here." Since he had his heart set only on Leah, he didn't know precisely which girls were courting age and which were older and already considered maidels.

"Got my eye on a couple of perty ones, for sure. And I s'pose I could be married again and livin' back in Ohio within a year's time." He went on to share that he'd been a widower for nearly two years already. "I had a right happy eighteen years with my Nancy Mae, kindest woman there ever was."

Jonas hadn't heard that a traded man could expect to return to his original church district, once married, but Eli was old enough to decide such a thing. "Seems we're in somewhat similar situations, both bein' older and hoping to marry."

"But you've remained single . . . after all this time." The question in Eli's eyes was evident, but he didn't press further.

Jonas felt no obligation to say why he'd never married. After all, he didn't know this fellow all that well, although he did know the Ohio bishop Eli had grown up under. Surely Eli was also a man of integrity, and a fine husband for any young woman in Gobbler's Knob.

Just then Eli asked if he could pour him some coffee, and Jonas was much obliged to accept. He followed his new friend back into the kitchen and thought unexpectedly of Emma Graber, his former, longtime landlady. His enduring interest in Apple Creek had much to do with the loss of his wonderful-good friends and the weekly Bible studies he had always looked forward to — a place of ongoing and keen spiritual interest, where he had regularly enjoyed the bonds of faith. Yet he must not allow his yearnings for his former life to thwart his Proving time, because the reward for fulfilling Bishop Bontrager's stern commands would be the go-ahead to make Leah his bride — and not a single Ohio friend was more important.

CHAPTER THIRTEEN

Jake stormed out of the barn following his attempt to speak to his father about the ridiculous notion of his returning to Ohio. Dat was determined for Jake to have nothing to do with the Ebersols, but no matter what Dat thought of his choice of a bride, Jake planned to marry Lydiann, *like it or not!*

The fury in Dat's eyes and the sound of the pitchfork scraping hard against the concrete floor of the barn had seared into Jake's memory, and all he could think of was running off his anger as hard and fast as he could, hoping to wipe the entire scene from his mind. The words flung at him by his father were as terrible as any he'd ever heard.

Running north, he headed toward the vast apple orchard, the site of numerous joyful days. *Much happier times,* he thought, not stopping to rest even when pain shot through his lower right side.

145

To make matters worse, he was befuddled with Lydiann, who'd surely fibbed to him yesterday, saying she was too ill to go riding with him last night when she'd looked hale and hearty standing there in the side yard, shaking her head as he pleaded with her to reconsider.

His mind in a whirl, Jake dashed through his father's orchard, his feet pounding against the dirt path in a relentless rhythm that nearly matched the beat of his heart.

Lydiann knew the longer she waited to break things off with Jake, the harder it would be for both of them. *It's horribly unfair,* she told herself in the privacy of her bedroom. *He needs to court a girl he can actually marry. . . .*

Thinking how innocent Jake was to the predicament they were in made her feel like crying, but if she gave in to tears, she'd never complete this terrible yet necessary task. The way things had been progressing, Jake would want them to start baptismal instruction next spring and then join church in the fall to be ready for the wedding season. She had seen the intensity of his affection growing in his eyes when he looked her way as they rode together beneath a sky dotted by silver-white stars and a shining moon, an affection that had in no way been quelled by their time apart. She'd also observed his discouragement last Saturday evening when she'd claimed she was too ill to go riding with him.

"It must be done this minute . . . I must figure out a way to do this gently," she whispered, taking out her best white stationery. Hardest of all was not telling him the real reason.

Moving toward the window, she looked out over the farmland and the east side of the meadow, wishing to goodness it wasn't hunting season so that she might have donned her heavy shawl and hiked up to the woods in search of the rare and beautiful honey locust tree she called her own. But no, she must simply write a few well-thought lines to Jake right here where she sat on the cane chair with Mamma Leah's Bible in her lap. She could not allow herself to think too hard about what she must write. Whatever her words, her letter would be sent on its way, along with her broken heart.

Monday, November 18

Dear Jake,
I hope you won't despise me for what

147

you're about to read in this letter. . . .

Early Tuesday afternoon Jonas and Jake had been out pruning apple trees before the snow flew when Jake suggested they return to the house to fill up several large Thermoses with cold water. Since it didn't take two of them to carry water, Jonas wondered what could possibly be on his brother's mind.

"Nobody knows it, but I hurried off to see your bishop first thing this mornin'," Jake confessed as they walked along the dirt path.

Jonas's jaw immediately tensed. "You didn't!"

"He's one perturbed man, I'd have to say."

"Well, I'm not sure we should be discussin' this."

Jake rolled his eyes. "If you ask me, sounds like he's got it in for both you *and* Abram Ebersol's family."

"You brought up my Proving?"

"I asked why it was all right for you to sell the furniture you made in Ohio but not here. Guess what he said to that? 'We follow the letter of the law here.' " Jake snorted.

"I wish you hadn't gone. It can only make matters worse."

Jake removed his hat and swatted it against his backside. "Well, then, why haven't you gone and talked to him yourself?"

"Because I'm followin' the Proving carefully, regardless of what is involved. Receiving the right hand of fellowship come spring is what *I'm* after!" Jonas felt sure his brother had stirred up a hornets' nest in his efforts to help. "Best not to say any more to anyone 'bout this."

"I thought you oughta know what you're up against, is all," Jake replied. "I came all the way home to speak my mind. That, and for one other important reason."

Jake didn't let on what he was thinking, but Jonas was certain Jake's main reason for returning was to get Dat's permission to marry Lydiann. "Time to get that water we came for," he said now, walking faster.

With a shrug, Jake followed.

I wish Jake had bided his time and kept his mouth shut, thought Jonas, heading glumly toward the well.

The afternoon mail had just arrived, and Jonas could hear Mandie hollering to Jake. "There's a letter for you!" Somehow or other, she always managed to be the first one out to the road this late in the afternoon, and she seemed to take great delight

149

in calling out the names of those who had received mail.

A large russet squirrel scampered across the barnyard and began filling his pouches with food for the winter. Jonas kept his eye on the bushy-tailed critter and headed for the well to pump a glass of water, too dirty from his barn work to enter Mamma's clean kitchen. All the while, he thought about the audacity of Jake, thinking it was his place to set the bishop straight. On the other hand, Leah had wanted to do nearly the same thing, though she'd had the sense to talk it over with him first . . . and to respect his wishes.

Some time later he spied Jake rushing out the back door, face as red as a beet. "What the world?" he muttered, turning to watch his brother make haste up the hill toward the springhouse. He decided to catch up.

What's got into him? Surely Jake could see him following, but he made no attempt to acknowledge Jonas. No getting around it, Jake was pigheaded when he wanted to be. *Much like Dat.* Jonas grimaced, but his impression softened when he was close enough to notice Jake's stiff jaw and trembling hands.

"All I ever did was love her. . . ." Jake stared at the ground.

Without speaking, Jonas placed his big hand on Jake's slender shoulder, immediately aware of the blow his brother had obviously been dealt. *Lydiann must have found herself another beau,* he thought, hoping he was wrong. *There's nothing worse than losing your sweetheart to another man . . . or assuming it to be so.*

Not wanting to pry, he squatted down to eye level with his brother, who'd perched himself on an old milk can, tears welling, lip quivering.

It must be a misunderstanding. He'd heard Jake speak fondly of Lydiann and assumed she cared similarly for him. So what had gone wrong?

At last Jake wiped his face on the sleeve of his shirt and raised his eyes. "I can't just let her walk away," he said. "She's the dearest, most beautiful girl I know."

Jonas listened, wondering if perhaps Dat had thrown a wrench in things.

Standing abruptly, Jake announced, "I have to talk to her. I won't let someone else come between us."

"Is it possible you're jumpin' to conclusions?" Jonas felt he should say this to help Jake think more clearly. *There's too much at stake to do otherwise.*

"No, there can't be any other reason.

Someone's come along and put doubts in *my* girl's mind. That has to be it!"

There was no talking sense to Jake now. "When did ya see her last?" Jonas asked.

Ignoring the question, Jake pulled out a folded letter from his pocket and slapped it against his hand. "It's all right here. Lydiann doesn't want to see me ever again. We're through."

Jonas inhaled deeply and felt as if the clock had been turned back to another time and place. "I'm awful sorry."

Jake coughed as if he was trying to choke back more tears. "I know she has every right to see who she wants . . . but we were gonna be married. We were in love. I'm sure of it."

"Best to let some time pass before you say or do anything," he suggested. "It won't be easy, but it's better to wait."

"We'll see 'bout that." Jake shook his head and slapped his hand on his thigh. "I'm not nearly as patient a man as you, Jonas."

Jonas wasted no time falling into step with Jake. They headed back toward the barn for afternoon milking, and along the way Jonas noticed a squirrel, possibly the same one as before, nibbling away on a seed or a nut. *Once winter sets in, Jake will be terribly lonely,* he thought, recalling the lengthy days and the long, long winters he had endured till surprising word had come of Leah's single-ness.

Too bad their father would most likely be a thorn in Jake's side, jumping for joy when word reached his ears — if it hadn't already — which would *not* sit well with tetchy Jake. And perhaps Dat would still eventually insist on Jake's returning to Ohio. Now that Jonas thought on it, such a thing might not be such a bad idea.

CHAPTER FOURTEEN

At breakfast the morning after receiving Lydiann's letter, Jake refused to reveal his anger or disappointment as he slid onto the bench next to Mandie at the table. Lacking an appetite, he did his best to eat the food Mamma served: fried eggs and potatoes, cornmeal mush, toast, butter, and strawberry jam.

He glanced across the table at his father. *Has Dat interfered with Lydiann and me? Is that what happened?*

Jonas mentioned something about helping their father shovel manure in the barn following breakfast.

"Jake'll help us." Dat nodded his head in Jake's direction.

Jonas and their father carried the conversation for the next few minutes, and Jake noticed an interesting camaraderie between the two. What sort of agreement had Jonas and Dat worked out, allowing Jonas to live here, yet court Leah? And Jake was mighty sure Jonas was doing just that, seeing Leah at least once a week. There would have been no other reason for him to move home from Ohio.

When it came time for the prayer following the meal, they bowed their heads for the silent blessing, waiting for Dat to make the guttural sound that signaled the end.

Mamma and Mandie talked of going to the mill near Grasshopper Level to have some corn ground into cornmeal as Dat, Jonas, and Jake headed out to the barn.

The minute I can break free, I'm going to Gobbler's Knob, Jake thought.

By the time Jake was able to get away, it was well after supper, but Jake was rather glad of the hour. This way he could stand out in Lyddie's side yard, a ways back from the farmhouse, and observe Abram and his family gathered in the kitchen for Bible reading and prayers. He *was* quite shocked when it came time for the silent prayer, since it was obvious Abram's lips were moving. Was he praying aloud? If so, this was something Jake had never heard of in their Old Order community, let alone witnessed, although he did recall Lydiann saying her father was most interested in reading aloud from the Bible every night.

He waited awhile till he thought Lydiann might be alone in the kitchen doing a bit of sewing, but when he gingerly knocked on the back door, it was Leah who came to open it and peer out at him.

"Could I . . . uh, talk to Lyddie right quick?"

Leah turned and glanced momentarily over her shoulder before turning back to him. "Is she expectin' you?" she asked softly.

"Well, no, she ain't."

She sighed loudly. "Honestly, Jake" — her voice was almost a whisper now — "I daresay it's too late tonight for an unexpected visitor." With that she lowered her head, as if pained; then she slowly pulled the door shut.

He felt as grief stricken as when he'd first laid eyes on the wretched letter. *Lyddie doesn't want to have anything to do with me!*

He wandered without a purpose now, shining his flashlight to find his way back to where he'd left his horse and open buggy parked some distance down Abram's lane.

Leah suspected from Jake's demeanor the night of his attempted visit that Lyddie must have put an end to their courtship — certainly Lyddie herself appeared morose

156

and kept close to home in the days that followed. Leah, meanwhile, attended to her housecleaning duties for Dr. Schwartz at the medical clinic and for his wife, Lorraine, at their big two-story house. She took her responsibilities seriously — dusting, mopping, and running the sweeper, as well as cleaning the bathrooms, leaving everything as sparkling clean as she and Aunt Lizzie strove to do at home.

It was midafternoon when she happened to see Mary Ruth coming in the door of the clinic, bringing tiny Ruthie for a one-month checkup. "Hullo, sister," said Mary Ruth right away.

Leah hurried over to peek at the sleeping bundle. "Aw, she's so sweet."

Mary Ruth smiled. "I think Robert's been spoilin' her."

"Ach, that's not possible with one so small." Leah took the baby in her arms. "Now, is it?" she whispered down to the infant.

Mary Ruth laughed and said her husband had decided there was no need for their firstborn to cry herself to sleep. "Not ever." Mary Ruth shook her head. "Which means one of us is either rocking her or walking the floor every night."

"I hope she doesn't have the colic like

Mimi did."

"Oh no, our Ruthie's not suffering any pain. Just getting pampered but good," Mary Ruth said.

"I'd be tempted to do the same, such a doll baby she is. Do ya ever just stare at her — so perfect and all — and nearly cry for joy?"

"Sometimes I do that." Mary Ruth stroked the wisps of hair on top of Ruthie's soft little head and began to share about the work Robert was doing with the young people at their church in Quarryville, mentioning that her close friend Dottie Nolt's son, Carl, was among them. "Carl's had quite the time of it recently. It seems his high-school girl-friend has jilted him."

Nodding her head in sympathy, Leah thought immediately of Lydiann and her sad situation. "Was Carl serious 'bout her, do ya think?" she asked.

Mary Ruth frowned momentarily, as if thinking what she best ought to say. "To be frank, I think Dottie is somewhat relieved, since this was Carl's first girlfriend and all. Still, as I understand, Carl's taking the breakup rather hard."

"Jah, where the heart's involved . . . there can be awful pain." Leah remembered Mary Ruth's grief after *her* first beau, young Elias

Stoltzfus, was killed, fifteen years ago now — ironically by a car Robert Schwartz was driving.

But Mary Ruth's thoughts must have turned to Lydiann, because she suddenly asked how their youngest sister was doing. "Has she been going to Sunday singings again?"

"I have no idea, but I doubt it," Leah said, wondering if Lydiann had indeed broken up with Jake, yet not comfortable volunteering more about so private a matter. Instead, she settled back with Ruthie nestled in her arms to listen to Mary Ruth chatter on pleasantly about the weather, church activities, and what color the tiny booties and blankets were she was crocheting for Ruthie.

It was as her sister was reaching for her baby, with Leah being careful to support Ruthie's head just so, that a thought crept into Leah's mind. Before she could even mull over the idea, she said it right out. "What would happen if Carl and Lydiann were reintroduced to each other?"

Mary Ruth's eyes widened and she began to blink fast. "What did you just say?"

"I was only thinkin' it might be nice for two childhood friends to meet up with each other again somehow. They used to have quite a bond when they were schoolmates

159

at the Georgetown School. Remember?"

"Well, I never thought I'd hear such a suggestion from you, Leah. Carl's most definitely preparing to join Oak Shade Mennonite Church — Dottie's said as much."

Leah had expected this sort of reaction from Mary Ruth, but she had no wish to explain her reasoning. "It might be nice for them to renew their friendship, is all. Nothin' serious, mind you."

Mary Ruth chuckled, touching Leah's hand. "Well, if you're sure about this . . ."

"You could start by puttin' a bug in Dottie's ear," Leah said. "Let her handle it the way she sees fit."

Mary Ruth agreed. "I think this just might put a smile on Carl's face."

Wish I could say the same about Lyddie, thought Leah, hoping none of this matchmaking would backfire.

Anything to take her mind off Jake Mast!

CHAPTER FIFTEEN

Mary Ruth was going about her usual preparations for a Friday evening meal when her husband came in the back door, looking pale as can be. "The president's been shot!"

"What?"

"Killed by an assassin's bullet."

"Oh, Robert!"

He reached for her hand. "People were standing around the sidewalks near our church, crying . . . a few came in and knelt at the altar. I suppose some will even think the end of the world is coming." He paused. "I can see why they might think that."

Tears sprang to her eyes. "This is just terrible."

"He was much too young to die. . . ."

"Makes me think how awful short life is." Mary Ruth brushed away tears and went to check on her little one, sound asleep in her cradle. She didn't bother to tell Robert she

161

had noticed Lydiann walking alone on the road earlier today, looking rather forlorn. At the time Mary Ruth had been running an errand with a friend and had merely waved, but she wondered now if it was possible Lydiann had somehow heard of the president's death. But how could that be with no radios in the house? Even with Lydiann in the midst of rumschpringe, Dat would never allow such worldly things.

"The vice president will take over President Kennedy's duties, of course," Robert was saying, "but our president was so well liked that his death will certainly leave a political hole for years, maybe even decades."

She recalled having studied the line of succession in high school, but understanding it and realizing its dire necessity were two separate issues. She could scarcely bear to listen as Robert described the sad scene in Dallas, Texas, today as relayed by an obviously shaken Walter Cronkite.

She recalled how President Kennedy's approach to war had disturbed her father, who, back during the election, had been rather outspoken against such a man leading the country, although he had refrained from voting. "I wonder what Dat will think when he hears this sad news," she said softly.

"I expect he won't say much but rather spend time in prayer for the Kennedy family," Robert offered. "And the nation as a whole."

They did the same as they sat down to eat their supper. Robert's eyes seemed to fall on Ruthie more often than usual throughout the meal, Mary Ruth noticed, and her own spirit felt numb, saddened anew by humanity's need of the Savior.

Lydiann rode with Abe to Saturday market in Georgetown, ready to keep occupied with customers. She, along with Sadie and Hannah, had stitched up oodles of pretty pillowcases and crocheted doilies and even some rather fancy placemats. Once Aunt Lizzie and Mamma Leah had contributed over a dozen pies, the enclosed family carriage was laden down with plenty of items to sell.

She tried her best not to communicate anything about her mood to her brother as they rode along. Truth was, she wanted to kick herself for sending off a letter to Jake instead of doing the kinder thing and breaking up with him in person. *He must think I've got myself another fellow!* That he might believe this of her hurt even more, and she thought again of how Jake must have opened the envelope in anticipation of a loving note, only to read words that had surely brought him heartache. How she wished she had never promised Mamma and Sadie to keep this secret to herself! Without his knowing the truth, her good-bye to Jake cast her in a heartless light, and poor Jake could never begin to understand her reasoning otherwise. Sometimes Lydiann wondered just how she would find it in herself to celebrate Christmas this year.

"What did ya think when ya heard 'bout the president gettin' shot?" Abe asked, reins held tightly in both hands.

"It's just horrifying, that's what."

He looked hard at her. "Ach, I wasn't the one doin' the shootin', ya know."

"I'm sorry, Abe." She dared not let on what was really bothering her or what she was contemplating just now. Abe would never begin to understand, and aside from the one time she and Jake had shown up at the house in the middle of the day, she was pretty sure her brother didn't know beans from applesauce about the state of their courtship. Maybe he'd put two and two together, though.

Abe spoke up. "Do ya want me to stay and help make change for customers?"

"That'd be right nice . . . if ya want." Time

to talk less pointedly. After all, this was her only brother and she must show him some respect, even though he was younger. Besides that, it was good of him to offer, as lippy as she'd been.

"Okay, then, I'll stay till noon or so and then come back for ya. How's that?"

"Dat will be glad for your help shreddin' cornstalks, I'm sure." That was all she said to him in answer, so quick was she to lose herself in gazing at the countryside. More weddings were coming up next week, both Tuesday and Thursday, and she tried not to think about how miserable she'd been the day of the one down at the Kauffman farm. At the time she'd begged off going, knowing she couldn't possibly plaster a smile on her face when it was all she could do to simply breathe.

When they arrived at market Abe helped her carry in the pies, but once the stand was set up and ready, he wandered about, talking to different friends and waiting for the doors to open to the general public.

It was during the first bustling hour that she happened to see Carl Nolt, along with his mother. Lydiann noticed their baskets were already full up with handmade aprons and other linens.

"I'm buying ahead for Christmas," Dottie

told her when the two of them came over to say hello. She turned to her tall, slender son. "You remember Abe and Lydiann?"

"Hi," Carl said.

Lydiann felt a bit embarrassed for her old friend and nodded, saying, "Hullo, Carl," as did Abe.

It was clear to Lydiann that Carl was miserable, and not from awkwardness. He looked as dejected as any boy she had ever seen — as bad as she felt, really — but she refused to stare.

Sometime later, when his mother was nowhere in sight, Carl came wandering back to see her. Abe shooed her off for a walk with her old friend, though her heart wasn't in it at all.

"Where have you been keeping yourself?" asked Carl, once they were outside and away from the stream of customers. Suddenly his smile was as big as it had been in the days before she'd stuck her neck out some years ago and insensitively questioned him about being adopted. He must have erased that conversation from his mind.

"I haven't seen you round much, neither." She felt uncomfortable around him, despite the fact they'd gone walking together plenty of times during seventh grade.

"How've you been, Lydiann?"

166

"Oh, fine, I guess."

"You don't sound so sure."

She avoided his eyes and made small talk, speaking only of insignificant things like the weather and all the folk at market. And she also mentioned how pleased she was with her new baby niece, Ruthie Schwartz.

Carl was kind, but he seemed almost too eager to visit with her, telling of his interesting experiences in high school while seemingly cautious not to be too excited about his adventure into higher education. He was no doubt well aware of the Amish stance on schooling past eighth grade. "I made a big mistake in the past year, though," he confessed. "I started seeing a girl I should've never given a second look."

She waited for him to continue, turning to glance his way. It was then she saw the hurt in his eyes.

"She and I . . . well, we're through."

"I'm sorry for you," she said, meaning it.

"What 'bout you, Lyddie? Are you seein' anyone?"

How to tell him without bursting into tears? "I was . . . jah, for quite a while. But no more." The lump in her throat threatened to make it impossible for her to speak, so she quit talking altogether. Carl wouldn't have known Jake, anyway, since Jake had at-

tended the Amish school over on Esben-
shade Road.

He stopped walking and grinned. "I have
an idea," he said more softly now. "How
would you like to go on a hayride with me
. . . for old time's sake?" He immediately
added that it was a church-sponsored youth
activity. "Just so you know."

She was caught off guard, not knowing
what to say — she was still too pained over
Jake to think of spending time with anyone
else, even with a former friend like Carl.
"That's awful nice of you, but I best not."
She also knew her father, if he got wind of
it, would not take kindly to the idea, no
matter that she, Abe, and Carl had grown
up playing together, thanks to Mary Ruth.
Dat would want her to be courted by an
Amish boy and eventually join the Gobbler's Knob church, not spend time with a
Mennonite.

After Carl said a kind good-bye, she
wandered back inside to find Abe acting
glad to see her. "We've sold more than a
third of our goods, snatched up in no time."
He gave her a sly smile. "Out chummin'
with Carl, ol' buddy, old friend . . . as they
say?"

"No need to get any ideas in your head
'bout that, little brother," she shot back.

But on the ride home, Lydiann thought again of Abe's reaction to her visit with Carl, and she began to wonder if she shouldn't consider going to singings again, if only for a little innocent fun. She hoped she wouldn't run into Jake there, but she truly needed the comfort of her many friends.

Hannah stooped low to pull out several of her numerous notebooks from the bedroom bookcase. Flipping through the pages of the makeshift journals, where she'd recorded bits and pieces of her life from the early teen years on, she felt unexpectedly self-conscious. As a wife and mother of three daughters with yet another baby on the way, she found herself amused at the childish things she'd written and wondered what she had been thinking back then, pouring out her immaturity onto these pages. Some of her own private thoughts struck her now as rather worthless, causing her to consider whether she shouldn't cease keeping a journal presently, although most of what she noted these days was about the cute antics of her girls or goings-on down at the Ebersol Cottage. She found herself wishing she might pass along the notion of keeping a diary to at least Ida Mae, who was showing some interest in writing, especially short notes to friends.

Glad for the stillness pervading the house on a Saturday of all things, the girls having gone over yonder to their Peachey grandparents', Hannah felt freed up to sort, taking the time to organize the notebooks according to year before she dusted the lower shelf.

That done, she moved on to dust the large bureau and the small table on Gid's side of the bed. Noticing a Bible there, she picked it up and opened it to the bookmarked page. She was surprised to see two underlined Scripture verses: *Is any sick among you? Let him call for the elders of the church; and let them pray over him, anointing him with oil in the name of the Lord: And the prayer of faith shall save the sick, and the Lord shall raise him up; and if he have committed sins, they shall be forgiven him.*

Reading the verses made her stop and think. The fact Gid had apparently marked these for a reason counted for something, although she was shocked to see such markings in the Holy Bible, of all places. Suddenly Hannah worried her husband might put a stop to her growing interest in pow-wowing. The idea made her almost frantic, and she was anxious to move forward with her planned visit to the Henners' as soon as possible. The minute, then, she finished dusting, Hannah would be on her way. *Nothing must stop me!*

CHAPTER SIXTEEN

From the vantage point of the buggy, Hannah could see the Henners' white clapboard farmhouse clearly from the road, despite the lofty sycamore trees and clusters of maples that created a formidable windbreak.

She turned into the long, narrow lane, stepped down, tied the horse to the post, and then made her way around to the back door. She knocked lightly, feeling hesitant, hoping not to interfere, yet desiring to have an opportunity to observe a healing. Despite the weeks she had anticipated such a visit with Zachariah or another healer, she didn't know if she would be acceptable to a seasoned *Brauchdokder.* If all went well and she was welcomed, she might learn about herbal potions, various chants, and formulas known only by local hex doctors.

Mary Ann came to the door with three small towheaded children at her skirt, her eyes bright. "Well, come in, Hannah." Over her shoulder, she called, "Zach, it's Preacher Gid's wife come to visit!"

"Hope I'm not a bother," Hannah said as she stepped inside. "I've been wantin' to get better acquainted with yous."

"Well, now's as gut a time as any." Mary Ann smiled warmly and motioned for her to follow, leading her through the long kitchen and into the front room, where the green shades were drawn, making the space extremely dark for midday. Zachariah was seated on a straight-backed chair, wearing gray trousers, black suspenders, and a long-sleeved white shirt, dressed as if for Sunday Preaching service. He looked up, somewhat bleary-eyed.

"You remember Hannah Ebersol, dear?" said Mary Ann, evidently assuming it was her husband whom Hannah was most interested in seeing.

"Come in." The healer waved to her.

"Hullo," said Hannah shyly, suddenly quite nervous in the presence of the man she had sought after, though still ready to receive as much as Zachariah might be willing to impart.

"Are ya in need of healin'?" he asked.

She shook her head. "Well, no, not today." She went on to explain. "I was a devoted patient of your *Grandmammi's* — several

173

times I visited her."

Zachariah's head bobbed up and down slowly. "I believe she spoke of you, jah." But the light went out of his eyes and he seemed preoccupied once again.

Now that she was here, she felt almost reluctant to stay as her eyes grew accustomed to the dimness. "I've been wantin' to ask you some things."

An uncomfortable silence ensued. Finally, without looking at her, he spoke again. "Along the lines of powwowing, do you mean?"

This is my chance, she thought. *Might be the only time I catch him alone.* She knew he had a good many patients all hours of the day and night.

"I've been curious," she said, asserting herself, "not in a prying way . . . but about becomin' a healer . . . like you."

He looked at her again, holding her gaze this time, as if sizing her up. For a long while she felt uneasy, but when he asked her to sit down she did. "Tell me more."

At last she had his attention. Glancing over at Mary Ann, she saw the young woman standing alone in the doorway, her small children having left the room, though exactly when Hannah did not know. "I don't know much 'bout sympathy healin', but I have a yearning to help others, startin' with my own little ones. I must say I do hunger after the gift."

Zachariah's blue eyes shone. "Your children, ya say. Are they sickly?"

"Not anymore, and with all thanks to your Grandmammi." She continued on, telling how Old Lady Henner had cured both herself and Mimi. "The ailments disappeared instantly. I was completely in awe."

Zachariah rose from his seat and beckoned for Hannah to do the same. Then, turning to Mary Ann, he asked if he might be alone with "the seeking woman."

Hannah was only now aware of a draft in the room as Zachariah moved closer to stand near her. "As a rule, the gift is passed to a younger relative, from man to woman, or woman to man, but in this case — since you are a willing vessel — I will consider you."

"Oh, I'm ready *now.*"

"Not just yet," he said. " 'Tis important for me to observe you amongst the People . . . in a crowd . . . see if folk are drawn to you, which is necessary."

Her heart sank. *Not a smidgen of hope for me, then.*

"Well . . . I've never been one to turn heads." She hadn't drawn attention the way

Mary Ruth and Sadie had in their youth.

"You're a creature of heaven — anyone can see that." He smiled, but it seemed out of place.

"What happens when the transfer comes . . . if I'm to receive it?" This she felt she must know, for she'd heard whispered talk indicating frightening things.

"When the moment comes," Zachariah said in a monotone, "you'll experience a sensation . . . some say like an electrical current from head to toe. I can assure you it is not unpleasant. In due time I will know if you are the one."

Standing in his presence, Hannah felt a great fatigue sweep over her.

"If it is to be so and you are to receive the healing gift, you will be given the necessary instruction, once the transference is made."

If it is to be so . . .

She bade him and his wife good-bye and made her way out of the house and around to the horse and buggy, aware now of an odd tranquility. Her breathing seemed slower and steadier than before she'd encountered Zachariah Henner alone. Deep down, she wondered, *Will they consider me special enough?*

Leah was startled out of sleep by a stone

hitting her window. Looking up, she watched a streak of light pass over her bedroom wall. For a moment she felt as if she were a teenager again, being courted by Jonas. *Well, of course, I'm being courted,* she thought, sitting up in bed. *Just ain't a girl anymore.*

Having been asleep for more than an hour already, she climbed out of bed, scurrying across the room. Quietly she lifted the window and leaned her head out. Jonas stood down in the yard, his flashlight shining brightly against the frosty ground. "Jonas? Are you all right?"

"Can ya come down?" he asked immediately, adding, "I'll wait at the end of the lane."

"I'll only be a minute." Closing the window, she slipped out of her long nightclothes and took down from its peg one of several clean work dresses, hurrying to dress in the dark. *What on earth would bring Jonas here at this hour?*

She hoped the unanticipated visit wasn't going to involve Jake or his interest in Lydiann, particularly as Jake himself had shown up here unannounced just last Wednesday night. With how miserable her girl had been the past few days, it did seem Lyddie had put the nix on things at last. She prayed it was so, yet she could not be sure, as Lyddie had stopped sharing with her as she used to — truth be told, her girl had nearly stopped talking to her altogether. As it stood, it was terribly awkward for her or Jonas, or both of them, to get thrown into the middle.

Tiptoeing down the long staircase, she wished she weighed even less than she did — every creak seemed amplified so late at night. She hurried through the kitchen and out to the utility room, where she slipped on some shoes to protect her feet from the frost.

When she met up with Jonas, his flashlight was off and his horse and carriage were parked quite a ways up the main road. He pulled her into his arms and hugged her till she thought she might pop. "I missed ya, Leah."

I can tell! She was awful glad to see him, too, and told him so.

When he released her, he reached for her hand. "I *had* to see ya tonight. Jake's out of his mind distraught over Lydiann. She wants to break up."

She felt herself stiffen. "Was there a letter from her?"

"Apparently . . . and there's no consolin' my brother. He's a mess, 'tween you and me."

Sighing, she fully understood Jonas's concern.

"I'm worried 'bout Jake. He's never seen anyone else — first love is quite intense, for sure, as we oughta know." He forged ahead without skipping a beat. "He's awful angry, like I've never seen him. Even so, I'm mighty sure Dat would be right happy, if he had any idea. Can't say that he does, though."

Knowing what she did and not being able to reveal it to her darling put Leah in an awful quandary. Feeling truly dreadful, she said as little as possible while offering her sympathy to his despairing brother. *Jake's behaving like Sadie did when she was a youth . . . and no doubt Derry, too,* she happened to think. Torn as she was on the matter, she wished she were not out here on the road with Jonas, juggling a rather one-sided conversation as she struggled to keep a terrible secret from the man she'd been separated from for so long. She despised being less than forthright, but what choice did she have? If she revealed Jake was Sadie's son, what might Jonas decide to do about his promise of love to *her?* Besides, such upsetting news was not hers to tell — not without talking first to Sadie — even though she wished she could be completely truthful with Jonas.

No, I must remain silent. 'Tis best he never know.

CHAPTER SEVENTEEN

Despite repeated calls from Mamma, Jake was late for breakfast. Presently Dat was hollering for the missing boy as Jonas stood near the wood stove, watching the scene unfold. Finally Dat went stomping up the stairs, but when Jake didn't respond to even that, Jonas assumed he was hiding out in the barn or elsewhere.

"What's gotten into him?" Mandie asked, getting up from the table where she had been sitting with a longing glance at the sausage and waffles, which were growing cooler by the minute. She headed for the back door and peered out. "I saw him outside earlier."

"Too cold out for him to just be wanderin' round," Mamma said, her face rather drawn.

"Ach, he'll come in when he's hungry," said Dat as he came to the table and pulled out his chair. He sat down with a disgusted harrumph. "I say we go ahead and eat."

Mamma sat quickly and bowed her head when Dat did. The silent blessing was shorter than ever before, and Jonas wasn't pleased at the thought of feeding his face when he had visions of Jake out in the haymow somewhere, or clear up in the back meadow, bawling like a wounded pup. Of course, it was his right to wail if need be. Jonas remembered too well the disillusionment that had come from being jilted, though in his own case the breakup had turned out to be the result of a complicated misunderstanding.

Some time later Jonas found Jake in the meadow clear on the other side of the orchard, where from the house, the sky appeared to meet the hillock. "Mamma's worried 'bout you."

Jake stared up at him from the ground, where he'd planted himself. "I don't feel like eatin' or anything else. Lydiann's called it quits with me. How do ya expect me to be hungry?"

Jonas sat down next to him on the frosty earth. "I say it's time you wrote her back — ask how it happened that she changed her mind."

"What gut will *that* do?" Jake got up and brushed off the back of his work pants. "She doesn't want to see me, so I doubt she'd even read my letter." He explained how he'd gone to Gobbler's Knob some days ago now, only to be turned away.

"Listen to me." Jonas's ire was building, and he felt it was his duty to persuade Jake to pursue his girl. "Disregard her letter." He grabbed Jake by the shoulder. "I've walked in your shoes. When you love someone the way you care for Lydiann, you must never just stand idly by."

Jake shrugged him away. "I ain't gonna beg her."

"Jake, I mean to help. I missed out on knowin' you all your life, for pete's sake. The most I can do is pound some smarts into your head." He stared at his stubborn little brother. "I know why you came back home. Think on it, Jake. It wasn't so much to give the bishop a piece of your mind 'bout *me*. You returned for Lydiann."

Jake looked down at his feet. "You're right. I know what I want." His head came up and his gaze met Jonas's. "And I won't let one letter change the direction of my life. I know what I'll do."

Amazed and relieved at Jake's sudden change of heart, Jonas headed with him down the wide brown pasture, brittle grass crunching beneath their work boots.

When the last plate was washed and dried that Sunday evening and Hannah felt too tired to stand any longer, she went to Gid's favorite rocker near the wood stove and sank into it. Sighing, she thought back somewhat discouragedly on her visit to the Henners'. To think she might not be "chosen," as Zachariah put it, made her even more desperate to secure the gift.

She'd nearly given in to sleep when Gid came into the kitchen, looking for some more coffee. "Oh," she said, getting up, "let me pour it for ya."

He looked at her, frowning slightly. "You're all in, Hannah. Go and sit some more."

"No, I best not rest too much 'fore bedtime."

"Soon it'll be time for evening prayers," he said. "And, just so ya know, tonight I plan to say some out loud."

Even though she didn't admit it, Hannah was right startled, and had she been a strong woman who thrived on speaking her mind, she might've asked, *What on earth for?* But she bit her lip and decided this strange announcement was further reason to keep her encounter with Zachariah to herself, at least for now. Thinking again of Zachariah's words, Hannah wondered if his observations of her with others would leave her wanting. She could try all she wanted to put her best foot forward, but the truth of the matter was, she had never been the sort of woman people were drawn to. She had few friends and was as shy a person as anyone she knew. And just now, with the cares of her own world and family responsibilities resting heavily on her shoulders, she could only hope she might impress either of the Henners the next time they were at the same church gathering or whatnot.

Breathing deeply, she tilted her head back against the chair and let herself go into the hazy realm of presleep, relieved to be free of pain where her wee babe grew beneath her heart.

Thank goodness, she thought, though not directing her gratefulness toward anyone in particular.

Blinking her eyes open, Hannah saw by the day clock on the wall that twenty minutes had already passed. Feeling guilty for having herself a catnap too late in the day, she rose swiftly and headed to the front room. There Gid was playing checkers with Ida Mae while Katie Ann read a storybook to

Mimi. *My contented and happy family,* she thought, standing silently.

At last Gid looked up. "Come and watch Ida Mae's king finish me off!" he invited. To this Ida and Katie both laughed and clapped their hands. Their father was clearly cutting up with them, even clowning a bit — the man was such a good father.

Once the game was finished and put away, the family gathered around Gid for the Bible reading. This night he read in English, from the New Testament epistle of James — the very underlined verses Hannah had seen earlier. In fact Gid read from verse thirteen all the way to the end of chapter five, emphasizing the words " 'The effectual fervent prayer of a righteous man availeth much.' " He went on to explain, after he finished the reading, what he thought it meant to pray fervently, and Hannah was taken aback by the break in routine, as well as the eagerness on the faces of their elder daughters. It was as if they were soaking up their father's every word — except Mimi, who had a most unpleasant look on her usually sweet face.

"Dawdi Abram prays out loud," Gid was saying now, "and I aim to do the same. I believe the Lord God has this in mind for us, no matter what the bishop might say."

Hannah wondered what the bishop might think if he knew of her husband's rather rebellious opinion, but when the time came, she bowed her head and hoped Gid would never ask *her* to speak a prayer in front of the whole family. She doubted she could pray in such a fashion by herself, let alone with people listening. If Gid knew the truth, he might be surprised to learn she had ceased her silent rote praying years ago.

"O Lord God and heavenly Father," Gid began, "I come before you in the name of the Lord Jesus, who spilled His blood on Calvary's tree for each of us. Humbly I ask for the Holy Spirit to guide us every day . . . to teach us your ways . . . that we might wholly belong to you. I beseech you for the strength and health of our bodies and minds. Make our hearts your dwelling place so that we may be found worthy on that holy day to stand before you without spot or wrinkle. In the name of Jesus our Lord, I make these petitions known. Amen."

Befuddled as she was, Hannah was quite sure she knew who must have encouraged her husband to pray this way: Gid had revealed himself that her own father, under the influence of Aunt Lizzie — and much earlier, Mamma — had brought him to this curious spiritual place. She would not think of inquiring further about such private matters of her husband, though, being that he was not only the patriarch of this house, but God's appointed one.

Much later, once the girls were tucked into one big feather bed, Gid sat down at the kitchen table and asked for a second helping of lemon meringue pie. Hannah was happy to serve him a generous slice, but the tone in his voice made her uneasy.

"We best be talking 'bout your visit to Henners'," he said, his face rather stern.

She came to stand near the table, her hands all of a sudden clammy. How did he know of this?

"Won't ya sit, Hannah?"

Quickly she did so.

"I s'pose you didn't understand why I said not to invite Zach and Mary Ann over for supper." He folded his hands on the table and regarded them for a moment before going on. "Frankly, Hannah, I've come to understand why there are folk among the People who won't go to a powwow doctor. And I believe most firmly now that my mother, your father, and Lizzie have been right all these years in stayin' clear of them."

Her heart sank. "I should've known you wouldn't approve of me goin'," she confessed softly, knowing she ought to offer an apology. "I just felt like I was bein' pulled there . . . wanting to be a healer myself 'n' all."

Gid's eyes widened, his eyebrows shooting up into his forehead. "No, Hannah. That's not what you oughta be seekin' after."

"I guess I haven't told ya because I was worried you'd feel this way." She must not go on trying to explain herself, even though it was all she could do to sit there and realize how much he disapproved of her. The concerned way he continued to frown made her wonder if his demeanor was beginning to change, his affection wane, maybe. But then, her own father had actually softened quite a lot since getting all caught up in Aunt Lizzie's view of God.

"You know I never cared one way or the other about powwowing," Gid said, "but now I've come to believe the teachings of the Holy Scriptures, 'which are able to make thee wise unto salvation.' "

"It surprises me that you're quotin' the Bible so freely," she said meekly. "Even Mimi looked troubled by your talk tonight . . . and she has no idea what's expected of us from the bishop."

He offered a smile, obviously unfazed by her comment. "Between you and me, I've memorized quite a lot of verses here lately — whole chapters — though not to boast. I do it because I've come to know the God of the Bible, Hannah, really know Him and something of what it means to be a servant of Christ Jesus, my Lord and Savior. And ain't it awful strange this should happen to me since becomin' a preacher?"

She wondered what on earth Bishop Bontrager might say to this admission, but she continued to listen as Gid shared his "unexpected faith," as he called it.

Then he said something else that truly caught her off guard. "I've been thinking, and I'd like to say this outright: Your twin sister is welcome to visit here with you anytime." He reached for her hand. " 'Tis high time to make amends on that count. I'm sure my harsh decision hurt both you and Mary Ruth terribly, and I'm sorry for that."

She was astonished at this change of heart. "You're sayin' it's all right for her to visit with me alone?"

He nodded and kissed her hand. "You've missed out on some important sisterly chats, I daresay. And the girls need to see both her and their uncle Robert more often, too."

She felt nearly scatterbrained with joy, and

she smiled her gratitude back at her husband, letting the pleasant expression on *his* face quiet her heart. In one short span of time she had been both reprimanded and rewarded.

"Mary Ruth might not know what to think, if she doesn't hear this directly from you," she ventured.

"Then we'll have them over for supper this week. How'd that be?"

"I'll drop a note to her tomorrow, first thing — invite her and Robert and little Ruthie." Hannah couldn't help wondering if Gid had gone a tad ferhoodled, forgetting the initial reason he'd given for her not to spend time alone with Mary Ruth: talk amongst the People. Supposedly, some were bothered by a preacher's wife having frequent fellowship with a Mennonite who claimed to have received salvation.

So what changed? That Gid was seeing things much differently these days was obvious. He'd admitted to a newfound faith. Was it the sort of one Mary Ruth and Robert also shared?

With all that Gid had opened up to her about, Hannah felt she ought to at least say something more about her trip to see the Henners. "I honestly wish I could say I'm sorry for visitin' Zachariah and Mary Ann," she said at last. "Shouldn't have gone without your consent, I know."

Gid finished off the last bite of his pie before he spoke. "Next time you have a hankerin' to visit a sympathy healer, come and talk to me first, won't ya?"

Quite unexpectedly Hannah began to feel awfully blue again as a wave of depression nearly toppled her in spite of her best attempts to stand. All this intense yearning for the gift — how could she simply turn it off? And what would happen if she were to be chosen, after all? Would Gid forbid her to accept?

CHAPTER EIGHTEEN

Finding out which Sunday night singing Lydiann would attend, if she was going at all, felt like searching for a lost boot in the depths of a forest. But Jake thought it through carefully, backward and forward, until he'd decided on what he felt was a good plan.

He waited till dusk to ride to Gobbler's Knob, about the time he assumed Abe would be taking his sister. Once in the vicinity of the Ebersol house, he tied up his horse within running distance and hid in the thicket not far from the entrance to the long lane. Waiting was the hardest part of all.

It was not but ten minutes later and here came Abe at the reins, driving fast, with Lydiann alongside.

Nearly breathless, Jake watched. His dear girl was in the Ebersol family buggy with her brother.

Which direction will they go?

He kept himself concealed as best he could till Abe turned onto the main road, heading west. Jake breathed more easily, knowing they wouldn't spy an abandoned horse and courting buggy just east of them.

His instincts had paid off, and he felt a boost of energy as he dashed back, ready to follow Abe and Lydiann, wherever they were headed.

When Lydiann noticed Jake sitting with a group of fellows from the Grasshopper Level church at the singing, she was at once surprised and instantly disheartened.

What's he doing here? she wondered, thinking surely he wasn't ready to begin looking for a new girlfriend. *Oh, how terribly awkward if that's true. . . .*

Quickly she determined not to look his way a single time more all evening long. She would have kept to that if he hadn't come walking right up to her following the actual singing part of the get-together. Different couples were already pairing up and walking or talking together within the large expanse of the swept barn floor. She even spied four young people sitting high in the haymow, one girl cuddling a midnight black cat.

"Hullo, Lydiann," said Jake, standing

much too close to her.

She stepped back slightly, heart in her throat. Oh, she'd missed him something awful! Yet seeing him now, she felt she saw something of Sadie in Jake's face for the first time, and she found herself all but too shy to speak.

"I got the letter you sent, and I don't believe I see eye to eye with ya at all." He looked down, fidgeting with his thumb. "Tell ya the truth, I think the whole thing is baloney, plain and simple, and I won't have any of it. So there." He was grinning now, holding out his hand to her. "Let's just let bygones be by—"

"No, you don't understand. I . . . *we* can't go on courtin'."

"Why not? I love you." He reached again to hold her hand, and she felt her body shiver.

She looked at him, hoping he hadn't seen in her eyes the apprehension she'd felt. She had planned this moment so differently, having already decided what she might say if she encountered him again . . . knowing she must speak the truth on her heart. But it was too late for that.

"Why are you looking at me that way?" He released her hand, the pain on his face unconcealed.

"I love you, too, Jake," she whispered. "What I mean is . . . I *did*. And if you listen carefully, I can explain why."

He grimaced. "What're ya sayin'?"

The promise she'd made to Mamma Leah and Sadie now struck her full in the face. How much easier to simply tell him the truth outright and let things fall into place as they eventually must!

She managed to move back, even turned away from him momentarily, hoping he might walk away from her and be done with it. But no, she felt his hand on her shoulder, spinning her around to face him yet again.

"If there's someone else for you, just say it to my face, Lydiann Ebersol!" He was talking much too loudly, and several of the other young people turned to stare their way.

"Jake — please!"

"There *is* another beau, ain't?" he said more softly. "Why else would ya write such a letter?"

"That's not the reason at all." She searched his eyes, his face. "If you knew the truth, you wouldn't be raisin' your voice." Tears spilled down her cheeks. "You'd be sayin' to me: 'Ach, Lyddie, I'm ever so sorry to hear this . . . and I hate it, too, something awful.' That's what you'd be sayin'."

Jake was shaking his head now, staring as if he thought she was a crazy woman. She should have backed away right then and run, but she couldn't make her legs move.

"What do you mean, that's what *I'd* be sayin'?"

"Oh, Jake . . . it's no use. . . ." She began to inch away, but he grabbed her arm, literally pulling her out of the barn with him, his face red.

"You're hurting me." She tried yanking away, and he tightened his grip.

"I won't let you go! I'll *never* let you go, don't ya see? How can you forget the promises we made . . . the love I thought we shared? Is it that easy to walk away?"

When they reached the tobacco shed, he loosened his grasp and stood there facing her in the light of the moon.

"It's not easy at all, Jake. I still care for you."

He reached for her and pulled her close. "What do you mean when you say such things? Tell me, what's in your head?"

Lydiann had no choice. Promise or no, she felt she would never be able to get Jake to understand unless he heard the whole story. So she pleaded with him to go and sit on the fence nearby, and she crossed her arms in front of her, breathing hard.

In that moment she remembered how Mamma Leah often asked God for wisdom, even under her breath sometimes. Drawing in lungfuls of air, she asked the Lord God above to help her say what she knew she must.

"We're both Ebersols, Jake" came the words.

His eyes narrowed, but he held her gaze without blinking or speaking.

"It's a long and knotty tale, but according to what I've just learned, you are not Mandie's twin brother, nor the natural son of Peter and Fannie Mast."

Jake began to shake his head, no doubt bewildered. She shivered, horrified by the things she had shared. She had broken her promise, but there was no turning back.

"Your mother is my sister Sadie." She sighed, not caring her tears were falling fast. "We can never, ever marry . . . 'cause I'm your aunt."

Then, as if it had finally sunk in, he gasped. "I've heard of girls makin' up stories to suit their fancy, but this? Lydiann, you best just come right out and say we're through for any other reason under the sun than *this* crazy, mixed-up one." He jumped down off the fence and began to pace in front of her. "I daresay you're as flighty as my father says all you Ebersols are." The tone of his voice had changed.

Quite unexpectedly, he turned to look at her again, coming too close for her liking. "But if you ever decide to stop tellin' fibs and want to fulfill your promise to me, I'll be waitin' for ya." With that he began to hightail it toward the barn.

"No! Wait, Jake!" She ran hard to catch up, nearly plowing into him when he stopped. "If ya don't believe me, go 'n' pay a visit to the doctor."

"Dr. Schwartz?"

"He'll tell you what's what." She turned away.

"All right." His voice grew stronger again, as if he was challenging her. "I'll do that. Right away tomorrow, in fact."

Her heart felt like the heavy stones Dat, Gid, and Abe dug up out of the fields this time of year, but Lydiann knew she must not look back. She had to keep walking all the way home, hoping against hope Jake would follow through with seeing Dr. Schwartz.

Before first light Jonas hurried out to the barn to get things rolling for milking, wondering how Jake felt after seeing Lydiann, if that was indeed where he had gone.

He was mighty sure Jake had taken himself off somewhere last night, most likely to one of the barn singings, looking all spiffed up in his for-good trousers, white shirt, and black vest.

So when Jake came dragging into the barn, looking down in the mouth, Jonas knew he had his work cut out, either getting Jake to talk or trying to lift his spirits while they hand-milked their several cows.

The morning had gotten off to a cold and windy start with the tinny tap of sleet on the windowpanes long before it was time to arise. With the approaching nasty weather and the knowledge that yet another November had come and was nearly gone without his marrying Leah, he wasn't in the mood for a sorry ending to Jake's courtship with Leah's youngest sister, as she was in most folks' eyes. Truly, Lydiann was Leah's first cousin, and he had never forgotten the surprising account of Leah's beginnings Abram had given him deep in the cornfield seventeen long years ago. Not a whit of it bothered Jonas enough to ever unduly ponder Lizzie's having conceived Leah without being married. People — young and old alike — made dire mistakes, ofttimes paying dearly for them their entire lives. Eventually Lizzie had become an upstanding woman in the eyes of the People, and what mattered most to him was that Leah had grown from a sweet girl into a precious and honorable woman.

All the same, if Jake had a hankering to talk now, Jonas would do his utmost to listen and encourage him to try and move forward with whatever good things his life had to offer, whether here or in Ohio. The pursuit of a wife, while important, was only a part of that. *Anyway, he's too young to marry even next year,* thought Jonas as he recalled his own midteen years and his near-constant yearning to spend time with Leah. *Seems like just yesterday. . . .*

With that thought, he turned his attention to somber-faced Jake, lest his own longings for marriage overtake and distract him.

Studying Jake, he realized again what a strong and gritty young man he had become, one who understood and thrived in the adult world of farming, tending to orchards and barn animals alongside their father these many years.

"I don't s'pose you'd care to hear a downright dreadful story," Jake said from his place on the old, three-legged milking stool.

Jonas cocked his head. "Speak your mind."

"I'll say it straightaway, but you'll never

believe this. Still, it's the reason Lydiann's givin' for our breakup."

Such a long pause ensued that Jonas nearly spoke, but a glance over at Jake's frowning, pinched face made him hold his tongue.

"According to Lyddie, I don't belong to this here family. *She* says I'm Sadie's baby son, all grown up . . . ain't a Mast at all." Jake looked right at him — clear through him, really. "Have you ever heard such a ridiculous thing?"

"There's no way she can believe that." Puzzled, Jonas wondered at the source of this tale. "Did you ask her how she came to think such a peculiar thing?"

"She seemed altogether sure it's fact — even said I ought to go 'n' see Dr. Schwartz 'bout it."

"What on earth?" Jonas mumbled, considering what this odd suggestion might mean.

"Truth is, Lydiann declares up and down she's my aunt, and 'cause of that, we can't court anymore."

Jonas glanced at Jake again. *Why would she say such a thing?* The thought disturbed him, but he forced himself to set the question aside for the time being. "The whole notion's absurd," he said.

"And a right *dumm* way to end our courtship if there's another boy she'd rather be seein'." Jake said this in such a fiery manner, the cows swooshed their tails and bellowed.

Jonas scarcely knew what to offer as consolation. "What are ya goin' to do?"

There was an awkward silence, and it seemed Jake might not answer. At last he replied, "I'm honestly thinking 'bout paying a visit to the doctor . . . just to show her up and make her give me the real reason."

"Ya really want to go 'n' do that?"

"I need to put all this to rest — and quick." He rose and walked to the barn door but looked back at Jonas. "Best not be sayin' a word of this to Dat and Mamma."

Jonas nodded, watching him leave. *It can't be true,* he thought.

Yet in the back of his mind, he recalled how Leah had shared her aching heart over her sister's sin — and Sadie herself had confided in him, as well, out in Millersburg the summer after she'd given birth to a supposedly stillborn baby. Come to think of it, he realized Jake *was* the age Sadie's son would have been, had he survived.

O Lord God in heaven, may this all blow over!

CHAPTER NINETEEN

The frosty weather printed roses on Abe's and Lydiann's cheeks as the two headed briskly toward the house, leaving afternoon milking chores behind. Sadie watched them from the window of the back door, smiling as they fell into step, their breath wafting up from their heads as they talked. The wind puffed Lyddie's long skirts out behind her, and Abe leaned his black felt hat into the wind, steadying it with his hand.

While she couldn't hear what was being said, she observed the lively exchange and fondly wondered what her own stillborn babies might've grown up to look like, had they lived. The memory of meeting her sole living child at market, the one and only time they had spoken, had emblazoned itself in her mind, though at the time she had been unaware of their relationship. *What would happen if Jake knew I was the mother who birthed him? What if he knew how much he was loved by a silent stranger?*

She opened the door for her younger sister and brother as they came up the back steps. Once inside, they began to remove their work boots and hang up coats and scarves, and she headed into the kitchen to make some hot cocoa. "Anybody need warmin' up?"

"I do!" Abe said, hurrying to the cookstove to thaw out. "It's too early for weather this cold, ain't?"

Lydiann, on his heels, responded with merely a nod of her head, though when Sadie served up two large coffee mugs of hot chocolate, Lydiann wasted no time in reaching for hers and blowing gently. She was so quiet Sadie wondered if she wasn't feeling well, but the brightness of her eyes and the flush of health on her cheeks told another tale.

Abe brightened when a second mug was offered, asking for whipped cream this time, to which Sadie happily obliged.

Sitting with them in her regular place at the table, she was taken with Abe's animated talk. "I'm goin' on a pest hunt here in a few days," he said, face alight. "We're gonna see who can catch the most rats and prove it."

"Ew!" Lydiann said suddenly, shaking her head. "You and your friends oughta find something better to do with your time than choppin' off rat tails."

"Why should you care?" he shot back. "I don't complain 'bout the quiltin' frolics and whatnot you hurry off to."

Lydiann scrunched up her face. "But pest hunts are disgusting."

Sadie spoke up, enjoying the banter between them. "Dead rats do mean less work for barn cats."

"So there!" Abe said, glowering in jest at Lydiann. "Wouldn't want them cats to have too many rodents runnin' loose, now, would we?"

"I don't care in the least," Lydiann whispered.

Abe continued, oblivious to his sister's solemn demeanor. "I daresay some of the fellas from Ohio are goin' with us — now, ain't that right fine?" He started rattling their names, and Sadie's ears perked up when Abe mentioned Eli Yoder. Evidently it was he who'd asked for some help from the young folk with the barn pests.

Abe leaned over and grinned right in Lydiann's face. "We'll make short work of 'em."

Lydiann simply slid her cocoa away from her and rose to her feet, leaving the room without saying a word.

Sadie wanted to get up and follow her in

the worst way, but Lyddie probably needed some time alone upstairs, which was where she was headed, and mighty fast, too, by the sound of her feet on the steps.

Abe was quick to verbalize concern. "What's gotten into her?"

Sadie raised her eyebrows. "You know her best, jah?"

"I'd have to say she's crazy in love," he spouted off. "But don't ask me how I know."

Sadie rose and began rinsing the mugs at the sink.

"I'm serious," Abe insisted, coming over to her. "Lyddie's a walkin', breathin' mess over the youngest Mast boy, if ya ask me."

"Nobody's askin' you, Abe." Just then she remembered Abe and Jake were acquaintances — no wonder Abe was so adamant about Lydiann's emotions. Turning, she placed a gentle hand on her brother's shoulder. "Don't be too hard on your sister, all right?"

He nodded, more serious now. "Jah, I s'pose."

Sadie sighed. "Ain't nothin' easy 'bout love sometimes."

Seeing the envelope with her name printed in Hannah's hand, Mary Ruth sliced it open with a table knife. She was pleased to discover a supper invitation from Gid and Hannah. "Well, *this* is interesting," she said, placing the note on the kitchen table for Robert to see when he returned from the church.

Just then a knock came at the back door, and she hurried to see who was there. "Dottie! Come in, won't you?" She took her friend's wrap and hung it on the row of wooden wall pegs. "So good to see you again."

"I can't seem to keep myself away from your baby," Dottie said, following her into the kitchen, where Ruthie's cradle was pulled close to the table. "Oh, just look at her." She stooped low and made over the sleeping infant.

"She got herself a clean bill of health from her grandfather at her checkup," volunteered Mary Ruth. "She's as healthy as the day is long."

"I'm not one bit surprised." Dottie eyed the little one longingly.

"She's still at that stage where she sleeps through most anything," Mary Ruth said. "Go ahead and pick her up if you wish."

Dottie sat in the rocker with Ruthie and began to hum softly.

"Babies bring out the hum in all of us." Mary Ruth laughed. "You should hear

Robert sing to her while he rocks. It's the dearest thing."

Dottie nodded, yet it was as if she was paying Mary Ruth little or no mind, her gaze was focused so wholly on Ruthie's peaceful face.

"How's your family?" Mary Ruth asked.

"Oh, Dan's keeping real busy; you know how he is. And Carl . . . well, he's some perkier here lately."

"Oh?"

Dottie looked up at her. "Between you and me, I think he had a nice, long walk with your little sis."

"When was this?"

Dottie told about the Georgetown Saturday market. "I just so happened to show up there with Carl."

"You didn't!"

Dottie smiled mischievously. "What can it hurt? The two of them were good friends until Carl went on to high school, you know."

"I wonder if Leah has any idea they talked."

"I say we leave things be. In time who knows what might come of their renewed friendship."

"True." Suddenly Mary Ruth remembered the note from Hannah and picked it up to show Dottie. "I honestly think my twin and I are about to renew *our* close relationship, as well."

Dottie took the note and read it. "Oh, how wonderful!"

"It's an answer to prayer, to be sure. The old bishop must have changed his mind — either that or Gid is simply doing what he believes is best for Hannah . . . and for me."

"Well, it's good news whatever the reason." Dottie rose from the rocker and began walking the length of the kitchen as Ruthie began to stir.

"Here, I'll take her. It's time she nurses again."

Smiling, Dottie handed Ruthie to her. "You're a fine mother, Mary Ruth. I hope you have a half dozen more wee ones."

"That's nice of you to say." She settled into the rocker while Dottie sat at the table, picking up the note from Hannah. "Isn't it interesting how the Lord works?"

"Especially when we don't try to rush things."

Dottie agreed. "Patience is more than a virtue, I'd have to say."

Mary Ruth thought of Leah. "For some, it's a way of life."

The breathy sound of Ruthie's suckle rose and fell in the quietude of the house, and

Mary Ruth smiled, thinking of Hannah yet again, eager to write an answer to her twin's kind supper invitation.

Henry saw Jake Mast coming up the drive, his feet pounding hard against the pavement in the way Derek had always run. He moved away from the window and walked to the door of the clinic, opening it for his grandson.

"Dr. Schwartz, I must talk to ya!" Jake announced as he came rushing inside.

It was virtually closing time, and Henry noticed Leah was pushing a dry mop over the hallway. By the intense look on Jake's handsome face, Henry was relieved the lad hadn't burst in thirty minutes before, when a patient or two might still have been in the waiting room. "Let's step into my office," he suggested as calmly as possible.

He closed the door and motioned for Jake to have a seat. Then, sitting at his desk, he noted again the intense concern registered on Jake's face and guessed what had precipitated this visit.

"I had to come here, Doctor . . . and I'm awful sorry, not makin' an appointment 'n' all."

"Quite all right." Henry felt his entire body go stiff.

"I'm having trouble believing what someone told me Sunday, so downright ridiculous it is." Jake's face was red. "I was told I should hear what you have to say about it, which is why I'm here."

"Go on, son." He felt the fire in his bones as he anticipated what was coming. He had lived this moment in his mind, projecting forward in time to this inevitable day. It was ground he had already walked with Leah, presently down the hall as she completed her cleaning duties.

Carefully he observed Jake, whose upper torso remained rigid as he sat inert but for his callused, restless fingers, which seemed unable to be still. Henry was caught by the sight, finding it curious that Derek's son should be so similar to Derek himself in this small way — superbly composed in one area, yet obviously out of control in another.

Jake got right to the matter. "Am I a Mast or an Ebersol?"

"I beg your pardon?" Henry asked. He'd expected to face that very question, but hearing Jake voice it here in his office still took him off guard.

"Who *am* I, sir? Someone told me I ain't who I think I am."

"Why, you're Jake Mast . . . you know that." But no, he must backtrack and start over, lest he cower and fall into his old, devious pattern. "What I mean to say is . . ." He stopped. This was not going well. "Jake, I have been terribly deceitful," he tried again. "For too long I have kept from you . . . and those who love you . . . the most vital information."

He paused to breathe deeply before continuing. "You are both an Ebersol and a Schwartz." His jaw was so tight he had trouble forming the words. "Let's begin with the night you were born, not so far from here."

Jake listened, eyes flickering open and shut, as Henry confessed the truth about everything, including Jake's connections to Sadie, Derek, and even Henry himself. He did not spare a single detail, describing the apparent stillbirth and the astonishing miracle that had occurred during the drive to the clinic, as well as his wrenching decision to give Jake to the Masts instead of to his rightful mother.

When he finished, Jake was frowning harder than when he had first arrived. "But . . . this — how can it be?" He stood abruptly, shaking his head. "My parents are Peter and Fannie Mast. Mandie's my twin." He paused a moment, looking around the room as if trying to get his bearings. "You must've gotten this wrong — ach, awful mixed-up. I'm not that boy. Surely you must have someone else in mind."

Henry rose to go to him. "You *are* my flesh-and-blood grandson, Jake — that's why I've kept you within arm's reach. But I also needed to know you were being nurtured by good Amish folk — Sadie's people." His throat locked up, leaving him with only his compassionate expression to attempt to atone for his sins.

"What proof is there of this?"

Henry reached for a framed picture of young Derek, turning it around. "This is your natural father. You're the spitting image of him at this age."

Jake held the picture and stared at it for a long time before speaking. "And . . . my parents don't know this?" His voice was thick with emotion.

Henry sighed. "No."

Jake shook his head sorrowfully. "What'll they say . . . or *think?*" He returned his gaze to Henry. "They must be told . . . soon as I get home."

It's unraveling, just as I feared, he realized. *I have no one to blame but myself.* He wanted to apologize again, to say he'd had no right to play God, but he couldn't utter the words at the look of distrust in Jake's eyes.

"No wonder Lyddie says I can never marry her," the boy said. "Himmel, no wonder!"

Henry continued, "If I could change what I did that night, I would. I *should* have returned you to your mother. Instead, I cruelly allowed her to believe her baby had died."

Jake's eyes gleamed with angry tears. "I met her once, did ya know? And I thought she was Abe Ebersol's sister, nothin' more." He shook his head, eying Henry with disdain before hurrying to open the office door. "Ach, my poor parents!"

Then, just as loudly as he'd come in, Jake turned around and declared, "I've never known what it means to hate another person till today — nor did I think I could be rude enough to say so!" At that he dashed down the hall.

Henry stepped out of his office as the clinic door slammed shut, and he almost bumped into Leah, who looked both pale and astonished. He required fresh air, not another painful discussion, but he lingered long enough for her to say, "Maybe you should follow him home, Doctor."

He looked at her incredulously. "Yes, that's absolutely the right thing to do." He tried to collect his wits. Leah was a bright woman, yet if he went to the Masts' home, as she suggested, what would he say? Henry glanced at her again, the unspoken question looming in his mind.

As if perceiving the reason for his hesitancy, she repeated, "Follow him. Please . . . don't let Jake attempt this revelation alone."

He hurried to grab his coat and hat off the coat tree. *My sins have more than found me out. It's long past time to come clean.*

PART TWO

For the Lord God is a sun and shield:
the Lord will give grace and glory:
no good thing will he withhold
from them that walk uprightly.

Psalm 84:11

CHAPTER TWENTY

Leah had once heard it said that, especially in late autumn, a person's cheerfulness was in direct proportion to the amount of daylight one might expect. Yet in spite of the sun's brilliance, she was worried nearly sick as she trudged home.

She opened the back door of the Dawdi Haus, calling for Sadie, whom she found folding a pile of clothes. "Ya best stop what you're doin'."

"What is it, sister?"

Leah looked about her to see if they were indeed alone. She felt uneasy telling Sadie what she must, but there was no need to withhold what she knew. "Lydiann broke her promise. She told Jake 'bout you."

Sadie held the dish towel she was folding in midair, her face turning nearly ashen as she stood like a slight statue.

"Jake knows who you are to him . . . that the Masts aren't his parents by blood." Leah paused to catch her breath, suddenly winded.

"How'd ya hear this?" Sadie's voice sounded unnaturally high.

Leah sighed. "I put two and two together," she said, telling how she'd overheard Jake's heated comment as he left Dr. Schwartz's clinic.

Sadie's lip quivered and she put her hand on her chest, as if fighting back tears. "Ya mean . . . ?"

"Jah, dear one. Jake knows the doctor's secret . . . and ours."

"At long last." Sadie reached for Leah's hand. "Time for rejoicing. The truth is out at last!"

Shrinking back, Leah shook her head. "No, this is a terrible thing . . . for all of us."

"It's the best news *I've* had in a long, long time — truly 'tis." Sadie stood tall, eyes shining with what Leah knew to be tears of gladness.

Leah, on the other hand, was terribly worried. Jake and Dr. Schwartz were on their way to tell the truth to Peter and Fannie Mast, and she couldn't help wondering how long before the news might overtake the whole community. What would this mean for the Mast family? For herself? How would all of this set with Jonas — that she had known for some time, even the night he'd asked pointed questions about Lydiann's letter to Jake? Yet she had kept the truth from her beloved, as well as, for a time, from her own dear Lydiann.

Emotionally torn, Leah dreaded what was to befall them, and the day and the season seemed darker to her than ever before.

Lydiann was out on the road with the team, running a sewing errand for Aunt Lizzie to Deacon Stoltzfus's wife, when she saw a cluster of bundled-up children walking home from the one-room schoolhouse. It seemed like only last week that she, too, had been among the youngsters returning home from a long day in the classroom.

She slowed the horse and called to them. "Any of yous care for a ride?"

All eight of them came running. "Can ya squeeze in tight?" she said, smiling as she remembered how cold it could be walking this time of year.

The children jostled into the buggy, several of them thanking her right away, before she realized she wouldn't be getting to the Stoltzfuses' anytime soon — not if she was to deliver the children to their individual homes.

"So . . . how many sets of brothers and sisters do I have here?" she asked, which brought a burst of laughter, the children catching on that she'd taken on more than she might have originally set out to do.

"Two Zooks," said one of the girls.

"Four Kings," said another.

"Mast twins," said one boy softly.

That comment befuddled her, and just when she was finally hoping to get her mind off Jake Mast. "That's three stops," she said, glancing over her shoulder. "Where to first?"

The oldest Zook girl spoke up again. "We aren't but a half mile from here."

When asked, the others said they were "just a bit farther." Lydiann didn't mind, really. She enjoyed listening in as the children chattered in Pennsylvania Dutch about their school day.

She heard one of the boys mention Carl Nolt. "He's taking some of us sleddin' when the first big snow comes."

She almost blurted out, *How do you know Carl?* but kept quiet, taking in the fond remarks about Carl, who seemed to be someone special to the children.

Well, and of course he is. She hadn't thought of his invitation to include her in his church autumn hayride much at all, but as considerate as Carl had always been, she shouldn't have been surprised at his offer. Still, it was much too soon to think about another boy.

Carl was only trying to get my mind off my woes, she decided, dismissing the notion he might have actually been asking her for a date.

At Leah's gentle yet wise suggestion, Henry had gotten into his car and had driven merely a short distance when he spied Jake running along the road. Stopping, he insisted Jake not travel on foot all the way home in the chilly air. "Let me drive you," he offered.

Jake shook his head, holding his ground. Henry continued to entreat him all the same, ever conscious of his own churning emotions — despising the confession that had led to such obvious antagonism in his own grandson.

After much persistence and suggesting that he, too, go and talk with Jake's parents, he was finally able to coax him into the comfort and warmth of the car.

Jake seemed to cling to the far right side of the front seat. "I have no need of your help with my family," he mumbled.

Henry drove without speaking, trying to overlook Jake's obvious antagonism. He imagined how incensed Derek would have been at hearing such earth-shattering news, comparing it to Jake's more tempered, yet plainly icy demeanor.

Since Henry could not begin to anticipate how the next few minutes might unfold, he concentrated on turning into the driveway.

"This ain't somethin' that oughta be kept quiet any longer," Jake said suddenly. "I've reconsidered: I'm thinkin' you ought to see firsthand what findin' out about your trickery will do to my parents . . . if they believe it."

Henry realized that no amount of spoken regret would remove the pain from Jake's face, nor the justifiable sting from his words.

They got out of the car and headed toward the back door, Henry trudging along behind Jake.

"You and your family bein' English makes all this even more complicated, ya must surely know," Jake said, nervously touching the brim of his hat.

Again Henry was appalled at his own lack of judgment. Had he never envisioned the excruciating scene about to take place here in Jake's childhood home? Why hadn't he foreseen this present heartbreak?

Vaguely he was aware of Jake telling his mother, "There's something important to be said to you and Dat and Jonas." Then Jake, terse yet evidently wanting to exhibit good manners, kept his wits about him and insisted Mandie go upstairs, "for the time being." To Henry's surprise she went willingly, glancing down at them several times as she ascended the long staircase. That done, Jake left the kitchen and hurried out to the barn to fetch his father and Jonas.

The awkward moments that followed seemed nearly endless as Henry stood near the wood stove with Fannie, who appeared to be trying her best to keep her attention on ironing Peter's long-sleeved shirts while waiting for Jake to return with the two men.

All too soon, though, what Henry had confidentially shared with Jake in the privacy of his office was being voiced aloud in the hearing of Peter, Fannie, and Jonas.

"Outrageous . . . if true," Peter said, the anger in his eyes speaking volumes.

"I'm afraid it is," said Henry, "though it's much too late now to offer an apology for my misguided attempt. I primarily had my family's potential embarrassment in mind." He struggled to keep his emotions in check, tempted to hide his long-ago decision behind some kind of purposeful rationale. "When Fannie gave birth to her stillborn twin boy, I knew both of you would be heartsick at the loss . . . and since Sadie had already experienced what she had assumed was the death of *her* baby — all in the same night — it seemed right, somehow, to place premature Jake in Fannie's welcoming arms."

Peter glared at him. "A deceitful deed."

Henry continued, digging himself deeper into a pit of his own making. "It was a most selfish act, one I wish could be undone."

Peter breathed loudly, as if he was about to erupt into a heated retort, but it was Fannie who began to weep.

After some time Henry offered to direct the dismayed couple to the location of their deceased son's grave, but Peter declared the notion "idiotic."

Turning toward the window, Peter inhaled loudly, and an uncomfortable silence fell on the kitchen.

Jake stood alone, his eyes forlorn, like those of a child suddenly displaced, and Henry was aware of the pulse pounding in his own aching temples.

Jonas stepped forward, going to stand with Jake, his arm resting on Jake's shoulder. "I say we're brothers, no matter what."

To this Peter deliberately turned, his face grave. "No, not brothers. And not my *son*."

He frowned briefly, eyes focusing on Jake,

whose face was drawn. "You're an Ebersol," he said brusquely, as if making a pronouncement of evil. "Pack your clothes and get out of my house immediately."

Jonas appeared stunned. "But, Dat!"

"Do not defy me." Peter moved quickly to Fannie, who was sobbing. "Come with me," he said to her, not looking back a single time at the young man whom they'd raised as their own. Clearly, he was theirs no longer.

"Dat, mayn't I speak to Mandie?" pleaded Jake. "Can't I have a minute to say goodbye?"

"Hurry up with it," said Peter, his back still to Jake and Jonas.

Henry's heart sank and his blood boiled, but he dared not utter a word: This mess was his doing. Even so, he could not fathom Peter's decision. *No, you ignorant man, you cannot renounce your son!*

"Listen, Dat," said Jonas. "If ya mean what you say, then I'll be goin', too . . . with Jake."

Abruptly Peter turned in the doorway between the long kitchen and the front room, his countenance surprised but no less unyielding. "Do as you must, Jonas." Then, looking Henry's way, he motioned with his head to indicate that he was also expected to exit now.

Bewildered at the unforeseen turn of events, Henry wasted no time in plodding toward the back door, making his way outside, tormented by what he had just witnessed . . . and the responsibility he bore for it.

What wretched thing have I done to this family?

CHAPTER
TWENTY-ONE

As discouraged as he'd ever been, Jonas headed out on foot with Jake. Both of them politely refused Dr. Schwartz's proffered lift, and they made their trek up the hill to Gobbler's Knob, toward the home of Eli Yoder, with only a pillowcase each, filled with a few essential items of clothing. The sun behind them, they discussed the tumultuous scene in their mamma's kitchen as the wind kicked up from a breeze to full-blown gusts.

On the way Jake expressed his disbelief at their coldhearted ousting by Dat, his voice quaking. "He can't be thinkin' straight . . . he just can't be." Their father had given them scarcely any time to gather up work trousers and an extra shirt or two, socks, and underwear. In fact, Dat had outright barked at them from the bottom of the steps, to Jonas's disbelief. This was a man he suddenly felt he did not know.

Jonas offered some halfhearted encouragement to his brother. "Dat's beside himself with anger, but I would hope he might come round in time." But after what they'd just experienced, he was not absolutely sure of that.

Jake's face remained taut and expressionless. "Got Schwartz and Ebersol blood in my veins . . . but it's Abram's blood that's the culprit in Dat's eyes," he muttered.

Jonas listened quietly as his brother ranted, his own head reeling. He could only imagine the enormous pain Jake was feeling.

"So this means I'm not part of my own family, then? Just like that, everything I've known 'bout my life and who I thought I was is dead wrong."

"Not everything, Jake."

"Aren't ya believing Dr. Schwartz?"

"It's a mighty hard thing, but I can't say differently." *What other reason would the doctor have for telling such a tale?* Jonas thought to himself.

" 'Tis unbelievable." Jake blew out an angry breath. "And to think I'm not welcome at the orchard house anymore . . ."

Jonas had long since come to both accept and ignore his father's intolerance toward Abram Ebersol and his family, though he wondered how Jake's being kicked out of the house might affect Leah when she found out — and surely she would — since she had become quite close to Sadie in recent years. With Jake's being Sadie's son, Jonas considered how such a relationship might play out over time. Still, he was hopeful for a sensible resolution to his father's initial reaction, unreasonable and shortsighted as it was.

"The worst of it is I can never marry Lyddie." Grief registered powerfully on Jake's face. "If only Dr. Schwartz had told the truth when Sadie gave me birth . . ." His voice trailed off to nothing.

They remained silent for a time, their shoes making the only sound as they plodded along the frozen road. Jonas didn't intend to bring up the idea of pressing forward with one's life — not at this difficult moment. There would be time for that later.

Jake glanced at him now, his jaw set. "I've never seen Dat so irate, 'specially not in front of Mamma . . . and Dr. Schwartz, too. What am I s'posed to do, Jonas?"

Jonas clenched his hands. All facts considered, Jake was going to have a rough time of it, starting with walking away from Sadie's little sister. "Well, we can only pray something gut will come out of the whole mess," Jonas said, wishing Jake might seek spiritual counsel from one of the brethren. But from whom? Gid, or even Abram? He would think on that and do a heap of praying on his own.

When at long last they arrived at Eli Yoder's, they were welcomed with a warm smile, even though Jonas told Eli precious little as to why they needed a place to stay for a while. He would share more later, if need be, but for now he was mighty grateful for the hand of friendship and a roof over their heads.

In the meantime Jonas was all too aware he was seeing Jake in a completely different light — which couldn't be helped as he struggled to get his mind bent around a Jake who was Sadie's son, as well as both Abram's and Dr. Schwartz's grandson.

I need to get away, thought Henry. Too many years without a vacation had taken their toll, too many years of waiting for the inevitable revelation of his sin — too many years, as well, of trying to protect his good name, only to lose it with his own disclosures.

And when the truth finally filtered out to all his patients — *if* it did — he preferred not to be in town. It crossed his mind that, if worse came to worst, he might end up being forced to take a vacation at an entirely unwelcome location, and he shuddered at the thought.

He trudged up the porch steps and entered the side door of the house. Instead of calling out, "Lorraine, I'm home," as he normally did upon returning, he went directly to the formal parlor, where he stood before the tall bookcase and opened the glass door. Pulling out the world atlas, he thumbed through the section for Switzerland, Italy, and Austria, deciding to take Lorraine on an extended getaway, a sort of second honeymoon.

It might be our last chance, he thought morosely.

Standing at the window, he looked across the way to the woods, noting a small clearing someone had made near the road where chopped wood had been neatly stacked. Seeing the firewood drove his thoughts back to hardworking Jake, who had cut firewood for him on several occasions.

I'll begin making travel arrangements tomorrow, he thought, taking the atlas with him into the kitchen. There he found a somewhat disheveled Lorraine cooking supper. "How would you like to go on a trip with me, dear?"

Her smile was unexpectedly spontaneous. "Really? Where to?"

"Does Europe interest you?"

"Oh, Henry . . . I'd like that quite a lot." She was silent for a moment, as if she wished to make a request but was reluctant to do so.

"What is it, dear?"

"Would you be interested in Florence, Italy?" she asked. "I'd like to see the cathedral and Michelangelo's famous sculpture of David."

He hurried to her side and wrapped his aching arms around her. "We'll go as soon as I can contact a travel agent to line everything up."

She looked surprised but pleased.

"Yes, it's high time we go somewhere special together. It could be an early Christmas present, come to think of it." But Henry dreaded spoiling his wife's happiness with the distressing truth he was compelled to reveal while they were gone from home. At least she would have ample time to process what he must tell her once they arrived in the Renaissance city, which was more than he could say for the now-cynical Jake and infuriated Peter Mast. It did not take any great intellectual enlightenment to understand that the mind-numbing news they had received today would take the Mast family a lifetime to recover from.

Such destruction I've wrought.

Word of Jonas and Jake's hasty move came to Leah's surprised ears at the Friday quilting frolic at Dorcas's house. Women folk sat around the large frame making small stitches to join together the colorful design they had pieced together some time ago when someone quietly mentioned that Eli Yoder had visitors.

"Jah, Jake Mast's been sent away," an older woman said.

"By his own father," added another.

At first Leah wondered why Jonas hadn't contacted her directly, though she assumed he was busy and would be sending word soon enough. Earlier in the week she'd heard from Dorcas that he was helping Tomato Joe with the removal of large rocks in the fields for pay and that he had been doing odd jobs for others, including her uncle Jesse Ebersol. Whatever had befallen him, Leah could not imagine why both he and Jake were now staying with the Ohio widower, and she tried not to show undue interest as she listened.

Leah glimpsed Sadie, who appeared distressed, and then looked at Lydiann, whose pretty face was screwed up as she pushed her needle into the quilt. *Such a trying time for poor Lyddie, especially,* she thought.

"Jonas is ever so kindhearted to go along to stay with Jake at Widower Yoder's place," Dorcas spoke up, making it apparent she knew somewhat more than the others.

Leah felt her chest tighten but was determined not to fret, even though, most likely, Jake's and Jonas's leaving the orchard farmhouse presumably had much to do with the doctor's confession. *Could it be Dr. Schwartz spoke openly with the Masts?* If so, it was surely the last straw for Peter Mast.

Where will it end? Leah worried, thinking of Jonas and what he must be pondering. The secret, kept only out of concern for others, was flying in their faces.

That afternoon after the frolic, Abe announced to both Leah and Dat that he and a group of boys were going on another pest hunt. "We'll be back after dark tonight," he said.

"We're all going over to Uncle Jesse's to visit tomorrow, so it'd be a gut idea if you're not out too late," Leah gently reminded her excited boy.

Dat nodded in agreement. "Don't get too rowdy, like some of the youngsters I've been hearing 'bout lately."

Abe flashed his winning smile and pushed his hands through his hair. "I won't be *that* late, you'll see."

"Well, nobody's gonna wait up for ya, son," Dat said, rustling this week's edition of *The Budget* as he looked up from his rocking chair.

Dat having had his say, Leah went about her work, putting the finishing touches on the apple betty she was making. Sadie had settled in beside her to peel potatoes, not saying a word.

After Abe had disappeared out the back door, Dat cleared his throat, as though to request their attention. When Leah turned to look, he said, "I want to talk about whatever is goin' on with Jake and Jonas Mast."

The direct reference to her beau took Leah momentarily off guard, but she quickly composed herself. "I've heard nothin' from Jonas, if that's what you mean. But I'd think he'll fill me in soon."

"Seems Jake was not only asked to leave his father's house but also told never to return," Dat said, as if he somehow knew firsthand.

She wanted to ask where he'd heard such a thing but waited to speak, not wishing to interrupt her father's pattern of thought.

Dat continued. "I have a mind to go over there to Eli's and see what's what." He shook his head. "Truth be told, it's bothered me no end this rift 'tween Peter and me. Ain't right." He paused. "All these years, well, it's just a shame."

"I think I know why Cousin Peter would send Jake away," Leah offered softly, motioning to include Sadie in the conversation.

"Jah, we both know," Sadie spoke up. "It's time to open the floodgates, I daresay."

Sadie's right. The secret's as good as out, Leah thought. *No point pretending otherwise.*

Sadie's voice remained at a whisper as she shared with their father the truth about Jake Mast, his own grandson.

When at last she had revealed every jot and tittle, Dat rose swiftly from his chair. His paper shook as he attempted to fold it, but he gave up struggling to do so and pushed the whole bunch of it onto the table. "I'm mighty shocked at this news. You mean to tell me I have a grandson I've never known?" He inhaled loudly. "Sadie, your son is alive?"

"Jah, Dat . . . 'tis quite true." Sadie's eyes were bright with tears.

Leah spoke up. "We should have told you

earlier, but —"

"Jah, you should've," Dat muttered, and Leah looked down at the floor, ashamed. "But what's done is done. And . . . it's best to leave every part of this in God's hands. He alone knows the end from the beginning."

Leah and Sadie nodded respectfully.

It was obvious how shaken their father was. He wandered through the kitchen and mutely came back to sit down as if the shocking news had impaired his ability to speak his mind.

The room was still as stone until he smiled. "Well, now, ain't it something? This might be precisely what we Ebersols and Masts need to bring us all together again."

Before either Leah or Sadie could respond, he headed outside for the barn, leaving much changed.

Leah rushed to Sadie's side and squeezed her but good. "You heard him, didn't ya? Your son — your Jake — might just be the one to cross the chasm of years."

Sadie bobbed her head slowly, apparently awestruck at the idea. "Well, ya know, Mamma always said, 'the tarter the apple, the tastier the cider.' "

To this both sisters burst into laughter. When Leah had wiped her face of bittersweet tears, she returned to her baking, adding the icing to the apple betty while it was still warm.

With nearly a week having passed since he and Jake took up residence with bighearted Eli, Jonas was quite eager to see Leah again. He sat down at the desk Eli had made years before and wrote a brief note, asking if he might visit her soon. He was reasonably sure the grapevine had begun to spread its creepers and Leah might already have heard of his and Jake's relocation.

Jonas had been mulling over what part, if any, Leah might have played in keeping the doctor's and Sadie's secret, at times even feeling the immediate need to ask her straight out why she hadn't shared with him her possible knowledge of Jake's roots. He recalled having asked Leah what had prompted Lydiann to write a letter breaking things off with Jake for seemingly no reason, yet Leah had remained silent on the matter that night, giving no indication of what was to come.

Now, if only she might be able to see him Saturday evening, it wouldn't be long before he and his darling would be able to clear the air on the matter, the Lord willing.

■ ■ ■ ■

One week to the day following his visit to
Dr. Schwartz's office, Jake received a letter
from Mandie.

Dear Jake,
How are you? I simply had to write!
Mamma told me the sad news a few
days ago, though I can hardly believe it.
How is it possible you and I aren't twins
or even brother and sister? I've cried
myself to sleep and gone through the
motions of my days as if in a nightmare.
This has to be the worst thing that could
ever befall me — a cruel joke.
In case you don't know it already,
you'll always be my brother, no matter
what. How can anyone change the fact
we grew up picking apples in the orchard
together, sledding down the steep hill in
winter, playing volleyball, husking corn
— all of that? Except for those long
months you were in Ohio, we've shared
all our lives so far together.
I know where you're living, because
Jonas has written to both Dat and
Mamma twice already. I wish I didn't
have to bear the pain in our parents'

eyes, especially Mamma's. Dat isn't himself, either. I can tell he's as upset as the rest of us, yet he is as stubborn as any man I know. Sending you away can't have made it easier on him.

And you, dear Jake? How on earth must you be feeling?

I hope you'll write to me and say what you're thinking these days. Will you go and see your first mother sometime? I would if I were you. Jonas will go along, maybe. He's the perfect choice for a visit to the Ebersols, seems to me.

With love — and I miss you something awful,

Your twin sister (in heart),
Mandie Mast

Jake handed the letter to Jonas, who was outside working on the shed behind Eli's house. "Read this when you have the chance." He turned away, not wanting to stand there and see the hurt on Jonas's face. He had already pictured Mandie's red and swollen eyes — Mamma's, too.

His *poor* mother, innocent as a daylily — what terrible things must be going through her mind! He longed to console her, to reassure her things would soon return to normal. Yet he wondered if that was even true, so topsy-turvy his life had become.

Mingled with grief over the doctor's deplorable deed, the misery of breaking up with the only girl he'd ever loved, and the loss of his family was the budding realization that eventually he must seek out Sadie Ebersol. Mandie was right that he needed to meet her: A few short minutes on market day were never going to be enough.

Leah was not one to jump too hastily to conclusions, but when a letter from Jonas arrived in the mailbox with her name clearly written on it, she assumed this was the word she had been awaiting. Opening the envelope out in the barn, high in the haymow, she discovered quickly that he wanted to see her again, "to talk."

There was no question in her mind that Jonas was out of sorts with her, because there was little else written, except a single comment about the weather having been awful cold — enough that he felt he should come for her in a borrowed, enclosed buggy.

Leah wished again that she and Sadie might have handled Jake and Lyddie's courtship differently. Dr. Schwartz must surely be thinking along similar lines where Jake was concerned, and she'd heard from Lorraine they were planning a rather long getaway overseas. *I'm not surprised he desires an escape,* she thought, assuming the doctor's conscience must be gnawing away at him.

Thinking back to Jonas, she realized he now deserved to hear her side of the story — with Sadie's permission, of course. Such a thorny problem all of this was. And would Jonas react like Lydiann, who, since hearing the truth, had been quite cold toward her? The detached state of affairs between her and her girl tore at her heart, but what could she do now?

Weary of secret keeping, Leah felt like calling for a meeting of the People to get the news completely out in the open as quickly as possible.

She rose from the corner of the hayloft, where she'd sat on the window ledge, and stumbled over a burlap bag covered with straw. When she opened it and looked inside, she was astonished. It was half filled with rat tails! *Proof of Abe's recent pest hunt triumph.* The discovery brought both a small smile to her face and a bit of trepidation to her heart. She would continue to pray for Abe's safety, since it seemed he was bent more on satisfying his curiosity than using his head. *He's all boy, that one.*

With the hope of marrying Jonas a year

from now, once he was past his Proving, Leah wondered how both Lyddie and Abe would manage without her here in Dat's house. She had considered asking Jonas his opinion on the matter but hadn't brought it up just yet, recalling the stumbling block the question of Mamma's children had been for Gid so long ago.

Yet, now that she thought on it, she supposed she *had* indeed followed through on her loving promise to Mamma. With Dat remarried and Sadie living next door in the Dawdi Haus, surely Leah would be free to marry her dearest love.

CHAPTER
TWENTY-TWO

Abram preferred the sounds in his house to fade to nothing come eight o'clock or so of an evening. He welcomed the tranquility and thought about making ready to retire for the night, but before doing so, he went and knocked on the neighboring door between the big house and the smaller one.

Grateful that Sadie was still up and dressed, he asked if he might come in and talk a bit.

"Why sure." Sadie took a seat after offering him one.

He brought up the weather and the numerous weddings coming fast and furious all this month, as many as fifteen on the same day. Then, at last, what he really wanted to say — the question foremost in his thoughts — came out. "Well, daughter, just how are you doin' with all that's swirlin' round you these days?"

Her lips broke into a gentle smile. "Findin'

out Jake's my very own?"

"Jah, that's what I'm meanin' to ask."

"Honestly, I'm as delighted as ever I've been. Jake's the grown baby son I thought I'd lost, and now he knows it. Jah, I'm right fine with that." She stopped for a moment and then continued, saying she was hoping — "even prayin' " — she might have a chance to get to know him one day.

Abram nodded, unable to stop looking at her lovely face, so peaceful she seemed. They talked quietly of all that had transpired since her return as a widow, until Sadie's yawns became so frequent he took them as a signal that he, too, ought to call it a night. "Well, s'pose I'll be seein' you at the breakfast table, first thing tomorrow, ain't?"

She stood when he got up from his chair and followed him to the doorway. "Denki, Dat . . . talking with me 'bout this means a lot."

Abram wasn't too much on fussing with compliments or niceties — he left that for the women folk. "Good night, then," he said before taking leave of his eldest.

Making his way up the staircase in the main house, he headed toward the spacious room he shared with Lizzie. His wife was already propped up in bed with pillows, wearing her long cotton nightgown, hair brushed out and hanging gracefully past her shoulders.

He slipped on his pajamas quickly and hurried to her side, reaching for the covers and top quilt before bringing up the subject still on his mind. "I shouldn't be sayin' this to you, prob'ly, particularly not at night . . . before fallin' asleep 'n' all."

She reached over and brushed his hair from his face. "What's on your mind, dear?"

"Seems we've got ourselves a grandson we didn't even know existed." He began to share with her the news of Jake Mast's true identity, telling all he understood about the situation.

"Ach, Abram . . ."

"Quite surprising, ain't it?"

"Oh, but how's our Sadie with all of this?"

"Chickens come home to roost, I daresay." He chuckled softly.

Lizzie nodded her head. "I of all people should know this. We're so blessed, *all* of us, with Leah's precious life. Seems the Good Lord can turn a sad and traumatic circumstance into something exceptionally beautiful, just as He promises. I don't see why it can't be the same for Sadie and Jake — over time, of course," she concluded.

"I would think they'd both want to get acquainted," Abram agreed.

"Hopefully, for Sadie's sake, they will." Lizzie squeezed his hand. "If she's anything like me, she'll be holdin' her breath for the day she and Jake can sit down together and talk. I pray, too, that Jake will forgive Dr. Schwartz for keepin' him from his rightful mother. Such a grievous thing."

Abram pondered his wife's tenderhearted words. "As the Scripture says, 'Judge not, and ye shall not be judged: condemn not, and ye shall not be condemned: forgive, and ye shall be forgiven. . . .' " Leaning over, he planted a lingering kiss on her cheek.

They talked for a while longer about what this revelation meant to them and to their family . . . and, eventually, all of the People. At last, too weary to continue, Abram put out the lantern and held Lizzie close till they both fell asleep.

Leah felt her heart in her throat as she waited at the end of the long lane for Jonas to arrive Saturday night. She purposely had come a bit early, knowing she might need time out here on the road to gather her wits before she saw him again. Except for after Preaching service, she had not been alone with him since his unexpected nighttime visit on behalf of poor, pining Jake.

Waiting in the cold, the darkness seemed

to envelop her as she looked toward the vast woods, fixing her gaze on the amber blush of windows — Gid and Hannah's log house. The blackness of the forest seemed exceptionally menacing tonight, and she shivered, turning to face the road.

Oh, Jonas, please understand. . . .

She heard a horse and carriage coming and braced herself, tightly winding her woolen scarf around the collar of her long winter coat.

Jonas halted the horse after making a slight turn into the drive to the house, and he rushed to her side. "Hullo, Leah. An awful brisk evening, jah?"

"*Wie geht's,* Jonas," she replied. "Wouldn't surprise me if it snows."

He admitted to expecting the same. "The air hangs heavy, ain't?" He helped her into the carriage and walked around to hop in on the opposite side, offering her the heavy lap robe as soon as he sat down.

She was aware of its warmth, Jonas having covered himself with it as he'd driven here. "Denki," she said softly, struggling already with tears that threatened to spill.

She was thankful he did not immediately bring up the topic of Jake, although she felt terribly tense awaiting it. They made small talk for a while and then Jonas asked,

"How's everyone at your house?"

"Oh, 'bout the same," she replied, pausing a moment before forging ahead. "Except for Sadie, who's on edge since . . . since . . ." She couldn't go on.

Jonas finished for her. "Since Jake discovered the truth 'bout who she is to him?"

She sighed, her hands clasped beneath the lap robe. "Jah," she said simply.

"Were you ever going to tell me?" he asked, his words gentle but probing. "Surely you've known longer than Jake."

" 'Tis as you say. Honestly . . . Sadie and I, we didn't think it through. When we found out last summer, we decided it should be kept quiet." She could scarcely go on.

"Seems unfair to Jake, considerin' his strong feelings for Lydiann."

She nodded. Her face felt numb, even frozen, not so much from the cold but from the pressure she endured within. "We didn't intend to cause him pain. Sadie wanted to get to know her son, but it was I who argued with her, wanting to spare your family all the pain they're goin' through now. In so doin', I hurt Sadie and everyone else."

Jonas fell silent for a time. When he spoke again, his voice was almost too low to hear. "You meant well. I can see that."

Leah felt like crying again. "But we should've told the truth right when we knew it was Sadie's son who was courtin' Lyddie," she said, adding, "I'm sure your parents and Jake must be havin' a terrible time."

"Terrible's one word for it," he said. "But sooner or later, if things had kept on, they likely would have suffered learnin' the truth. Placing Jake with them was Dr. Schwartz's doin', not yours."

"True . . . though, actually, Jake was sent to Ohio because of Sadie and me, because I confided in Gid what we knew 'bout Jake's courtin' Lydiann. Oh, Jonas, we were so terribly worried they might fall in love and want to marry."

They rode for a time without saying more, and finally, when they reached the edge of Gobbler's Knob, before the road wound down the long hill toward Grasshopper Level, Jonas pulled off, heading north a ways. This being a less-traveled road, she wondered if he might find a place to stop, but he didn't, and she was relieved.

Some time later, he turned to her. His eyes searched hers, and his slow and kind smile made her wonder, *Has he forgiven me?*

Lightly he covered her gloved hand with

his own. "I have to say one more thing, love."

She held her breath, listening intently.

"If Jake hadn't been sent away to Ohio, I never would've had the chance to meet him, and you and I would still be separated by hundreds of miles."

Leah swallowed hard. "Oh, Jonas, I'm awful sorry I didn't tell you the night when ya came inquirin' about Jake and Lyddie. So many things were goin' through my mind." She stopped to catch her breath, longing to be in his arms once again.

"You mustn't blame yourself." Then, as if reading her mind, he reached for her, gathering her into his welcoming embrace. "We'll muddle through what's ahead, helpin' Jake all we can. We'll pray, too, for a healing 'tween our families, ain't?"

To this Leah agreed wholeheartedly, glad they'd had this frank talk after all.

Jonas veered the horse around and headed back to the Ebersol Cottage, while Leah continued to ponder.

CHAPTER
TWENTY-THREE

Monday, December 9

Dear Diary,
Today I had to string up a line in the kitchen to dry the washing because of the sleet making down outside. Not sure how many days we'll have like this, seeing as how winter's arrived early in Gobbler's Knob.

The cold, wet weather draws our little family round the wood stove every night now. Gid reads from his big Bible and talks to the girls about Old Testament stories, taking time to read from the New Testament, as well — sometimes even reciting nearly a whole chapter from memory before sharing his thoughts on various verses. Ever so strange this is, but I've kept my lips closed. It's painfully clear that some of what Gid's been teaching us will contradict what happened yesterday, following the common meal after Preaching. That's when Zachariah and his wife came over to me and whispered that I've been chosen to receive the healing gift by the laying on of hands. I must either dismiss this and never say a word to my husband or accept it as God's will for me and keep mum.

I'm in something of a quandary, because I know Gid would be mighty upset if I went ahead without his blessing. Still, I am tempted to follow through, with the hope he might someday come to see things the way I do . . . and the way his own father does. But though I long for the gift Zachariah Henner is eager to pass on to me, accepting it would be disobedient. Yet how will I ever overcome my depression without such power?

At least the wee one within me is active, kicking hard at times. I am greatly relieved to feel as strong in body as ever I did with both Ida Mae and Katie Ann. Come April, there will be another little Peachey in this house. I do hope it's a boy, and so does Mary Ruth. She said as much when she and Robert came with their own darling bundle for supper at our house recently. Gid was ever so good to allow my dear sister and me to go off by ourselves awhile to talk quietly, even if "the love of the Lord Jesus" was nearly all Mary Ruth wanted to chat about. All the same, I feel so happy to have Mary Ruth smack-dab in the middle of my home — and life — again.

Respectfully,
Hannah

No matter where he happened to be when the first snow of the season flew, Jonas was immediately called back to his boyhood, when he would watch the timid flecks' descent through the pallid sky from the wide windows of the milk house or barn. And as winds stirred the tops of trees — a sudden and steady squall out of the north — falling snow would soon become a flurry of white, making the view of his father's farmhouse murky.

This day and the heavy snow it brought reminded him of some of the worst blizzards ever to hit Lancaster County. But when his youngest sister showed up at Eli's in Dat's open market wagon, he felt certain something more terrible than a snowstorm was threatening his family's orchard house.

"Come in from the cold!" He held open the back door as Mandie hurried inside.

"Ach, you best be returnin' home with me, Jonas . . . something's wrong with Mamma," she cried, her distress plain on her face. "She's up in bed, sobbin' her eyes out."

"Sit down and talk more slowly," he said, glad that, at least for the moment, Jake was out in the shed with Eli. "Take a deep breath and begin again."

She placed her hand on her chest. " 'Tween you and me, Jonas, I heard Dat and Mamma quarreling somethin' awful early this morning . . . over Jake and, well . . . all of that."

"What happened?"

"Mamma was sayin' it was wicked to send a boy away they'd raised as their own, 'don't matter the circumstances.' " Mandie wiped a tear from her cheek. "But Dat said this is all 'bout trickery, and there's no getting round it. Jake simply doesn't belong to us, and what's more, he's one of Abram Ebersol's grandchildren . . . and that's that."

She stopped to dab her eyes with a handkerchief. "Mamma's beside herself missin' Jake, but Dat's standin' firm on his decision." She hiccupped twice. "I'm scared

Mamma's gonna be sick over this . . . I fear she is already."

"What're ya sayin', Mandie?"

"She's got herself an awful cough and a fever, and I've heard tell of folk comin' down with a bad flu when, well . . ."

"I understand." He recalled his own emotional upheavals following his loss of Leah years back. "Do ya want me to try talkin' to Dat, maybe?"

"No need for that now," she replied. "Dat left after breakfast . . . said he was goin' down to the Beilers' farm auction."

"Jah, I went for a time myself but don't recall seein' him there."

"Well, that's where he was headin' hours and hours ago."

He sat down next to Mandie on the kitchen bench.

"Oh, this is just horrid!" She was wailing now, and he put his arm around her shoulder.

"You mustn't take this on yourself, sister . . . ya just can't."

"But what can be done?" She raised her head and looked at him. "Dr. Schwartz's switchin' babies has touched each of us, and I don't see how we'll ever get over it."

"The Lord God sees this here mess from on high." He patted her arm and led her to the sink, where she flung cold water on her tear-streaked face. "I daresay we oughta be prayin', beseeching God for His mercy on us all," he said.

Mandie turned around and stared at him. "I want my twin brother back, is what I want. What can God do about that?" With this she headed for the front room and stood at the window for a while, still weeping.

Jonas refused to interfere with what he hoped was a silent prayer for Mamma, Dat, and Jake. He went to the utility room and pulled on his boots, pushing down his old black felt hat on his head. Soon he heard Mandie's footsteps coming his way. "I'll follow ya home," he said, "and I'll try to console Mamma . . . and help with milkin', too."

"Denki." She gave him a little smile and threw her woolen scarf around her neck.

Jonas didn't bother to take the time to tell either Jake or Eli where he was headed. "Let's get goin', then."

By suppertime temperatures had fallen at least fifteen degrees, and the cold seeped into Jonas's bones as he finished carrying the milk cans to the milk house. He, along with Mandie, had looked in on Mamma, who was still upstairs in bed, sound asleep, completely exhausted from having wept much too long, Jonas guessed. Mandie had placed a hand on Mamma's forehead and was convinced her fever, if she'd had one, was nearly gone.

Mandie made him a supper of corn chowder and corn bread, also setting out a variety of jams and his favorite apple butter, too. He was grateful to sit down at the large family table and warm up a bit before his ride back to Eli's. "I'm sure Dat will be home before it's too dark," he said.

"What if he doesn't return?" Her eyes began to glisten again.

"Dat isn't one to shirk his duty," Jonas offered. "I could go lookin' for him if you're worried."

"No, he'll come back when he, well . . . gets here."

Jonas frowned, studying her. "Has he done this before?"

With what seemed to be grave reluctance on her part, she nodded her head. "Dat's got himself a weakness for moonshine," she whispered. "It's caused Mamma her share of sadness. He started drinkin' after he sent Jake off to Ohio . . . once he learned another son was in love with an Ebersol girl. The news must've opened some old wounds."

Jonas had never known his father to have trouble with alcohol and found Mandie's point of view to be quite perceptive for her age. Then again, she had lived here in this house for all the years of his absence. Since his return home, he had occasionally suspected such of his father, but he'd hoped he was wrong.

"The hate Dat carries for the Ebersols has been eatin' away at him, I think. He gets miserable 'bout how he's treated Mamma's cousins; then he goes and drinks."

"Where, though? Where does he go?"

"Who's to know, but there *are* plenty-a male cousins who like to imbibe. Our bishop might not know this, but it's quite true."

He thought on this and realized where his father might possibly go to guzzle liquor — Dat's Amish doctor friend, Zachariah Henner. The man was some years younger but had a keenness for spirits, both whiskey and otherwise — Dat himself had told Jonas as much. Perhaps strong drink was the reason for the rumors that Zachariah was linked to white witchcraft, as some in the area referred to Henner's powwowing. "I'm sure Dat will be home, and soon," said Jonas.

Mandie thanked him repeatedly for helping with the milking and for sitting down to supper with her. "You don't know how much I appreciate it." She walked him to the back door and out to the horse and carriage.

"Will you be all right?" he asked. "Or do ya want me to stay till Dat returns?"

Mandie shook her head. "It's fine, really. But he'll be mean as ever. Mamma and I have learned to keep to ourselves till he sleeps the stupor away," she confided in a near whisper.

Jonas's heart ached to hear of the dark times his mother and sister suffered. "I'll check on you and Mamma tomorrow at dawn."

Mandie's lower lip quivered. "Ach . . . Jonas. What on earth did we ever do before you moved home?"

"Now, let's not be thinkin' backward, jah?" He leaned down and kissed the top of her head. "Go be with Mamma. When she wakes up, tell her I love her."

She bobbed her head in agreement, and Jonas clumped out to his cold horse and now-white carriage through the ankle-deep snow, concern for his family bending him low.

Jonas found Eli in the kitchen with Jake, both men cleaning up the supper dishes in total silence. He was especially grateful for Eli's reading of God's Word as the three of them gathered near the wood stove afterward. When Eli closed the Bible and bowed for a silent prayer, Jonas prayed for his father, who was out somewhere in the bitter cold, possibly traveling home intoxicated. He also prayed for both Mamma and Mandie, so vulnerable there at home alone.

Later, when Jake had gone upstairs to bed, Jonas began reminiscing with Eli about a few mutual friends in Ohio, as well as his memories of joyous Sunday-go-to-meetings. "I admit to missin' the brethren in Apple Creek, too," he said. "And what a man of the Word our bishop was . . . studied it like he might kick the bucket tomorrow, he was that spiritually hungry."

Eli pulled on his wiry, thick beard. "Jah, I'd have to agree on that — missin' solid preaching, and all." He went on to relate one of the more lively discussions on Scripture he and several of the ministers had enjoyed, "not too long before I joined up with the group of men to be swapped with those from here."

"You must've been eager to marry again, deciding to do such a thing — leaving your home 'n' all."

"I'd hate to go through the rest of my life

without a wife." Eli paused, squinting his eyes. "I miss Nancy Mae a whole lot, and if I can be so blunt, the nights can be awful long at times."

"What caused your wife's death?"

"Leukemia . . . it took her mighty fast, which was a blessing, really. She didn't suffer like some."

"This life can be full up with misery." Jonas reflected on the trial this good man had endured. "But it makes us mighty anxious for the next, ain't so?"

To this Eli nodded emphatically, and Jonas felt a growing fondness for the ruddy-faced widower. The woman who would become his new bride would be blessed indeed.

CHAPTER
TWENTY-FOUR

Saturday dawned with a stony sky and icy showers of rain mixed with snow. In spite of the dismal day, Lydiann volunteered to run an errand to Georgetown for Leah and Aunt Lizzie — anything to get out of the house and breathe the brisk morning air to clear her head. It had been nearly three weeks since her encounter with Jake at the singing, and she'd not heard from him since.

Just as well. No sensible reason to hang on to a love that was never meant to be. She was actually looking forward again to attending singings and seeing old friends and making new ones. More than ever before, she needed the social connection with other courting-age young people, and she recognized that she was beginning to slowly make a turn in her mind — and in her heart. Even though her soul felt void of hopefulness as far as romantic attachments were concerned, she knew she must go ahead somehow with her life. And stopping in to visit with cheery Mary Ruth and her pretty baby was one way to do so.

While they sat visiting in Mary Ruth's cozy house, Lydiann laid eyes on the first real piece of evidence that her former school chum Carl Nolt *did* want to get to know her better. The proof came in the form of a handwritten invitation sent to Mary Ruth, who said she'd been wishing Lydiann might drop by to see her.

"He sent it here?" She found this curious and for a moment felt her cheeks warm with the knowledge. A quick scan of the short note left her secretly pleased — Carl was asking her to consider going with him to a church activity, a get-together on the Saturday evening following Christmas.

When Lydiann revealed to her sister what he'd written, Mary Ruth wore a fine smile. "Well, why don't you go? You might have the best time."

"Just why do ya think that, sister?"

"He's a wonderful boy, and the two of you used to have such a good friendship. One evening with him and his friends is nothing serious, mind you."

Sipping her warm tea sweetened with raw honey, Lydiann listened as Mary Ruth continued to sing Carl's praises, finding it a bit amusing. Still, if she were forthright with her sister, she would tell her not to hold her breath on this invitation. Lydiann would not be accepting, because she was not at all ready to forge a new relationship, old friends notwithstanding.

In the heart of the ancient town of Florence, Henry and Lorraine Schwartz had come across a picturesque restaurant with only a half dozen tables visible through its windows. The menu posted outside the door boasted of several courses of superb Italian dishes, pasta a staple with each meal.

"What do you say, dear? Shall we?" Henry asked, hoping his wife might agree, so appealing was the tiny place set back on the narrow, winding street tucked between rows of Gothic-style buildings.

"Why, it's just delightful." Lorraine was obviously pleased, and he was relieved.

They made their way inside, the smiling hostess ushering them to a table for two near an inviting fire. *"Buon appetito!"*

Enjoy the meal, the woman had just said, but Henry could not imagine it. Not unless he changed his mind and did not reveal his long-held secret to his wife as planned. Despite their charming surroundings, at the present he was feeling rather wretched, knowing their vacation was drawing to a possibly disastrous close.

Wine bottles of every conceivable vintage and from every region perched on shelves above a narrow mirror encircling the room just above the chair rail. His gaze caught the reflected glints of candlelight from each table, like miniature echoes in the mirror. *Haunting reverberations of the past* . . .

After he had ordered for both his wife and himself, Henry sat straight as a board in his chair, eyes fixed on Lorraine. She looked particularly lovely in her favorite ruby red two-piece day dress as she sat smiling across the linen tablecloth. He inhaled deeply. "I've been wanting to tell you about Derek's illegitimate son for quite some time."

Lorraine frowned. "Beg your pardon?"

The plunge taken, he returned to the beginning of the story, recounting Leah Ebersol's frantic knocking at their door, followed by the delivery of their very own grandson — apparently stillborn. That is, until a miracle occurred. . . .

Lorraine listened quietly, her composure seemingly intact, even though the shock of his tale was registered in the seriousness of her expression. When he had finished, she leaned forward and, instead of censuring him as he thoroughly deserved, said, "I never forgot the sight of that forlorn Plain girl sitting out on the porch steps, waiting for Derek."

He nodded. Neither had he.

"Ah, Henry . . . you know, I always suspected Derek had an ulterior motive for enlisting in the army the minute he turned eighteen."

Woman's intuition, he thought. Evidently Lorraine had sensed something amiss on a subconscious level all this time. He said, "I'm sure you've seen Jake Mast coming with Fannie and his twin sister, Mandie, for annual checkups and such."

"Maybe so," she replied, still remarkably composed.

She inquired about his reason for giving baby Jake to the Masts instead of revealing the sad truth that their son was stillborn. He struggled to explain his thoughts that night, his panicked decisions, until finally she reached across the table and covered his hand with her own. "I wish you had confided in me. Perhaps between the two of us, we might have come up with a more satisfactory solution. One that might have had poor Sadie's blessing."

Again he nodded, ashamed by her calm reaction. Why *hadn't* he sought the advice of his sensible wife? Sadie could have been told the truth and spared much heartache, and she might have desired to raise her baby. Or perhaps a legal adoption could have been arranged, such as the one Henry had made on behalf of a young patient who'd also found herself in the family way around the same time. That baby had ultimately been placed with their close neighbors, Dan and Dottie Nolt.

"You crossed the line, Henry," she said softly, her gaze on their entwined fingers. With a look of sudden concern, she raised her eyes to meet his. "Might you be arrested for this?"

"It's a worry, yes," he admitted, sorry to have put his wife in such a dreadful position.

Lorraine squeezed his hand and glanced away, and when the waiter came around with the first course, Lorraine shrugged as if unwilling to continue further discussion.

Henry sighed. Though years too late, he had at last apprised his wife of the truth.

Even if she forgave him, he knew the worst remained ahead. He must live each day unaware of what the present, or the future, might hold. And if word of his offense reached the ears of the wrong people . . . *Or the right people,* he thought sorrowfully.

He shuddered, attempting to dismiss his

fears. Having just toured the Cathedral of Santa Maria del Fiore and seen with his own eyes the awe-inspiring genius of Michelangelo, he would have much preferred to pretend the problems he'd created at home did not exist. There would be plenty of time to contemplate the disturbing prospects in Gobbler's Knob upon his return.

Jonas and Gid worked closely in the blacksmith shop, Jonas paying careful attention to Gid's patient instruction on shoeing a horse. He watched as Gid pulled each horse's leg up through his own and held it clamped between his knees. Jonas was fairly sure that if he could prove himself a reliable worker, he might be asked to continue his temporary employment here, because Tomato Joe was too busy with the work of farming and butchering to attend to all the steady blacksmithing help his father-in-law required.

Jonas kept the bellows going steadily, all the while observing even the smallest details of the trade as, one by one, the horses came through. As he did, he wondered how things were at his father's house at this hour. When he'd returned to visit with Mandie and Mamma earlier this morning, he had encountered his father, whose bloodshot eyes and overall rumpled appearance confirmed Mandie's suspicions. Jonas did not ask where Dat had disappeared to the day before, but Mandie whispered that he had indeed stumbled into the house awful late, quite *gsoffe* — drunk — at that.

His drinking surely feeds his animosity toward Abram, thought Jonas. On this he could only speculate, but the fact remained that Dat had a serious problem in his inability to forgive and accept Abram and his family, as well as in his obvious need to drown his troubles in alcohol.

I wish I could help somehow, Jonas thought, wondering, too, how long before his father might come to realize he *must* receive Jake back into the fold of his household. But if or when that might take place, Jonas had no way of knowing. After all, Dat's rift with Abram and his family had dragged on for nearly two decades.

The day was almost indistinct from all the others Sadie had spent doing heavy cleaning for Dorcas — this time the family was preparing for out-of-town company from Berlin, Ohio. Cousins on Tomato Joe's mother's side were coming in by train on Monday; a Mennonite driver would meet them at the station. Since Dorcas hadn't been feeling well, Sadie had volunteered to help redd up, even going so far as to wash down walls and mopboards and cook ahead several meals.

Weary now, Sadie picked her way through the snow and ice on the shoulder of the main road, always on the watch for horses and sleighs or buggies, a number of which were certainly out this Saturday night before a no-church Sunday tomorrow.

She kept a steady pace, her thoughts on her son and what he might be dealing with. What she wouldn't give to hear his voice again, to see him! A nagging worry skittered through her mind, and she feared Jake might up and return to Ohio, never to be heard from again. If so, she would not have the chance to know him at all.

Several horse-drawn sleighs passed by, each carrying young courting couples. She tried not to let the pain of wishing show on her face . . . the *we* of them and the loneliness of herself. The trees ahead stood black and shadowy against the steadily falling snow as she plodded along, one heavy foot following the other.

She whispered to heaven, petitioning the Lord not so much for her own happiness as for Jake's. *Let him someday know not only my love but the acceptance of those who raised him, as well.* A lump rose in her throat and she found herself fighting back tears.

Just then, like a distant echo in the darkness, she heard a man call her name. "Sadie?"

She did not turn to look because she thought she might be daydreaming. Was this the memory of her precious son's voice? Was it her mind playing tricks, as it had so long ago?

"Is that you, Sadie?" This time the call came more urgently.

She turned to see a slow-moving enclosed buggy with two people inside.

Eli Yoder? She squinted to see through the snow. The driver was indeed the handsome widower.

"Hullo?" she returned, hoping her voice might carry to where he held the reins.

"Care for a ride?" Eli asked as the carriage all but stopped right where she stood, trembling with cold and with the awareness that not only was Eli offering her a ride when the Ebersol Cottage was not so far away, but Ella Jane Peachey was sitting there next to him, prim and proper.

What an odd thing for him to do, she thought, but she found herself accepting and saying, "Denki," before she thought over what on earth she truly ought to say.

Eli hopped down and came around to help her to the left side of the carriage, lending his hand. Her heart sped up as she placed her own gloved hand in his, suddenly very aware of his attentiveness to her.

Eli stood outside the buggy, waiting for her to get settled into the seat next to his date. He made a quiet comment about Sadie's remembering Ella Jane, and with that went back around to the right side to climb in and move them forward.

Sitting there, Sadie wondered why she'd said yes to the ride. But no, she knew all too well. She had hardly dared dream such a thing might happen, assuming she'd already had her share of male attention during her lifetime.

She found it painfully humorous that Eli should proffer a ride, no doubt prompting as much uneasiness on Ella Jane's part as excitement on hers. Yet Eli was obviously interested in spending the evening with Ella Jane. *Eli and Ella . . . won't the People get their tongues tied if they marry?* She smiled at her foolish thought, rejecting it just as quickly; she must be respectful, even in her private thoughts.

When Eli directed the horse to turn right onto her father's long lane, piled high with snow, she wondered what she ought to say when the carriage came to a halt. How far would Eli bid his horse to go?

"There we are, now," he said, bringing the mare right up to the shoveled walkway that led to the back door. He stepped down to come around and help her out, standing for a moment at the end of the walk as she managed to extend her thanks before turning to make her way toward the door.

All the while, her heart continued its euphoric new rhythm, and she wondered what Ella Jane must be thinking . . . or feeling.

CHAPTER
TWENTY-FIVE

Tuesday, December 17, saw the return of Henry and Lorraine from their ten-day excursion. Tired from their long flights, they unpacked and ate supper, scarcely speaking a word to each other. Both retired to bed before twilight, relatively disoriented from having traveled through several time zones.

Henry was unable to immediately fall asleep, however, again recalling the calm nature of his wife's reaction to the news of Derek's son. Henry had been completely astounded when he realized she was not at all condemning or taken aback by the revelation. *Lorraine's so much more than I imagined her to be.*

Nodding off at last, he gave in to a fitful slumber. His dreams had him lost in a cornfield maze, the distorted stalks taking on the shape of Amishmen who whispered accusations as he attempted to find his way out. With no exit in sight, Henry fell and landed on the ground, his hands pressing deep into a freshly dug grave.

Sadie wasted not a speck of time worrying how Ella Jane Peachey might feel if she knew Eli Yoder had sent the letter Sadie was reading this minute. *He wants to see me again . . . alone!*

Though she was torn on whether to share the exciting news with Leah, Sadie felt it best not to respond too quickly to Eli's invitation. For her own sake, he must not think of her as overly hasty in replying, but rather she would take several days before she wrote a polite answer. This meant the earliest she would be riding with him again would be the Saturday after Christmas, a day that now felt an eternity away. *All in God's timing,* she told herself, most joyful at this unexpected turn of events.

Ascending to her bedroom, she removed her head covering and each of the hairpins holding her bun to let down her hair, so long she could sit on it. *Am I still pretty enough to be courted?* She began to brush her hair, counting the strokes as she and Leah often had as youngsters.

When she finished, she sat on the bed and purposed in her heart not to get her hopes too high about Eli, although she knew she already was in danger of exactly that.

Breathing a prayer for guidance, she rose and went to the dresser. The small hand mirror lay on top, and she reached for it, holding it up to her face. "I will not let pride get in the way of God's will," she whispered to her reflection. "I will follow Leah's path . . . askin' for the blessing of the Lord."

No matter what happens. . . .

That Wednesday Lydiann made five loaves of bread — including two for Dorcas Zook and her family, and one for Hannah's — never once uttering a word to Mamma Leah all morning, although she truly wanted to. She longed to tell Mamma of her visit with Mary Ruth and of feeling a twinge of enthusiasm for Carl's invitation, even though she'd declined it. But an impenetrable wall prevented her from saying what was on her heart, as if her disappointment and aggravation at not having been told sooner of Jake's connection to Sadie kept her from saying anything now.

All that aside, Lydiann busied herself in her work, recalling how delighted she'd felt while little Ruthie lay in her arms, aware of the stirrings within her heart toward her beautiful niece. It was then the terrible truth struck her that Jake Mast was as directly related to her as was darling Ruthie.

Shuddering, she was more than relieved Jake had not contacted her again. Glad, too, that he must be settling into his own awareness of their kinship . . . and realizing there were many other girls to pick from at singings and other social gatherings.

She glanced up and caught Mamma's eye. The right words skipped through her mind, but she remained mute, simply unable to make herself say them.

"I love ya, Lyddie," Mamma said, eyes bright now with tears.

Nodding helplessly, she felt more and more ridiculous as she stood there, silently gawking.

"I best be sayin' this again, dear one. I was wrong not to tell ya right away, and I'm terribly sorry."

The dam broke inside, and a sob caught in Lydiann's throat as she flung her forgiving arms around her. "Oh, Mamma. I never should've treated you so."

Jonas was grateful for the hope of steady work at smithy Peachey's blacksmithing shop, especially as Christmas was fast approaching and he had not decided what to give Leah. Having never fulfilled his promise to her of an oak sideboard for a wedding gift, he decided on that, knowing he could easily pay his weekly room and board to Eli, as well as purchase the necessary wood and stain to make Leah's keepsake. But before he took the time to gather up the materials to create the piece, he must seek out the Grasshopper Level bishop, Simon Lapp, to inform Dat's bishop about his family's potentially dangerous home situation.

The minute he completed his work for the day, he headed straightaway to the older gentleman's abode. Halting the horse in the side lane, he was surprised to see Bishop Lapp emerge from the house. "Ach, ya must come in, and quickly, Jonas. Get yourself out of this cold," the man said, greeting him. The stocky bishop apparently remembered seeing him following Jonas's return from Ohio, and Jonas was thankful to have grown up under this highly respected man's leadership.

"I won't beat round the bush," Jonas said quietly once the bishop had shooed his wife out of the kitchen. "I'm here about my father." Warming his hands by the fire, he continued on to tell about his father's recent drunken late-night return home.

The bishop acknowledged his awareness of the standoff between the Mast and Ebersol families, but he didn't indicate he knew of Dat's hankering for strong drink.

"I don't want to speak out of turn, but I'm concerned." Jonas explained some of what Mandie had observed, as well as testifying to having seen with his own eyes his father's obvious hangover. "It may be that liquor has made my father do things he might never have thought of doin' if sober, or maybe his rage and unacceptance has caused him to dull his sensibilities in drink. One way or the other, he has a problem. Actually, *all* of us do, because of it."

Bishop Lapp tugged his long, untrimmed beard. "If he drinks as much as you assume he does, I wouldn't be surprised if there's something he's tryin' to forget." He paused. "Now, Abram Ebersol, he's kin to your father, ain't so?"

"Actually, it's my mother who's the blood relation . . . to Ida, Abram's deceased wife. Abram has since married Ida's younger sister, Lizzie Brenneman."

"Ah, Lizzie . . . the name rings a bell." The bishop's ears seemed to perk up. "There was a-plenty of tittle-tattle flyin' round about this Lizzie years back, but Bishop Bontrager and I squelched it right quick . . . with some help from Abram and Ida."

Jonas knew precisely what he meant: Lizzie's pregnancy with Leah. "Well, I'm wonderin' what can be done to bring peace to the families."

"Hard to say." The bishop fell silent, folding his hands as if in prayer. Then he continued. "I'm reluctant to say this, but I've heard comments from your father that he believes one of Abram's daughters is . . . well, something of a bad seed."

Bishop Lapp was thinking of Leah, of course, because of Lizzie's sin. "He has no right to say such a thing, but, jah, I know what he thinks," Jonas replied, his neck hot. "Truth is, Leah is just the opposite of that. She's everything gut, and I hope my father might know this someday."

"Someday meaning you plan to marry the woman?" No doubt Bishop Lapp had been adequately filled in by Dat.

"I'm more than happy to say that, jah, I am." Jonas eyed him a bit suspiciously. The thought had crossed his mind on several occasions, but now that he was faced with the opportunity to pose the question, he pressed on. "Would you also happen to know anything 'bout the Proving I'm under?"

Bishop Lapp appeared grim. "Well, sadly, I believe I do. Maybe I oughtn't admit it, but there were quite a few heads put together on that. Your bishop and your father —"

"My *father*, you say?" Jonas interrupted, startled. His parents were not even members of the Gobbler's Knob church district, which he'd chosen to join as a teenager preparing to marry Leah. That his father should confer with Bishop Bontrager made not one whit of sense.

"Might be best to leave things be, then."

"Keep me in the dark, you mean?" Jonas felt terribly bold. "Please, I must know more. It's important — has been for years. The hard feelings between my father and Abram have gone on too long . . . and now the problem's even thornier." He didn't feel as if he should blurt out the news about Jake, but he'd obviously gotten the bishop's attention, for the man leaned forward now, frowning, his blue eyes intent on him.

"If you must know . . . it was your father who went to Bishop Bontrager nearly the minute after you presented yourself that first day you returned home. He was the one who put the idea of a lengthy, if not nearly endless Proving in Bontrager's mind, hoping to break your will to marry as you wished by takin' away your ability to work with wood. Naturally, that fell right into Bontrager's way of thinkin'. And now with the church membership having voted to give their approval, I'm afraid you'll have to bide your time."

Jonas was aghast. "My *father's* behind much of this?"

"You asked, and I told ya . . . a mistake, I can see now."

"But I wish to make Leah my bride next fall, which is one of the reasons why I want to see things set right between our families."

"Your father thought he could thwart your marryin' her. If you break under the demands of your Proving, you'll never be reinstated as a member and thus be unable to marry in your church district . . . separated forever from this woman." The bishop sighed loudly and shook his head. "With both your father and Bontrager in cahoots . . . well, it's a shame for you. That's what." He eyed Jonas. "Oughtn't to be this way."

Jonas understood fully for the first time what he was up against — the stern Gobbler's Knob bishop had found a like mind in Jonas's own conniving father.

Frustrated by what he had learned, Jonas attempted to put his feelings aside for the time being, as there was something else he wished to discuss with the sincere man. Putting his hands in his pockets, he pondered how he should say it. "Things being as they are, I wonder if it wouldn't help my sister and mother if you paid frequent visits to Dat . . . maybe beginning as soon as you can ride over there." As he saw it, the only clear way to prevent his father's habitual imbibing was to keep him far away from the drink that looked like water but kicked like a mule.

The bishop gave his word he'd go and see what could be done.

Jonas thanked him and hurried back to his waiting horse and carriage. The animal had more than a dusting of snow covering his mane and back. "Let's get goin'." He reached for the reins.

As he rode over the deserted, snow-packed roads, he was aware of increasing tension in his neck and jaw. *Dat and Bishop Bontrager have joined forces to keep Leah and me apart?*

He could scarcely get past Simon Lapp's words. His own father had gone behind his back, suggesting such a difficult Proving — one tailor-made to trip him up but good.

CHAPTER
TWENTY-SIX

Immediately following breakfast on Friday, once the children were sent off to school in Gid's big sleigh and the kitchen was spotless, Hannah sat quietly to write in her diary. She began by recording the weather, but try as she might, she simply could not keep her mind on it, so she headed back into the kitchen to bake a two-layer spice cake and several dozen chocolate-chip cookies.

That done, she felt lonely yet again and went to the bedroom window to peer down the hill at the Ebersol Cottage. Was Gid off working with Dat today, or perhaps Tomato Joe and Jonas Mast? She'd heard from her husband that Jonas was spending lots of time lately at the smithy's shop, helping out for pay.

If Gid's occupied for now, I'll go and visit the Henners, she decided then and there. Not daring to give it a second thought, lest she change her mind out of respect for her husband, she hurried to find her warmest coat, snow boots, and knitted mittens. She hoped she could borrow her father's enclosed buggy for the trip, having noticed from afar the horse and carriage already hitched up at the end of the mule road. Now all she must do was make her way down the long, lonesome hill through the ice and snow to the carriage.

She overheard Gid's voice in the barn when she arrived, but it was Dat who was coming out and heading toward the house with something of a limp. "Mind if I take the buggy for a little bit?" she called to him.

"Just be sure 'n' be back before dinner."

I'll be home plenty before noon, she thought, climbing into the right side of the buggy. *And if all goes well, I'll return with the healing gift.*

Having sat at the same table as Zachariah and Mary Ann, enjoying sticky buns and hot coffee for a good half hour, Hannah was eager to get on with talk of powwowing. She didn't want to seem forward, but she was curious to know exactly how the power was transferred from one person to another, and she was anxious to move ahead before she lost her resolve. Already she'd begun to feel prickles at the back of her neck — as though she was doing something wrong.

Zachariah began to speak affectionately of his grandmother and her lifelong fascination with powwowing. "She received the transfer from her elderly uncle, a bad-tempered deacon," he said with a slight chuckle. "Or so the story goes."

Mary Ann was frowning slightly, as if to say, *Don't tell all you know, Zach.*

Yet he continued. "*Mammi* Henner kept many diaries . . . hundreds of pages of 'em. Recently I looked back and discovered she

           e for healing, how
           n the table, and
           .ble it was, seein'
           hers — even local
           d her place, night

           nking of her own

           so keen on havin'
           He did not ask her
           o, but he studied

her, and the intensity of his gaze made her feel weak. It was as if his eyes spoke their own secret language, and she shivered.

He leaned forward, his elbows on the table. "You can be one of us."

The haunting words seemed to hang in the air.

"Are you ready to receive from me, Hannah Ebersol Peachey?"

Why is there such force behind his eyes? Just now she felt truly frightened — nothing like she'd expected. Maybe it was because she had always been somewhat unnerved by male Brauchdokders.

She trembled within, feeling panicky . . . even sick. The thought of Zachariah's hands touching her head or her shoulders — or whatever he had in mind to do to pass the gift to her — made her almost frantic. She'd come here for understanding and for the gift she had so respected in Old Lady Henner, only to feel as if she was being led down a long gray burrow that was closing in around her spirit.

The prayer of faith shall save the sick and the Lord shall raise him up. . . .

That Gid believed this wholeheartedly, there was no doubt in her mind. *I've gone against my husband in this. I've sinned against my dear Gid!*

"No," she whispered, barely able to utter the word. "I'm *not* ready." She rose abruptly, mumbling, "I changed my mind," and forgetting to offer her pardon for leaving the table that way.

She made a beeline to the back door, pushed it open, and headed out just as it dawned on her she'd left her wrap, scarf, gloves, and even boots indoors.

"Puh!" she said to herself, catching her breath.

At that moment she spied her husband at the end of the walkway. Gid stood with his back to his horse and sleigh, frowning in disbelief. "Hannah, what the world are ya doin' *here?*"

She nodded, acknowledging his presence, yet was incapable of speech.

Scarcely was Hannah able to make out the silhouette of Gid and his sleigh ahead on the road, the squall of snow was so dense. She followed him in Dat's enclosed buggy, thankful for the slightly warmer carriage but still suffering the sting of her shame.

She was as low as she'd ever felt in her life, defying her husband as she had. And she had no idea how Gid would go about disciplining her — surely he could do just that, being the anointed man he was.

Leah carefully topped each mug of hot cocoa with a dollop of whipped cream before carrying the tray of steaming cups over to the table. "Here we are."

291

When Lyddie spied the special treat, a full smile appeared on her face. "This looks delicious!"

"I daresay it'll warm us up a bit." Leah settled down where she normally sat at mealtime, looking fondly at her girl. "You seem so peaceful today."

Lyddie nodded. "I've had some time to think 'bout what happened with Jake. The shock of all this knowin' . . ." Her voice grew softer. "I know he'll find himself a nice wife someday, but I wouldn't be surprised if he returns to Ohio for that."

Leah listened, wishing she could absorb every speck of pain still evident in Lydiann's voice, although her countenance wore a noticeable resolve. "Maybe it'd be a smart idea for Jake to put down some roots in a new place."

"Except then he wouldn't be anywhere near either the Masts or Sadie." She sighed. "And I think he'd miss Mandie terribly."

"Jah . . . that *would* be painful for him," Leah said, knowing firsthand how it felt to lose connection with a loved one.

"It's kinda strange, really," Lydiann said. "To think the girl he thought was his twin is actually someone he *could* marry — but, pity's sake, who'd want to, them growin' up together! Meantime the girl he loved turns out to be an aunt, of all things. Why, there must be times he wishes this was all a mixed-up dream . . . just as I do."

"I know . . . that's why, however necessary, it was so difficult, knowin' what a mess this would make for both you and Jake — and to think of stirring up such pain for him, as well as his family. Imagine raising a boy, only to discover he wasn't yours at all!"

They sipped their hot cocoa and continued to talk heart-to-heart. All the while Leah kept thinking how thankful she was for Lydiann's ability to share her thoughts this way. *Very grateful, indeed.*

At dusk Jonas pulled off the main road onto the Henners' treelined lane, hoping to goodness he might not be seen and mistakenly assumed to be a patient of Zachariah's. Coming this late had been a good choice, he decided as he headed to the back door and knocked.

When Zachariah greeted him, Jonas made note of the man's scrutinizing milky blue eyes and the way he carried himself . . . as if he thought he was rather important.

Not wanting to stay longer than necessary, Jonas preferred to ask his questions while standing in the outer room connected to the kitchen, and he politely refused Zachariah's invitation to come in and have some black coffee. He could hear the voices of young children and Zachariah's wife's gentle prodding. But so as not to detain the family from their evening time together, he simply asked outright about his father's visits here. "Does he come regularly?"

Zachariah nodded without hesitation. "Both for back treatments and otherwise."

"For fellowship, too?"

"Oh, we like to talk whilst enjoyin' a drink, jah."

Obviously, Zachariah was not attempting to hide anything. "I believe my father has a problem, and I'm here to ask you not to encourage him further by offerin' him whiskey when he visits in the future."

Zachariah sighed loudly, folding his arms across his wide chest. "Well, now, I can always recommend coffee if you'd rather." His reply gave the impression he wasn't too interested in kowtowing to a nosy son's demands.

"This is hardly a joking matter," Jonas said. "I'll take you at your word on the coffee. Much obliged!" He turned to dart down the back steps, mighty glad to breathe in the crisp night air and hoping Zachariah was trustworthy.

CHAPTER
TWENTY-SEVEN

Upon moving in with Eli, Jonas and Jake had learned of Bishop Bontrager's special allowance regarding the shed behind the widower's house. The small space had been converted into a makeshift woodworking shop, something that was of little consequence to the People here, since Eli had long ago joined his Ohio church district and wasn't planning to stay put in Gobbler's Knob, anyway.

It was nearly two o'clock on the Saturday before Christmas when Jonas stepped back from his handiwork, crossing his arms as he admired the attractive sideboard he'd put together in a matter of days. "A fine gift indeed," he said in the quietude of the shed. "Nearly as perty as Leah is herself."

A knock came at the door and he jumped. Turning, he saw Gid at the window, waving and wearing a tentative smile. "Ach, it can't be locked . . . must be stuck," Jonas called out, hurrying through the wood shavings to yank open the door.

"Hullo," Gid said right quick. "It's been a while since we talked privatelike."

"Jah, and it's gut to see you," said Jonas.

Gid eyed Eli's fancy tools . . . and the sideboard. "What's this you're makin', Jonas?"

"A Christmas gift for my bride-to-be."

Gid nodded, scratching his beard. "Can't help but wonder what the bishop might say to this."

"I wouldn't think it's a problem, but I s'pose I should've gotten the go-ahead all the same." Jonas felt rising frustration. "Guess I assumed since it's a present, and plain as can be, it would be all right."

Gid looked around Eli's shop. "Must be a mighty big temptation livin' here."

Jonas wished he could convince Gid he hadn't moved in with Jake for the purpose of using Eli's fine tools. There was no denying he was irresistibly drawn to woodworking — cherry, oak, walnut, maple, and cedar for lining chests — every variety of wood caught his eye, and in a big way. Yet he'd promised to put all that behind him during his Proving, both as a means to earn money and a regular hobby — anything to find favor with the Gobbler's Knob church, and all for the sake of marrying Leah.

"I'm afraid I have no choice but to mention this to Bishop," Gid was saying. "Much to my dismay."

Jonas would not plead with Gid to keep quiet. It wasn't as if he'd forgotten his promise or wanted to disrupt the Proving in any way; he'd simply let his great eagerness to please Leah at Christmas overtake him. "I understand," he said.

"On second thought, might be best if *you* went to him 'bout this. The consequences might be less severe thataway."

"Not a bad idea." Prior to today, Jonas had thought that if things didn't work out here in Lancaster, he might try to convince Leah to marry him out in Ohio — except that would cause her to be put under the shun, as well, which would never do. And as close as she was to Lydiann and Abe, as well as her other sisters and father, it was unlikely Leah would ever consent to leave. He loved her too much to present such a maddening choice, so Jonas was keenly aware he was in something of a dilemma at the moment, and the knowledge left him miserable.

Gid commented on the blizzard as he moved toward the door. "An awful ugly day out."

"Best be careful goin' home."

Despite the nasty weather, Jonas made his way to the house to put on his heaviest coat and muffler as soon as Gid was gone. He went and hitched up Eli's sleigh to the only remaining horse, as both Eli and Jake were down the road, visiting friends in Eli's buggy. *No sense waiting for a sunny day to tell on myself,* he decided.

The road was snow-packed, with drifts on either side, and the white stuff was thick in the air as a fierce wind whipped it, making seeing nearly impossible twenty minutes or so into the trip. He had a mind to turn around, but another five minutes would get him to the Dawdi Haus where Bishop Bontrager and his elderly wife resided, next door to their married grandson Luke and his wife, Naomi, and family. Jonas recalled it had been Naomi who was Sadie's troublemaking sidekick back when they were both caught up in rumschpringe, though Naomi had obviously become a good and faithful church member over the years. And he knew from Leah that Sadie had gotten herself straightened out for the better, as well.

Pulling into the lane now, Jonas could hardly make out the Bontrager farmhouse till he got right up next to it. *I'll stay just long enough to tell about the sideboard and then hurry back to Eli's.*

Tying the horse to the hitching post, he clumped up the walkway that led to the smaller addition built onto the main house. Suddenly he felt unexpected anger well up in him as he realized how put out he was with Bishop Bontrager . . . not to mention his own father. To think the two had conspired against him!

If he didn't get ahold of himself and settle down, he might say some things he'd later regret. So he briefly hesitated at the back door, inhaling the frigid air several times before knocking firmly.

The bishop's wife answered, all bent over, leaning on her cane. "Oh, hullo, Jonas." Her eyes and nose were puffy and red. "Are ya here with bad news for this ol' woman?" She shook her head, tears welling. "Didja happen to find him?"

"Who?"

"Why, *der Mann* . . . he's gone missin' out in this terrible blizzard."

Jonas stepped inside as she motioned for him to do so. "I'm here to pay him a visit. I thought surely he would be at home."

She studied him; no doubt she'd overheard her husband speak not so fondly of him through the years. "He's been gone for hours out somewhere in this storm. But . . . there are others already lookin' for him."

Hobbling over to the wood stove, she picked up the coffeepot. "Wouldn't ya like some hot coffee? Warm yourself a bit?"

"No, I best be goin', but denki!" He opened the door and waved his good-bye. "If the bishop is lost, I'll join the search."

Sadie was thankful for the tranquility of the Dawdi Haus, especially this snowy evening. Having completed all her chores, she curled up on a rug near the wood stove and read Mamma's old Bible. She enjoyed the Old Testament love stories, especially the one of Isaac and Rebekah. Actually, she liked reading all the biblical accounts of courtship and marriage and found herself daydreaming once more. *If God wills, I'd like to be a wife again. . . .*

She contemplated Rebekah and Isaac's meeting that fine day out in the countryside as Rebekah came riding on her camel. *What things were in her heart and on her mind? Did she wonder if Isaac would find her pleasing . . . even pretty? Had she ever wished to be cherished by a man?* Sadie remembered how dearly loved Harvey had made her feel during their short marriage.

Nearly embarrassing herself with such idle thoughts, she wondered if Eli was thinking ahead to one week from today, when he was to pick her up right at her door — and not under the covering of night, but during the afternoon.

Sadie couldn't deny how excited she was. Since their meeting was to be the Saturday right after Christmas, she thought about making a card for him, with tatting gently glued on. *Jah, I'll do something nice like that.*

Snug by the fire, she turned again to the first book of Moses to reread the heartwarming account of Isaac and Rebekah's marriage arrangement.

Jonas might have discovered Bishop Bontrager's toppled buggy an hour or so sooner had it not been for the deep banks of snow. Thankful he had taken the sleigh, he maneuvered through the narrow opening that had become the only passable lane on the road, until he spotted the unusual shape of one particular drift. From what he could tell, it was not as tall and windswept as others he'd scrutinized while riding through the blinding snowstorm. Halting his horse, he went to investigate, pushing mounds of snow away. A shattered carriage lay buried beneath.

Desperately he searched for the elderly bishop, seeing no evidence of either a man or an injured horse thus far. Further investigation caused him to conclude that the broken hitch, as well as the smashed carriage, must have occurred when an automobile struck from behind. Jonas hoped the driver of the car had stopped to assist the bishop, taking him to get medical assistance, if necessary. He couldn't imagine anything less on the part of their English neighbors, although there was no way to know who had been out driving in this storm. Still, he continued searching for more clues, his face, hands, and feet growing more numb by the minute.

Moving snow away with his gloved hands, he was determined to find evidence this *truly* was the minister's carriage. And when, at last, he came upon a red Thermos with the initials *B.B.* printed on the side, Jonas assumed he'd found exactly that.

Not so eager to go on with his search, except for the possibility of finding a wounded bishop, he turned to head back toward his horse and sleigh and stumbled over something large — a piece of the buggy, maybe?

Stooping, he swept more than a foot of snow away and let out a gasp — lying on his side was the bishop. Jonas shivered into the wind at the shock of seeing him, yet he touched the man's neck, hoping for a pulse.

Upon further probing, he realized how very stiff, even frozen, the man of God was.

Not waiting another moment, he began to drag him toward Eli's sleigh. With all the energy he could muster, Jonas hoisted Bishop Bontrager up and onto it, laying him out, face up. *Toward the heavens.*

The ride was insufferably cold as the exhausted horse pulled the sleigh back toward the Bontrager home. *Our longtime bishop . . . dead three days before Christmas.*

There was no way to know precisely what had transpired this bleak and ferocious night, and Jonas was downcast about returning the dead man to the bishop's frail wife. The darkness of the evening and the merciless gale seemed to thrust him through the long, snowy tunnel, and he sent a plea for help heavenward.

CHAPTER TWENTY-EIGHT

The days following the bishop's death included the strenuous process of digging out from persistent, heavy snows, as well as getting word to the People of the bishop's fatal accident. Then, the funeral itself. While there was still plenty of snow on the ground, the day was sunny with no breeze at all, as if the wind had blown itself out. Folk from both the Georgetown and Gobbler's Knob church districts turned out in droves for the Preaching service and the burial, though Jonas hadn't noticed Bishop Simon Lapp anywhere in the crowd of men who waited outside before filing into the Bontrager homestead or who stood together at the graveside.

But he *had* seen and talked with Preacher Gid, spending a few private moments with him during the time the large pine box was carried from the front room of the house out to the wide front porch for the public viewing. Gid took the opportunity to thank Jonas. " 'Twas a kind and generous deed, riskin' your life to search for the bishop."

Jonas said that, despite the circumstances of his Proving, he felt it was only right for him to have located the minister. When all was said and done, he harbored no malice toward Bishop Bontrager. *No point in that.*

"I wanted you to know, too, that I haven't said a word to the other preacher, nor Deacon Stoltzfus, neither . . . 'bout the sideboard you made."

Jonas perked up his ears. "But I thought —"

"It's clear you have no intention to earn money from it — a Christmas present to your soon-to-be bride, plain and simple." Gid's breath was like a spiral of smoke. "All that Proving business will need to be discussed at the next ministers' council, I'm thinkin'."

Jonas was relieved to hear it. "Denki."

"No need to thank me." With that Gid walked away, waving his black hat.

It had been a long and tiresome day by the time Jonas and Eli returned home from the bishop's funeral, and the fire in the wood stove was dying down to embers. Now it was long past time to turn in for the night,

305

but Jonas was still sitting in the kitchen listening to Jake pour out his feelings. It was apparent he had been brooding for some time, although he only this minute had declared that he wanted to meet Sadie. He said it with much certainty, as if his grief at their father's rejection of him had turned into an iron-willed determination to forge new ties.

Jake raked his hand through his dark hair. "Don't ya think that if Sadie had known I lived the night I was born, she would've kept me?" He was staring a hole in Jonas. "Just think how everything would've been different if she had."

"What makes you say this?"

Jake stared at the braided rug for a while before he spoke. "You should know what I'm gettin' at. You love her sister Leah, who's a kindhearted woman, raisin' Lydiann and Abe like they're her own. So I'm thinkin' something of Leah must surely be in Sadie." He paused again, frowning. "If I could have even just a short time with her."

Jonas wondered if Jake's interest stemmed from their being here at Eli's, missing out on their own family Christmas dinner and gift exchange. Mandie had been the only one to hint at them coming over for Christmas, and Jonas felt it wise not to simply show up unwelcome. Like Jake, he also felt somewhat displaced this cold and wintry evening.

"I'll be seein' Leah tomorrow," Jonas offered. "I could ask her what she thinks of you visitin' with Sadie."

Jake leaned forward, nearly falling out of his chair. "Ach, would ya? I'll take a bath and put on my for-gut clothes."

"I have no doubt you'll tidy up, but I think it best if you not get your hopes set on this. It's such short notice . . . and I'd hate to see your feelings smartin' on Christmas."

"Oh, I'm sure Sadie will *want* to see me again." Jake rose and walked to the window. "What a mighty *feiner* day!"

Not certain what to say to his overly eager brother, Jonas got up and went to the window, peering out at the stars. "I pray this isn't a mistake."

But Jake insisted it was not. "The mistakes are in the past, don't ya see? Old things are passed away. . . ."

"In more ways than one," whispered Jonas, thinking now of Bishop Bontrager, gone to his eternal reward.

Abe was the first one downstairs for breakfast, and Leah greeted him with a delighted smile. "Happy Christmas Day!"

307

"To you, too, Mamma!" He surprised her by kissing her cheek. "I smell waffles."

"Jah, and not just any waffles — chocolate waffles served with hot syrup or whipped cream, take your pick."

"That's easy. I'll have both." He went and sat right down at the table.

" 'Let patience have her perfect work.' " Leah smiled.

"You're the most patient person I know." Abe picked up his fork and knife and clunked them on the table. "I ain't even half as long-suffering, Mamma. I've been waitin' all night for a taste of your Christmas waffles."

How could she deny such a wonderful boy? "All right, then. Get yourself over here." She motioned him over.

"Really, Mamma? You're goin' to tempt me, ain't so?"

She removed a freshly made waffle and placed it on the large serving platter. "Count to five slowly and pull off a piece. Tell me if there's too much chocolate or not."

The twinkle in his eye surely reflected hers. "Aw, you can *never* have too much chocolate!"

"All right, then. Go 'n' call your father and Aunt Lizzie . . . and Lyddie, too. I'm ready for our Christmas breakfast."

She watched him dash to the stairs, thinking all the while what a wonderful-good day this would be. But it was knowing she would see her beloved beau in a few hours that made Leah's heart beat faster.

Leah held her breath as Jonas's buggy fairly flew up the lane. *He's here!* She hurried down the steps and tried to contain her exuberance, but it couldn't be helped.

"Come in, son," Dat said in his big voice, greeting Jonas at the back door. "Leah's in the front room."

That was all she could make out as Aunt Lizzie also offered soft words of welcome. Soon Jonas was coming through the doorway and into the large room, not nearly as toasty warm as the kitchen, but more private at least.

He rushed to her, giving her a squeeze. "Blessed Christmas to you, love."

"Happy Christmas, Jonas."

He comically pulled her away from the view of anyone who might be peering into the doorway, grinning at her as he reached for her hands. "I've missed you something terrible. And I have a surprise for you, but you'll have to ride with me somewhere to see it."

"Oh? Where to?"

"You must wait 'n' see."

"All right." She nodded, but she could scarcely wait, feeling as thrilled as a young girl.

"Should I give you a hint?" he teased.

"I thought you said I had to wait. What's this guessin' game?"

"I love you to pieces, that's what."

Her heart pounded with his nearness. "We best go 'n' see what pies are left, jah?"

A flicker of disappointment came and went on his face, but she knew he would enjoy one of the tasty pies she, Aunt Lizzie, and Sadie had busied themselves making. Pecan, apple mincemeat, pumpkin, lemon sponge, and chocolate cream all awaited, so she took him by the hand and led the way to the kitchen.

They spent time visiting with the rest of the family, some of whom sat at the table for second and third helpings of dessert, not minding at all sampling the many sweets.

Sometime later, when afternoon milking rolled around, Dat, Abe, and Lydiann excused themselves, and Jonas mentioned he and Leah were "goin' for a quick ride." Leah rose and kissed Aunt Lizzie and Sadie on the cheek before rushing to find her warmest wraps, cheerfully following her beloved out the back door.

On the ride to Eli's place, Jonas recounted for Leah the day he'd gone to visit the bishop. Leah's heart went out to him as he described the hazardous search and the ultimately terrible discovery. He shook his head as though reliving the ordeal.

"A car struck him . . . that's what you think?" Leah was horrified.

"Well, there's no way to check that — no skid marks, not with all the snow." He reached around her. "But it's Christmas, my dearest, so let's not talk of this anymore. I'm sorry."

" 'Tis all right. Poor man . . . it was his time." She believed in the sovereignty of the Lord. What came to bear on a person's life was simply the will of the Almighty One.

They rode along, Leah sitting smack-dab next to Jonas, surrounded by the crisp late afternoon air and the serenity of snowy white.

Jonas pointed out some deer tracks along the roadside. "They must know 'tis hunting season."

"The clatter of gunshot must frighten them," Leah said, wondering if Jonas, who was not a hunter, was aware of the old shack where local men, particularly the English, went for shelter or to reload their rifles and fill their stomachs with food and drink. It had been a long time since she'd roamed the woods high above the Ebersol Cottage, and even longer since her last visit to the old shanty, where she'd heard the surprising tale of her beginnings from Aunt Lizzie, who'd happened upon her there. But she did not utter a word about the place just now — not on the Lord's birthday.

"My father and brothers had been plannin' to go huntin'," Jonas said out of the blue. "But I doubt they will now.

"Leah, there's something on my mind, but I hesitate to bring it up." Her interest piqued, she waited for him to go on. "It seems Jake has an idea . . . and I'm only sayin' this on his behalf."

"Oh?"

"He'd like to visit with Sadie sometime. What do you think of that?"

The words inched into Leah's mind, but she didn't have to think too hard, knowing her sister as she did . . . and the cry of her heart. "Honestly? I say it's a perfectly wonderful idea. When should it be?"

"Well, you might think this too sudden, but Jake was hopin' it might happen yet today, bein' it's Christmas and all."

"Tonight?" She could scarcely believe her ears.

Jonas nodded. "You and I could bring Jake back with us, if you think it wise, and you could go and see how Sadie feels 'bout it."

She almost laughed but squelched it. "Oh my, Jonas. Let me tell ya . . . there's no need to be askin' Sadie anything beforehand. I know what she'd say." She sighed. What an amazing turn of events. "There's not a single doubt in my mind." She became so excited she could hardly sit still.

"I wanted to do the right thing, you know. Be mighty cautious."

She fully understood. "Thank you for being so considerate, but I'm sure nothing would please my sister more."

When they arrived at Eli's, Jonas took her around the back to the shed, where, when he opened the door and lit the lantern, she gazed at a most beautiful furniture piece.

"This is for you, Leah." He slipped his arm around her.

"Oh . . . it's ever so perty!" She assumed it was an engagement gift, but he quickly told her it was for Christmas. To this she said, "Ach, are ya sure?"

He pulled her into his arms. "It's been the longest time since I promised it to you."

She leaned her head against his strong

chest. "I don't think I've ever been so happy."

"Jah, I know that feelin', too, my dear."

She stepped back and went to explore the wood and sheen of the lovely sideboard, Jonas right by her side as she touched it and peered into its drawers. "You should be makin' furniture like this all the time, ya know." Instantly she realized what she'd said and wished to take back her remark, hoping against hope she had not been thoughtless.

"Maybe I will again someday." He reached for her hand. "I'm biding my time."

She leaned into his tender embrace. "Denki, Jonas . . . for the lovely present."

After she'd inspected every inch of the sideboard, Jonas asked if she wanted to go to the house to talk with Jake. She was a bit reluctant to leave behind her Christmas surprise, but quite eager to see Jake, as well. To think of Sadie spending time with her son on this most blessed day made Leah feel ever so joyful.

What will dear Sadie say when she sees her son?

CHAPTER
TWENTY-NINE

Just when Sadie was thinking she might feel a bit lonely tonight, she heard the back door spring open and became aware of Leah's voice. She also heard Jonas and assumed he was coming in to get warm before heading back into the cold.

Leah came running into the front room, her cheeks flushed and eyes wider than usual, and Sadie immediately wondered what was up. "Stay sittin' right there, Sadie . . . I have a surprise for you!" Then she turned and headed toward the kitchen.

In a few moments she was back in the front room again. "Sister, ya best close your eyes, all right?"

She would play along with Leah's game, whatever it was, but she felt nearly like a child doing so, what with Leah's goings-on. "I've got my eyes covered, you silly."

After a moment's wait she heard the sound of footsteps — and a young man's voice. "Hullo, Sadie . . . a happy Christmas to ya."

When she opened her eyes, there stood Jake, tall and smiling. She could not speak, so astonished she was. "Oh goodness!" she sputtered.

"I've been wantin' to meet you." His brown eyes shone and he looked slightly embarrassed.

Leah and Jonas, who had been standing in the doorway, inched back, leaving her alone with her son. "Please sit with me," she said at last, her heart racing with absolute gladness.

"I hope I didn't startle you by comin' uninvited."

"Well, jah . . . you certainly did. But never a more welcomed fright!" She literally stared, taking in every aspect of his handsome face — eyes, brow, nose, cheeks, mouth, chin — until she realized he was just as curious about her, too. "Well, I guess it's not polite to stare, is it?"

They both laughed, and she blinked back tears, nearly overcome with emotion.

He looked at her fondly. "Ever since I heard 'bout you from Dr. Schwartz . . . well, my grandfather, I knew I had to see you again." He paused before continuing. "I wouldn't have known of you if it hadn't been for Lydiann."

"Most important is we're here now, Jake, sittin' and talking together, ain't so?" She opened her heart wide and began to tell him many of the things she had longed to say all this time. "Losing you the night you were born was out of my hands. I would've kept you, because I wanted you so desperately . . . to raise you and love you dearly, in spite of my unmarried state."

She felt the tears running down her cheeks. "I always felt in my heart you might be alive somehow. I truly did." She didn't refer to her recurring dreams in those first months of a baby's cries, but her remembrance of them caused her to weep.

"I didn't want to barge in on you tonight . . . but I'm mighty glad I did," he said gently.

When Sadie had composed herself, she went on. "I believe you're much like I was at your age. Nothing stood in my way if I had my heart set on it." She reached for his hand. "Denki, ever so much, for takin' this brave, even awkward step. I can't tell you what it means to me."

"Thank *you* . . . for sharin' what you did."

"I am very happy." She said it with the utmost reverence.

"We daresn't wait so long to see each

other again, jah?"

"Why, sure, as soon as you'd like."

He placed his free hand on hers. "Happiest Christmas, jah?"

"Oh my . . . the best ever, Jake. Truly."

He rose slowly, and she felt compelled to stand, as well, wishing she might hold him near, wanting to protect him from further pain, desiring only what was best for him, but she spared him more choked-up words and tears.

With a deep breath, she put on her brightest, most delighted smile, following him through the kitchen, where her family sat around the table playing quiet games, their heads politely bowed. She happened to notice Lydiann's head bob up quickly before going down again.

Poor, dear girl. She thought of the unfortunate short-lived courtship with Jake, thankful she'd heard recently from Leah that the worst of Lyddie's sadness was already past.

Soon both Sadie and Jake found Jonas and Leah in the utility room, holding hands and looking as happy as she'd ever seen them.

"Good night, Leah, and happy Christmas," Jonas said.

When it seemed appropriate, Sadie thanked Jonas — and Leah — for making it possible to meet with her son. She found it difficult to keep her eyes on anyone but Jake, hardly able to get her fill. "A most wonderful night!" she declared.

Leah came and stood near, and together they watched Jake and Jonas head outside, the two men turning to wave their good-byes yet again.

Seems like nothing short of a miracle, thought Sadie, her heart brimming with joy.

Cozy in her log home, Hannah sipped hot cocoa as she watched the girls play with their new games. Gid sat nearby in the front room, close to the fireplace. Such a fine day they'd all enjoyed together, having made the short trek across barren fields to Gid's parents' to partake of the Christmas feast with Tomato Joe and Dorcas and their children, as well. A later visit to the Ebersol Cottage in the early afternoon had treated them to more pie and cookies. A busy sort of Christmas Day, yet Hannah would not have traded their comings and goings for anything.

Out of the blue, Gid spoke of the bishop's death and how there would most likely be an ordination for a new bishop come spring. "We'll draw from the older, more estab-lished preachers from both the Georgetown district and here."

"Who'll oversee us in the meantime?" she asked.

"The Grasshopper Level bishop is the nearest, so I'm sure it will be Simon Lapp — a most compassionate man, I must say."

"You won't be considered for bishop, then?" Hannah said.

"People would look on me as too young, which is quite all right by me."

She was glad to hear this, because when the ministerial lot fell on a man, it was a most solemn thing. To back away and not receive the ordination was to meddle with the sovereignty of God and seen by some as a bad omen.

Gid reached for her hand. "Don't worry over the ordination, Hannah, but be in an attitude of prayer."

In that moment she wanted to say once more how sorry she was for her recent disobedience. "I was ever so wrong, Gid."

"No need to cover old ground," he replied. "All's forgiven."

She nodded, tears unexpectedly springing to her eyes. She would not seek out Zachariah further, having promised Gid she would not. "I don't know what got into me that day, goin' to the Henners."

"Well, I think *I* do. You're much too curious, that's what." He was teasing her, but now his face grew more serious. "And it's high time for me to apologize to *you,* dear."

"Whatever for?"

"I s'pose it must've seemed I was more concerned 'bout Mary Ruth's Mennonite influence on you and our family over the years than I was the powwowing you were so bent on. But I was sorely wrong on that point."

She was quite surprised to hear such a thing coming from Gid. "Mary Ruth brings joy to everyone."

"Jah, your twin's cheerful nature is bound to raise a person's spirit."

"For sure and for certain." She was most grateful for her husband's understanding and love this blessed Christmas . . . and all year through.

Mary Ruth sat by the fire, rocking Ruthie to sleep. She smiled across the room at Robert, who sat on the sofa reading the Bible. She didn't want to break the peaceful stillness of the moment, so she sang a gentle lullaby. The traditional carol was one the children sang at church.

"Infant holy, infant lowly, for His bed a cattle stall . . . oxen lowing, little knowing Christ, the babe, is Lord of all."

As she sang, she thought of Hannah, who,

while seeming to have experienced relief from depression and despondency for some time now, still appeared to be spiritually lost. *Will my twin ever open her heart to the Lord?*

She knew she would not cease praying for just that — not as long as she was living and breathing. Surely Hannah would come to find Jesus real and near to her someday. Mary Ruth sighed. She knew too many Amishwomen, several of whom Hannah was well acquainted with, who suffered from a melancholy spirit. Often she prayed for Hannah to be free of the darkness that seemed to surround her, so she might spread light to others in similar need, perhaps. *Too many such women live in bondage.* She was glad her twin at least was blessed with a kind, God-fearing husband. It was for Mary Ruth to simply put her trust in God's sovereignty, praying each of her family members would experience saving grace in the Lord's perfect way and time.

When Robert closed the Bible, he patted the pillow next to him. "Come sit with me, love."

She went willingly, placing Ruthie in his arms and snuggling close to him. "What a special day, jah?" She laughed softly as the Dutch word slipped out unexpectedly.

"Once Amish, always Amish, you used to say." Robert kissed her head.

"I daresay," she replied. "Well, maybe just simple and Plain."

"Which is just the way I like you."

They sat gazing into the face of their precious sleeping daughter, reminiscing on the day spent between Dat's house and the Schwartzes'. "Your parents seemed quite taken with Ruthie," she said, touching her baby's dainty hand.

"Yes, and with each other, as well," said Robert. "Did you happen to notice?"

"I did, actually." She hadn't said anything before but was glad Robert brought it up. "What is different between them, do you think?"

"With Dad that can't be easy to know. He's as tight-lipped as they come. But they must've had a wonderful time on their trip overseas."

"There's a shared something or other . . . a special *knowing* between them."

"All for the good, I trust," Robert said.

Feeling tired, Mary Ruth was content to simply lean her head on her husband's shoulder, aware of the occasional crackle in the fireplace and the sighs of their little one, nestled in Robert's embrace.

"I know it's a long way off, but I'd like to

have our families here for dinner next Easter," said Robert.

She sat up at the suggestion. "Maybe we should invite the Masts, too. See if they'll surprise all of us and accept an invitation for a change."

Robert chuckled. "After all these years, I wonder what it would take for Peter Mast to change his mind about your father."

"I think his grudge has more to do with Leah . . . and Aunt Lizzie, maybe."

"Well, he'll have to come around quite a lot in his thinking if he's ever to attend Jonas and Leah's wedding," Robert said, surprising her.

She looked at him, not sure what to say. "You sincerely think Peter and Fannie would not attend the marriage of their eldest son?"

Robert shrugged. "Something's got to give, sooner or later. People shouldn't willingly go to their graves filled with such hate — at least not if I can help it."

"What can you do, Robert? Seriously."

"I don't know what the Lord has in mind, but I've felt compelled to pray about it more frequently, and I won't stop until I get an answer, one way or the other. Prayer changes circumstances, you know."

"And people, too." She found Robert's

sudden concern about the longtime clash between the Masts and the Ebersols to be quite curious. "I felt so sad when Cousins Peter and Fannie didn't come to Mamma's funeral . . . sad for them and for Dat."

"At this point, I doubt Peter even remembers what triggered his aggravation with Abram in the first place."

"Perhaps." Mary Ruth wished something could be done about it. Just what, she had no idea, but she would join her husband in praying for God's answer.

CHAPTER THIRTY

"Listen to this," Jake said on Friday as he read to Jonas another letter from Mandie.

Jonas was all ears where he stood clearing the breakfast dishes from the table. He, Eli, and Jake had been taking turns redding up the kitchen, each drawing lots to see who would cook which day, as well.

"Seems Dat's got himself a 'certain visitor' every evening now, followin' supper . . . and sometimes right after the noon meal, too." Jake looked up from the letter. "Can ya guess who?"

Jonas was sure he knew. "Bishop Lapp?"

"Well, now, how did ya know that?"

Jonas wasn't about to say. Fact was, Bishop Lapp was apparently interested in dealing with problems head-on, whereas it seemed Bishop Bontrager had been more inclined to create them, at least where some folk were concerned.

Jonas had told Jake nothing concerning

the frank visit with the Grasshopper Level
bishop, and maybe he never would. At least
it sounded like some progress was being
made at the Mast orchard house, especially
if Dat wasn't riding off to get his daily quota
of the hard stuff, what with the man of God
showing up to keep him regular company.

Sadie couldn't have suppressed her smile
even if she'd wanted to when Eli Yoder
showed up at her back door the Saturday
afternoon after Christmas. "Hullo," she
greeted him. "Would ya like to come in and
warm up a bit?"

"Mighty nice of you," he said, a twinkle in
his eye.

Once he was seated at her table, she
poured hot coffee for them both, all the
while utterly aware of his endearing smile
— like a moonbeam on newly fallen snow.
She noticed the notched cut of his red hair,
slightly squared off at the ears, evidence of
his Ohio roots.

They exchanged comments about his
enthusiasm for woodworking, as well as
their individual time spent in places in Ohio
familiar to both, discovering several people
they knew in common from the Millersburg
area. "Ever get a chance to walk along Kill-
buck Creek?" he asked.

"Oh jah, and it ain't such a little creek, either, is it?"

"Well, in some places, it is plenty wide and deep — nearly like a small river." He lifted his coffee cup to his lips and drank. Then, setting it down again, he smiled. "This is right gut coffee."

"Denki."

They talked of Christmas, and Eli described how both Jonas and Jake had helped "cook up a fine feast." Hearing Jake's name mentioned made her miss him, but Eli was back to speaking of Ohio. "Did you happen to get over to the Swiss cheese factory near Berlin?"

"No, I didn't stay in the area for long. One young fella from the Millersburg church district introduced me to the Indiana man I eventually married."

Their conversation was slow and quiet, and she found herself perfectly content to sit with him, conscious of the heat in the belly of the stove, as well as the gentle warmth of the hot coffee she drank.

During a lull in their conversation, she presented him with her homemade card and was surprised when he handed her one, too. "Why, thank you," she said, feeling her cheeks warm at his attention.

When they'd finished their coffee and

Sadie had taken the cups and saucers to the sink, she reached for her heaviest coat. Quickly Eli offered to hold it while she slid her arms inside.

They walked to his enclosed buggy, and she was thankful they were no longer youngsters. No need to endure this brisk night in an open courting buggy!

"Awful nice spendin' time with you, Sadie," he said.

As Eli helped her into his carriage, she felt as if her heart might burst with joy.

Leah had a kettle going for tea and cups set out on a tray when she went in search of Sadie Saturday evening.

She found her sister happily humming as she worked by gaslight in her tiny kitchen. "We must talk," Leah said softly. "I'll bring us some tea over here if you'd like."

Sadie looked up from the pot of vegetable soup she was making. "Sure, I'll be glad for some hot tea." She added shyly, "I had a visit with Eli Yoder today."

"Oh, what lovely news!" Then and there Leah knew she had to admit to having seen Sadie and Eli make their way out to his carriage. "I hoped, all the while you were gone, that you'd have yourself a real nice time. Did ya?"

"Oh my . . . jah." Sadie did not volunteer anything else, and Leah guessed she wanted to hold this memory close for a while before revealing more. "Well, sister, what's on your mind?" she asked after a brief lull.

Leah hesitated, not wanting to spoil Sadie's present contentment. "It's just that I've been considerin' Jake quite a lot." She paused. "I'm wonderin' if you think it might be time for folk to know he's your son."

Sadie folded her hands on the table. "All the People, ya mean?"

"Mary Ruth and Hannah and their spouses in particular."

Turning her head, Sadie looked at the cookstove and icebox. "I've thought the same, to tell the truth. 'Tis next to impossible livin' with the knowledge of something so . . . well, wonderful, and havin' to keep it to myself." Sadie looked back at her, tears glistening. "Jake's such a fine boy, Leah. Truly, he is. I can't tell you how happy I am."

Leah felt she understood at least something of her sister's emotion. "It was nice seein' the two of you visiting together. Did my heart gut."

"One of the best moments of my life." Sadie got up for the honey jar and asked, "How do you think we should go 'bout telling Hannah and Mary Ruth and Abe? I don't want to wait and have word leak out through the grapevine . . . which it could, ya know."

"Ask Dat," Leah suggested. "Either he or Aunt Lizzie will have something to say 'bout it."

Sadie smiled, although her chin still trembled slightly. "The worst is behind us, jah?"

Reaching for her hand, Leah closed her eyes. "Oh my, let's pray so."

Every corner of the morning sky twinkled gold as Jake and Jonas worked methodically in the kitchen on New Year's Day, chopping vegetables and cutting up stew beef for their noontime meal with Eli. Jake was fired up and eager to say what was on his mind, and as Eli was gone from the house, now was as good a time as any. "I say *everyone* ought to know the truth 'bout me."

Jonas didn't immediately respond, although his quick intake of breath and the serious look in his eyes made it clear he had an opinion.

"Seems like a falsehood to me for folk to continue thinkin' I'm Peter Mast's son, don't ya think?"

Jonas regarded Jake quietly, nodded his

331

head, and then unexpectedly went and adjusted the flame under the black kettle. "Too bad the secret was ever kept at all . . . but then, I wouldn't have known you as my brother, would I?" he said at last. "I can't imagine what Mandie or Mamma or any of our siblings would think if you weren't a part of our family. I do mean this, Jake. What's done is done and should be left alone." He paused to reach for the lid and placed it firmly on the kettle. "And something else . . ." He turned toward Jake. "You must forgive Dat. The sooner you do, the sooner you'll get past all your disappointment toward him. That's not to say I blame you for feelin' the way you do."

Jake shook his head and sat down at the table. "I would never think of doin' such a thing to my son — true kin or not. It helps some knowin' that Sadie never would've given me up if she'd had any say."

"I believe you're right."

Jake stared at the tray filled with the sourdough sticky buns a neighbor lady had brought over earlier as a New Year's surprise. He muttered to himself, not persuaded that he shouldn't go about telling the world — *his* world, at least — the news.

Jonas spoke up again. "Maybe Dr. Schwartz is the one you need to consider forgiving first."

Jake wasn't surprised at Jonas's pointed words. Unfortunately, both the doctor and their father had been terribly at fault in his case, though the latter was of more concern at present. A month had come and gone since Dat had asked him to leave, with nary a note or visit all this time.

How long will the silence continue? Jake wondered with a heavy heart.

When a knock came at the door, Henry jumped, startled from where he had dozed off while reading the newspaper, enjoying the tranquility of the house.

It had been that sort of afternoon — one in which to recover from having overindulged in Lorraine's fine New Year's Day dinner of prime rib with all the trimmings. His wife had not gone to all that trouble simply for him, however. Robert, Mary Ruth, and their peach of a baby girl had come to spend a good portion of the day, much to both Lorraine's and Henry's delight.

He rose gradually to see who might be stopping by for a visit, and upon opening the door saw three uniformed men. He instantly tensed and thought Peter Mast had decided to press charges, having abandoned the nonaggressive posture Leah had been so adamant was the Amish way.

So this is it, he thought, imagining how Lorraine would react to his being hand-cuffed and arrested today, and just when the two of them had begun to click far better than they had in many years. No doubt in his mind, his luck had run out.

"Are you Henry Schwartz, father of Sergeant Major Schwartz, Derek L.?" one of the men asked.

His breath caught in his throat. These men were not here to charge him with a crime; they weren't policemen but military personnel. "I beg your pardon?"

The man asked again, "Is your son Sergeant Major Schwartz?"

Henry trembled, realizing at that instant why this man with intense gray eyes wore the badge of a military chaplain. He stood like a piteous sage of sorrow right here on the front porch.

"Yes, Derek is my son," he said as terror filled his soul.

"On behalf of the U.S. Army, we regret to inform you . . ."

Henry clutched his chest, scarcely able to breathe. *Derek . . . my boy . . . dead.*

More words cut through the fog fast descending on him. "Your son's body will be sent home with a full military escort within four days." It registered in Henry's brain that the military was already doing an investigation into Derek's accident, but the thought seemed somehow unrelated to him. Henry's sense of things and the world as he knew it had utterly changed.

CHAPTER
THIRTY-ONE

The Bullfrog Inn was smoke-filled and noisy with men making merry. Henry had slipped out of the house some time after breaking to Lorraine the news of Derek's tragic death at his army base in Ft. Carson, Colorado, where he had been assisting in conducting predawn live-fire exercises. Not at all familiar with the military and its war games and drills, Henry could not envision the scenario, and the pieces of information the chaplain had given him did nothing to quell the string of questions from Lorraine's trembling lips. They would have to wait two weeks for the official account to understand more fully how their son had died.

Henry's chest ached now as the devastating knowledge of their loss seeped into his mind and soul. Before ever telling Lorraine, he had gone alone to the clinic, grieving there in the privacy of his office for a while, dry heaves shaking him to the core.

When, at last, he was able to return to the house, he found his wife awaking from a nap. He went to her and said the painful words, holding her near as she wept.

After quite some time, they talked a little of Derek's disconnection from them in recent years, so complete he had ceased answering even his father's letters. Now they would never know what unforgivable deed they had committed against him, if indeed the fault lay with them at all. When Henry voiced this thought to Lorraine, she shook her head and pleaded with him not to say such things. "Derek chose his way . . . his own path. You mustn't torment yourself for the choices our son made." Yet Henry was shaken in knowing the day of reconciliation for which he had long held out hope would never be.

Even as they talked of funeral plans — Henry insisting the service be small, with a private viewing for family members only — he was scarcely able to grasp that their long-estranged son was gone from them forever. Henry had felt an urgent need to "breathe some fresh air," and Lorraine kindly encouraged him to do so. His feet had led him here.

Now that he stood inside the door of the local tavern, he was beginning to feel guilty for having left his wife to mourn alone. Not having any appetite whatsoever, he slipped into a chair at a corner table to order a single beer. His emotions — a vast array this night — ran deep, and for the first time in his life he was uncertain how to repress his reaction to despair.

Henry sipped beer from a tall glass and recalled the day he and Lorraine had brought their second baby home from the hospital. He allowed himself to remember the joy — and his great pride — at welcoming another son into the family.

He recalled Derek's childhood days as a curly-haired tot, inquisitive and playful. Derek had always been so clever and bright, though somewhat boastful about his accomplishments as a Tenderfoot in the Boy Scouts.

One late-summer evening when Derek had begged permission to spend the night in the highest crook of a towering tree in their backyard, Henry had taken Derek's side against the more protective Lorraine, and in the end the boy had gotten his way. Their son had hoisted an old pillow and a blanket to the uppermost branches, where he had slept blissfully beneath the leaves.

Henry wondered what sort of relationship they might have had if Derek had made even the slightest attempt to keep in touch as an adult. What if his son *had* responded to letters from home instead of ignoring them since the Christmas of 1949, the last time either Henry or Lorraine had seen him? Henry had continued to write, only to be pierced afresh by Derek's indifferent silence.

The chaplain had indicated Derek had never married, his next of kin being his parents. Henry had no reason to doubt it, but this brief glimpse into his son's life had come as a surprise, especially because of Derek's previous fondness for the ladies.

He thought of Lorraine again. Not wanting to leave her alone too long, he was rising to leave when he noticed Peter Mast sitting across the room, the only Amishman present. Wandering over somewhat hesitantly, he offered a greeting. "Happy New Year, Peter."

He was only partially convinced Peter had motioned for him to sit at the table, but Henry pulled out a chair to do so and the bearded man frowned. "I wouldn't have expected to see *you* here, Doctor."

"Likewise, you." Henry nodded, eyeing Peter's nearly empty glass. "Alcohol appears to be the drug of choice. Folk delaying their resolutions for one more day."

"I daresay you carry enough guilt around

for two or three men." Peter raised his tumbler.

Henry stared at this man, incredulous at his contempt. He recalled that Derek had actually worked for him as a teenager, often bringing home Fannie's excellent jams to Lorraine at her request. Peter had changed for the worse over the years; his rudeness was unlike the polite, even dignified manner of the Plain folk Henry treated up and down the Georgetown Road and beyond. "I'm here because Jake's father is said to be dead," he muttered at last.

Peter leaned back in his chair and let out an odd chuckle. "I shouldn't be surprised . . . there are prob'ly more than a few who wish me an early end."

Stunned, Henry looked at him. "Not *you*. My son Derek . . . the father Jake never knew. Nor, scarcely, did I." He formed the last words with difficulty.

"Well, then, we've both lost sons, seems to me. Mine's as gut as dead."

Henry shook his head. "You and Fannie raised Jake as your own. He *is* yours."

"I'm no fool, Doctor. Jake's got your blood in his veins — Abram's, too. He ain't mine at all."

Henry was appalled. "Jake has your values . . . he accepts your principles as his own.

340

What more could a man want?" He wished the same could be said of Derek. *If only he had embraced a sense of family loyalty, if nothing else. . . .*

"I was deceived and my family's in shambles for it." Peter got up and stood at the table, fire in his eyes. "I don't know who to blame more — you or that scoundrel Abram." He planted his fists on the tabletop, his head lunging forward, but he did not utter another word; the look in his eyes made plain his utter disdain.

"What are you talking about?" Henry shot back. "Abram is as innocent as you were. And as ignorant of Sadie's pregnancy as you were to Jake and Lydiann Ebersol's courtship."

Peter deliberately turned and walked to the bar, apparently snubbing him. Henry stayed seated, reflecting on their blunt conversation. Peter was clearly a wounded and angry man, and when Henry saw him returning with a shot glass of whiskey, he decided he cared for not an ounce more of either Peter's company or strong drink.

Getting up from the table, Henry left without offering even a good night.

News of Derek's death swept through the village from the west end to the eastern side of Gobbler's Knob. Friends and neighbors of the family and schoolmates of Derek who remembered him from before he enlisted called the Schwartzes or sent their condolences in the form of flowers, cards, and hot dishes. Even the Ebersols sent a sympathy card, signed by Leah on behalf of the family, and both Leah and Sadie dropped by for a short visit with a large fruit basket, not saying much more than how sorry they were.

On the day of the family viewing, Robert and Mary Ruth accompanied Henry and Lorraine to the Strasburg funeral home, along with, at Henry's personal invitation, Jake Mast. Now, as Henry stood in the portal to the visitation room, his eyes focused on the open, flag-draped coffin. His breath caught in his throat and his chest felt as if it might cave in.

Struggling, he made an attempt to compose himself lest his grief overtake him. He looked at Lorraine, slumped in one of the formal-looking wingback chairs, with Mary Ruth hovering near. Yet before he could make his way to her, Robert motioned to him. His son was standing next to Jake, whose usually ruddy complexion was now as pale as a white sheet, and the two spoke quietly to each other.

Henry went to them, and the three moved slowly to stand before the casket together. Henry's throat closed at the sight of Derek's face. *How much older he looks,* he thought, recalling the youthful days before Derek's enlistment.

Jake stood silently, hands folded. "I daresay I didn't expect to meet him . . . like this," he said, his voice cracking.

Robert put his hand on Jake's shoulder. "None of us could have imagined it." He gave a slight smile. "Your being here today is a gift to our family."

"I wish I might've known Derek . . . somehow or other." Then, clearly shaken, Jake stepped away, going to sit by Lorraine.

Henry followed him. "I want you to know . . . your natural father was a fun-loving young man."

Robert pulled out a folded handkerchief from the inside pocket of his suit coat, coming to Jake's side again. "My brother had a real spirit of adventure, too. You would've enjoyed that."

Henry suddenly realized they were attempting to offer thoughtful comments — even going overboard somewhat — largely for Jake's benefit. He felt sorry the boy had been placed in such an awkward position, attending a viewing for a father he'd never known. Making the best of it, Henry encouraged Jake to go with him to the small alcove, where a guest book lay open on a marble podium.

Henry picked up the plumed pen and handed it to Jake. "Why don't you sign your name first?"

After Jake did so, Henry scrawled his and Lorraine's names on the line beneath. *Dr. and Mrs. Henry Schwartz.* His hand shook slightly as he returned the pen to its holder.

His heart sank as he watched Robert and Mary Ruth encircle Lorraine, who was crying softly. *Dear Lorraine.* She had taken the startling news about Jake in her stride. But now, here in this hushed, floral-laden place, she had completely lost her composure over Derek.

He felt torn between wanting to comfort his beloved wife and a sense of duty to remain with Jake. Henry was, after all, responsible for bringing the boy here — a day to say hello and good-bye in a single, overwhelming breath.

Sadie needed time to think, but she didn't want either Leah or Aunt Lizzie to know what was bothering her. She paced in front of her bedroom window, wondering why she felt numb when she thought of Derek

Schwartz's death. *He was my first love. Shouldn't I feel sad?*

She recalled the unspeakable grief she'd suffered when Harvey had died, how she'd fallen into a deep pit of despair but concealed it as best she could.

Not so now. With Derek she felt only the sadness one might when hearing of a stranger's death. In all truth, it had seemed as if Derek had already been dead to her for years on end, his abandonment had been so complete.

And now he *was* dead, never to reconcile the loose ends of his life here at home, or to know his son, which, as she pondered it, might be better for Jake. At the same time, though, Derek would never have the opportunity to make amends with her — nor his parents, whom he had continually rejected, according to Leah, who'd on several occasions lent a sympathetic ear to a dismayed Lorraine.

No, Derek's time to make peace has simply run out.

CHAPTER
THIRTY-TWO

All of Gobbler's Knob experienced winter's brazen settling in, and there wasn't anything anyone could do to stop it. Often from January through early March, the dark and distant hills would be shrouded in banks of haze nearly every dawn. The People would endure frigid temperatures and howling winds, warming themselves by drinking hot apple cider and cocoa, or black coffee, the brew of choice, and taking comfort in cobblers, apple dumplings and crisps, and the ever-popular creamed, chipped beef served at church gatherings.

Leah would long, as she did every winter, for the fairest season of all. This year the spring thaw would precede the solemn period of fasting and prayer as baptized church members examined their lives and motives in hopes of finding blessed unity. Then, and only then, would the spirit be right for the ordination of another bishop.

Everyone knew that disharmony and friction during these days would mean postponing an ordination. Only once it was determined the People of Gobbler's Knob were in one accord could they "make a bishop," according to the qualifications of their Ordnung.

It was well into February when Lydiann confided in Leah about having attended "several Mennonite Bible studies." Despite the source, Leah felt she could hardly discourage her girl from learning more about God's Word. After all, Mary Ruth's unique experience had changed her life for the better, just as faith had altered the lives of Mamma and Aunt Lizzie and, eventually, Dat. And by the number of quilting bees Lydiann was taking part in with Mary Ruth lately, Leah believed Lydiann had found additional comfort in spending time with her older sister, as well as baby Ruthie. A blessing, indeed.

The month of March brought various sales and property auctions for retiring farmers, and Smitty Peachey let it be known officially that he was turning over his blacksmithing work to both Gid and Jonas. Leah was reasonably pleased for her husband-to-be, although she held to her secret hope that Jonas might one day be allowed to return to woodworking. For now, however, the work of a smithy in a well-established shop seemed both rewarding and financially smart for a man about to take a bride.

Leah wasn't the only one of Abram's daughters with matrimony on her mind. Sadie, too, had whispered recently of Eli Yoder's keen interest in her. "I wonder if he might just ask me to marry him," she said to Leah, her face glowing as they worked together in the kitchen.

Leah pinched the rim of dough on a pie plate. "What'll you say if the time comes?"

Sadie put her head down, speechless now, her cheeks blushing, and her uncharacteristic reaction spoke volumes.

Leah leaned her head against her sister's. "I'm ever so happy for you . . . for both of us, really." She thought of how things had begun to settle down in their lives — for the most part, just since the bishop's death, sadly enough. At present Jonas was looking for a house to rent or buy, though both knew they would not marry till the wedding season began . . . still nearly eight months away. The demanding work of plowing, planting, and harvesting prevented anyone from enjoying the privilege of an all-day celebration until November.

"What would you think if I moved to Ohio

. . . if Eli and I were to marry?" Sadie asked unexpectedly.

"Goodness' sakes, I didn't think I was goin' to lose you again." Leah sighed, not wanting to think about the dismal notion. "Does Eli want to return home?"

"His family expects him to go back to them with a bride. Honestly, it was the only way he would consider comin' here in the first place."

Leah didn't want to overreact, but she was already starting to feel glum. "Is there no other way — I mean, if you were to accept Eli's proposal?"

"Ach, we haven't gotten that far. It's just a feelin' I have that he might propose . . . but I could be wrong."

"Well, I hope you're not," Leah said, meaning it. "Time for you to have some ongoing happiness."

Sadie laughed. "Look who's talkin'!"

Leah smiled back. "Oh, Sadie, I've always been happy . . . just in a different way, I 'spect. Serving my family has brought me the greatest joy, even in the midst of difficult times."

"You ain't tellin' me anything there," Sadie said. "I've seen ya pourin' out your life, and it's been lonely and nearly exhausting for ya even during the best of times.

349

Because of that, I've been askin' our Lord to return some of the selfsame kindness back to you."

"Ya must quit prayin' for blessings when the greatest reward is simply doin' for others."

Sadie shrugged. "Still, can't I ask God to give you and Jonas a whole houseful of children? That'd be wonderful-gut, ain't so?"

Opening the oven door, Leah checked on her pies. "First things first. Let's just pray Jonas will be voted in as a church member once again."

"Surely he will."

"You'd think so after all he's sacrificed to follow the Proving."

The sisters fell into a companionable silence until Sadie left the room for the Dawdi Haus, saying she wanted to finish her monthly letter to her former sister-in-law in Indiana.

Leah turned her attention to setting the table, thoughts of cooking and baking for Jonas filling her head. *Thank you, dear Lord, for bringing us this far.*

Saturday, March 14

Dear Diary,

Tomorrow marks the day of the council meeting when the People will vote to reinstate Jonas or not — and the day we cast lots for a new bishop. Bishop Simon Lapp of the Grasshopper Level district will be on hand, of course, as he has been overseeing our church since the death of our former bishop. Such a difference there is between him and Bishop Bontrager!

Bishop Lapp is more open-minded, I'd have to say, and Gid has become interested in discussing his opinion on church matters with me. All in all, much has changed in my husband since he became Preacher, and I have come to respect his wishes, even on matters I never dreamt we'd see eye to eye on. Truly, there is no longer any desire in me for the powwowing gift. And I have dear Gid to thank . . . him and the way the hair on my neck stood up the last time I visited Henners.

With baby soon to arrive, I've been sewing some infant sleeping gowns here lately. They'll do fine for either a boy or a girl. Oh, how we all look forward to having a new little one in the house!

Respectfully,
Hannah

■ ■ ■ ■

Years ago Henry had decided he much preferred the outdoors and the wide, open sanctuary of nature to the stuffy walls of a church edifice. But months had passed since he had last gone to look after the Mast baby's grave on a Sunday morning, and the snows had drifted high over the vacant meadow.

The more he considered it, the more he recognized that coming clean with Jake and Peter and Fannie Mast had appeased his conscience somewhat, although Henry still felt appallingly responsible for the boy's current displacement. He had even contacted his grandson to let him know that, if at any time he was in need of accommodations, he was always welcome to occupy Derek's former bedroom, the current guest room of the house.

He and Lorraine had been elated when, in January, Jake had accepted an invitation to supper. What a fine time they'd had together. In some surprising way, it was almost as if they had Derek himself back in the youthful form of his only child.

Robert and Mary Ruth, too, had opened their home to their nephew for the first time, with Henry and Lorraine looking on while Jake held his cousin Ruthie, his eyes wide with happiness as he had comically talked in Dutch to her. Little Ruthie had seen fit to coo back "in English," as Robert had joked.

But it was Lorraine's obvious affection for Jake that impressed Henry most of all when, one day, she'd revealed that she had included her grandson in her book of prayer requests. Her kindhearted reaction to Jake made Henry feel he was beginning to fall in love with her again, even at this late stage of their lives. So much so, in fact, that he had given in to her repeated invitations to attend church. It seemed everything pulled them closer these days, even their shared grief over Derek.

For these reasons, then, Henry planned to go with his wife this Easter Sunday, willingly accepting the confinement of a conventional house of worship.

I've actually come to anticipate it, he thought, knowing how pleased Lorraine would be . . . and was already.

Danny Stoltzfus, who ran the general store over near Ninepoints, was a jolly, stout fellow who'd never met a stranger. He called out his usual cheerful greeting when Eli held the door open for Sadie, its bell jingling to beat the band. They slipped inside to warm up some before indulging in a root beer from the large box of ice-cold soft drinks found in the corner of the store. "Hullo, Eli!" called Daniel, eyeing them both.

"How's business today?" Eli removed his black felt hat and pushed his hand through his hair.

"On the downturn, I'd say. Most everybody's home gettin' themselves ready for Preaching tomorrow."

"Jah . . . most." Eli turned to smile at Sadie.

She felt a thrill rush through her, all the way down to her toes. She followed him to a small table and sat down while he went to the deep icebox to retrieve their sodas.

"Been gettin' all your mail delivered these days?" Daniel asked Eli, coming around from the counter.

Sadie nearly laughed at Daniel's remark.

"Well, now, how would I know *that?*" Eli replied.

"S'pose you're right. How would ya know?" Now Daniel was the one giving it a chuckle.

Eli was grinning as he brought a frosty root beer to her, placing the opened bottle on the table in front of her. "There ya be." He sat across from her on the delicate matching chair, nearly too small for Sadie, let alone a husky man like him.

Daniel had the good sense to leave them be, turning to step behind the counter.

"How's he know you, Eli?" she whispered.

"Oh, I helped put up those shelves behind the counter," he said. "Long 'bout the third week after I arrived in Gobbler's Knob, I heard tell of Daniel's need, so I got myself down here and helped out."

She found this interesting. "And our former bishop didn't give you a tongue-lashin' for it?"

"I doubt he even heard." Eli smiled, setting down his root beer and curving his hand around it. "Figured I wasn't staying round here longer than to find me a wife and return to Ohio. Least, that's what I thought back then," he said, his voice softer.

"Oh?" She felt she might need to hold her breath.

"Now I'm lookin' to settle down in these parts . . . that is, if you'll have me for your husband, Sadie."

Surely he knows how I feel! But no, she best not make her response quite like that. "Will I have ya?" she repeated, scarcely able to keep a straight face when this was all she'd been hoping for.

"Jah, that's what I said, Missy Sadie."

She smiled her sweetest smile. "Well, jah, I think marryin' you'd be real fine and dandy." Then, right away, she said what she'd been pondering for some time. "Since Leah's never married, well . . . what would ya say if we wait till she and Jonas get hitched first?"

Eli's grin filled his whole face. "First of December, maybe?"

"Whenever you say." She nearly startled herself, sounding so compliant. But Sadie knew this man across from her with the most appealing twinkle in his eye was surely God's will for the rest of her life.

Chapter Thirty-Three

Leah felt as if the pony and cart were flying, not making contact at all with the reality of pavement. The church vote was in. They'd had their unanimous say: Jonas was now permitted to fellowship with the People — to participate in every respect as a full-fledged voting member.

The membership meeting following the Preaching service this Easter Sunday had been a true relief from the past six months, and Leah savored the vision of Jonas wearing a broad smile as he was given the hand of fellowship by the ministers.

The whole Ebersol family was overjoyed and had stayed behind for seconds on dessert at Deacon Stoltzfus's house, where Preaching had been held. Undoubtedly they would soon head home in the family buggy.

For the moment Leah needed some time alone. Time to think and talk to God, thanking Him for this most wondrous blessing.

Jonas and I can be married for sure, she thought, urging the pony to full speed.

She wondered when to bring up with her father the subject of Abe and Lydiann and where they ought to live. Should they join Jonas and Leah, or remain with Dat and Aunt Lizzie at home? With the rift between her and Lyddie fully healed, Leah certainly didn't want to appear to turn her back on either Lydiann or Abe, even though they were both well on their way to becoming young adults.

She delighted in her homeward thoughts, almost pinching herself at the remembrance of the People's vote for Jonas today.

Aware now of a team coming toward her, right down the middle of the road, Leah slowed the pony a bit.

What on earth?

She leaned forward, straining to see if the driver was at the reins, but she couldn't tell because the enclosed gray buggy was too far away. The horse looked to be galloping recklessly out of control, and the closer it came, the harder she tried to see if there was a driver inside. Or was this runaway horse pulling an empty carriage?

"Whoa!" She drew back on the reins of her pony. Once she'd come to a complete stop, she got out and swiftly tied him to a tree trunk right quick before going to stand in the road, waiting, hoping to flag down the horse.

Straightaway this time she saw the driver was slumped over in the front seat, his head bobbing as the carriage raced along. *He must be terribly ill . . . maybe unconscious.*

She knew she had to be extremely cautious and quick or she could easily get tangled up in the buggy wheels and be run over. Recently there had been an account in *The Budget* about a mishap where a church bench wagon had zigzagged down a hill. The driver had been thrown, and the wagon wheels had run him over, causing his death.

Yet with no one else to turn to, Leah must try her best to bring the horse and carriage to a stop, lest the man inside be terribly hurt or even killed. *Dear Lord, help me!*

But as the animal approached, it did not slow at her command. She noticed one of the reins dangling loose, dragging on the road. *If I can just grab it,* she thought.

With desperate resolve, she lifted her skirt with one hand and stooped and snatched the rein off the road with the other.

"Ach!" she groaned, and was immediately snatched off her feet, losing her balance. She fell to the ground, clinging to the rein as she was dragged along, screaming out in pain.

"Whoa!" she called again and again, sobbing as she did, yet refusing to let go of the rein.

The horse, whose head was pulled hard to the left, began to slow, and then, as if by a miracle, came to an abrupt stop.

Thanks be to God, she prayed silently, thankful to be alive.

She lay whimpering in the road, catching her breath. Then, little by little, she cautiously inched up to stand and saw that her dress and apron were tattered and filthy. Instantly she was terribly aware of a sharp, shooting pain in her rib cage, and she held her side.

Hobbling up to the sweating and panting horse, she spoke softly to him, hoping to keep him still. Then she reached for the bridle and slowly led the animal off the road and tied him to a tree trunk. *I can't let this horse go wild again!*

Turning, she crept to the buggy and gingerly climbed inside to check on the man, who was clearly dazed and still limp in his seat. "You all right?" she asked.

He muttered something she couldn't make out, and as he raised his head, the glazed look in his eyes suggested he might be intoxicated. She gasped. "Why, you're Cousin . . . Peter Mast, aren't you?"

The man nodded slowly, trying to sit up straight now. "Jah, I'm Peter. Who might *you* be?"

What with the ongoing ill will between this man and her family, she didn't know whether she should say. But just when she gathered enough courage to do just that, Cousin Peter's eyelids drooped closed once again.

Surely he's drunk. She'd heard something of Peter's weakness for strong drink from Jonas, and a whiff of the man's breath confirmed her suspicions. Quickly she pinched her nose at the reeking odor.

Leah took another long look at Peter, who'd caused so much trouble for herself and her family, and knew there was only one place to take him. *Dat will know what to do,* she decided, taking charge of both reins while Peter leaned like a sack of potatoes toward the right side of the buggy.

She got down and untied the horse and then returned to the carriage. She slapped the reins against the horse's haunches and managed to get it turned around and headed back toward the Ebersol Cottage. All the while Leah prayed she might not pass out from the sharp pain in her throbbing left side.

It'll never do to have two of us fainted away as if dead — not with this horse!

Mary Ruth delighted in the fellowship around her and Robert's table as their guests lingered long after the Easter feast was finished. Along with Robert's parents, they had included Dan and Dottie Nolt and their jovial Carl. And although she would have loved to have her entire family there, as well, Mary Ruth understood how important the Amish Preaching service and common meal following was to Dat and Leah and the family — especially on this most important day, when it was expected Jonas would be reinstated.

"The meal was absolutely delicious," Robert whispered to her. In her opinion, however, it was not so much the tenderness or the flavor of the roast leg of lamb and springtime vegetables that mattered, but the lively table discussion regarding today's sermon. To her amazement and delight, even her father-in-law, who in the past had shown no interest in Scripture or sermons, spoke up about the disciples' renewed zeal in spreading the Gospel following the death and resurrection of Christ.

But it was the profound comment made

just now by her dear Robert that stood out most to her. "The power that brought Jesus Christ back from the grave is the same power that today can meet our every need — body, mind, and spirit."

Lorraine was nodding her head and smiling. "Yes, and I don't believe the Lord ever calls us to accomplish tasks greater than that very power."

Mary Ruth wanted to say something, but she held back, listening now as Carl spoke up. "I say it's our purpose as Christians to use God's strength to extend His love to others — to everyone we meet."

They talked awhile longer, Robert taking out his Bible to look up several verses as Mary Ruth poured more coffee for everyone.

At one point Dottie clasped her hands together, glancing around the room. "God is at work in so many hearts."

Mary Ruth knew exactly what she meant, and, later in the kitchen, she whispered as much to Dottie. "It excites me to see hungry souls being drawn to God's saving grace. To have my father-in-law at church . . . what a blessed Easter!"

If only there was some slight indication on Hannah's part of yearning toward the Lord, Mary Ruth thought. Still, it wasn't necessary for anyone but God to know the condition of her sister's spirit, for He alone was the discerner of heart and intention. Mary Ruth knew she must continually put her faith and trust in that.

By the time Leah arrived home with Peter and his horse and carriage, she could scarcely get out of the buggy for the pain. She inched her way out, very aware of the snoring gray-haired man slouched in the front seat.

Teetering up the walkway, she reached for the back door, pulling it open with all her might. Once she'd caught her breath, each one an agony, she called as loudly as she could. "Dat! Aunt Lizzie! Somebody help!"

Immediately Dat came running out. "What's a-matter, Leah?" But one glance at her and he was hollering for Lizzie. "Come right quick!" Then to Leah, he said, "Daughter, you're awful hurt!"

"I'll manage," she said, pointing toward the carriage. "There. Cousin Peter's out cold."

Dat rushed over to have a look-see.

By then Aunt Lizzie and Lydiann were outside, as well, looking worried sick. "Oh, honey-girl, you're all *skun* up . . . what happened to ya?" Aunt Lizzie asked.

"I tried to stop Cousin Peter's runaway horse. Wasn't so easy."

"Well, for goodness' sake!" Aunt Lizzie motioned wide-eyed Lydiann to support Leah's other side, and they helped her into the house before Lydiann ran to find Abe.

Meanwhile, Dat stayed in the carriage with Peter, trying to get him to come to, no doubt. Leah could hear him talking rather loudly even from where she stood in the kitchen. Cautiously she eased herself down, settling onto the wood bench with some assistance.

She tried not to cry, but she just hurt so badly. "Someone needs to go 'n' get the pony and cart," she gasped. "Left 'em out on the road a bit east of here. The pony's tied to a tree."

"Ach, don't worry yourself," Aunt Lizzie chided, dabbing Leah's face with a cool rag and calling for Sadie, who was in the Dawdi Haus.

"What the world?" Sadie exclaimed, joining them in the kitchen. When she was told what had happened, she said, "We best be gettin' Leah off to Dr. Schwartz."

"No . . . no, I'll be all right," Leah whispered, but she wasn't so sure.

" 'Tis for your own gut," Sadie insisted.

About that time Dat came into the kitchen

nearly carrying Peter, who remained in a stupor. "Here's a man in dire need of a warm bed and a good night's sleep," Dat grunted.

Sadie gawked at Peter and looked back at Leah. "Where'd ya find *him* like this, and on Easter Sunday yet?"

"Does seem just awful . . . what a thing to be doin' on such a blessed day!" Lizzie whispered.

Lydiann returned with Abe now, who soon was helping Dat to navigate Peter to the downstairs bedroom. In short order Leah heard them easing him onto Abe's bed, both shoes clunking to the floor, and she imagined Dat's frustration at having their drunk and bad-tempered cousin here in this peaceful haven of a house.

But when he returned to the kitchen, Dat appeared not at all angry but thanked Abe for a "strong set of arms" before sending him off to bring back the pony and cart.

"Maybe Abe should go 'n' let Fannie know Peter's stayin' the night here," suggested Aunt Lizzie.

Dat agreed. "Jah, Abe, do just that, but first get the pony and cart home and then take one of my drivin' horses and a regular carriage, since it's makin' down rain now. 'Course, maybe this means Fannie'll actually let you in."

An unspoken message passed between the two, and Leah thought Dat must be wondering if Fannie would agree to hear what Abe had to say about her husband's situation.

Abe went out the back door, and Dat said to Lizzie, "When Peter awakens in the mornin', I want Leah nearby." He went and sat beside Leah, touching her bruised face in several places. "It pains me to see ya like this."

"I'll be all right," she said.

Dat looked directly at Aunt Lizzie. "Our daughter's a brave one, she is." He sighed too loudly. "Riskin' her life to save the old man's . . ." He might well have said "the old scoundrel's," but there was no resentment in his voice. "You women look after Peter, here — see that he doesn't roll out of bed and hit his noggin."

More caringly, Dat said to Leah, "You and I are goin' to go 'n' see if anything's broken. There'll be no puttin' up a fuss."

With the stinging pain in her side growing ever worse, Leah went willingly.

"This here horse's gonna get himself a mighty gut workout tonight," Dat declared as he and Lizzie helped Leah into the Mast family buggy, its being already hitched up and ready to go.

"Be ever so careful, Abram," said Lizzie.

"I'll take care of her . . . and so will Dr. Schwartz," reassured Dat.

Aunt Lizzie waved as the horse turned at the top of the lane and headed back toward the road.

"I hope they won't fret over me," Leah said, trembling now.

"Well, sure they will." Dat glanced at her and adjusted his black hat. He grunted. "Just think. We get Jonas voted back in, and somethin' like this happens."

Leah held herself together around the ribs, unable to quiet her shaking. She fought to steady herself on the ride up the road to the clinic, already pained at the buggy's jostling. *Dear Lord, help me bear this in silence.*

Lizzie and Sadie sat with Lydiann near the wood stove, leaning an ear toward the downstairs bedroom, but all they heard was the sound of loud snoring. "He'll sleep it off and not know where he is, come mornin'," Lizzie said.

"It's kinda funny Peter Mast should awaken here, ain't so?" Lydiann squelched a giggle as she opened the family Bible. Since attending Mennonite meetings, she liked to read first in German and then in English.

"Well, Mamma should be smilin' above, don't ya think?" Sadie said.

"I should say so." Lizzie rose to pour herself another cup of hot coffee. "Care for more?"

Sadie shook her head. "I've had my fill."

They worried aloud over Leah — all brush-burned and scraped up — yet marveled how she had been spared dire injury and even death. "The Lord was with her, that's for sure," said Lizzie.

"Ain't that the truth," agreed Sadie, a tear in her eye.

After a time, they began to recount the Preaching service and the members' meeting in soft tones, careful not to mention anything that shouldn't be discussed before Lydiann, as she had not yet joined church. But Leah and Jonas were foremost on Lizzie's mind. "Our girl's gonna have herself a weddin', seems to me," she declared.

" 'Bout time," Lydiann spoke up, eyes bright and a smile on her face.

"Too bad November's seven months away yet," Sadie said.

Lizzie nodded, wishing it weren't so. "But there's plenty of farm work to be done . . . sowing and reapin' come first round here.

The time of celebration will arrive soon enough." She sighed, thinking ahead to the smile of sweet bliss on Leah's face as she stood next to her Jonas. "A mighty happy day for us all."

Sadie was nodding. "Happiest ever."

Would be even more so if the Masts gave us the time of day, thought Lizzie.

CHAPTER
THIRTY-FOUR

Frustrated to be stuck in the corner of the kitchen, away from the cookstove, Leah twiddled her thumbs while Sadie and Lizzie made breakfast. Dr. Schwartz's X-rays last evening had shown a fractured rib, and he'd ordered her to take it easy. Leah was trying her best to follow through on his advice, and she felt terribly confined at being wrapped securely around the middle. There was no way for her to help much with spring housecleaning now, either at home or the Schwartzes'.

Aunt Lizzie poured coffee and brought her a full cup with a heaping teaspoon of sugar and a few drops of rich cream already added. "Who can know what a day will bring, jah?"

"Jah, for sure," whispered Leah, breathing carefully, glad for the delicious coffee — something hot to sip on a rainy day.

Lizzie stood near. "I'm awful sorry you're

hurt, honey-girl."

"Ach, I should be much better in six or seven weeks, Dr. Schwartz says."

"Till you're mended, I'll tend to all of your chores," Aunt Lizzie insisted.

"Oh, you mustn't fuss. I'll be bakin' and cleanin' in no time, you'll see."

"I say you let yourself heal first."

Leah smiled despite the painful spasms in her chest. Dear Aunt Lizzie, always looking out for everyone else. Just listening to the lull of Lizzie's gentle chatter made her relax some — that and the pills Dr. Schwartz had given, urging her not to wait until the pain crept up again before taking more.

She was thankful that other than the broken rib she had been merely bruised and scraped up on her arms, since, according to the doctor, there would be no scarring.

Aunt Lizzie kept glancing at her with pity.

"You're too worried 'bout me," Leah chided.

"Oh, now . . . I'll worry if I want to."

Just then, breaking the stillness, Dat rushed into the kitchen. "Peter's wakin' up," he announced in a hushed tone. "Come with me, daughter," he said to Leah, helping her up.

She did as she was told, slipping her arm through the crook of his as they made their way to Abe's bedroom.

They found Cousin Peter sitting up in bed, still fully dressed in wrinkled clothes, his hair standing on end.

"Gude Mariye!" Dat leaned over to offer a handshake.

Peter ignored Dat's good morning and his extended hand. He looked first at Leah and then at Dat. "What am I doin' *here?*" he growled.

Dat paused, inhaling slowly. "Sleepin' off your drunken stupor, looks like to me."

"In *your* house?" Peter's face turned red as he swung his long legs over the side of the bed.

"Ain't a single foe under this roof," Dat said calmly.

A flicker of recognition crossed Peter's eyes as he fixed his gaze on Leah and frowned. "You were in my carriage yesterday."

She nodded.

Dat spoke up. "Leah might've been a goner if she hadn't stopped your runaway horse. It was a true miracle of God she wasn't run over by the buggy wheels!" He went on to describe her fractured rib and many scrapes and bruises, embarrassing Leah no end. He surprised her even more by saying, "Here's your Good Samaritan,

Peter." Dat motioned for her to come closer. "I'd have to say my Leah spared your hide."

The three of them stood looking at one another, but mostly Peter stared at Leah, which made her feel utterly uncomfortable. At last Dat motioned for her to leave, and she went gladly, wondering if her father's sharp words to Cousin Peter would help or hinder the long-standing feud between them. Time would surely tell.

She hobbled out to the kitchen and sat at the table to rest. She was both surprised and pleased to hear Jonas's voice as he entered the back door.

"Ach, be gentle with her," Aunt Lizzie warned him.

That didn't stop him from coming near, wet through though he was from the rain. Lightly he touched Leah's bruised face.

"You best be stayin' for breakfast if you want to hear all 'bout it," Aunt Lizzie said, carrying a second large platter of bacon and eggs to the table.

"Mandie told Jake and me late last night you were hurt. I prayed as soon as I heard."

"Everything happened so fast. And Dat took me off to the clinic right away." She mentioned his father was still here. "He's talkin' to Dat now," Leah whispered as they went to sit together at the long table.

"Well, isn't *this* progress?" said Jonas, smiling. "They're talkin' to each other at least — all 'cause of what you did."

She shook her head. "Anybody would've tried."

Aunt Lizzie laughed. "I ain't exactly sure of that." She went back to tend to her pancakes. "Plenty of women folk wouldn't have taken on a wild horse *and* a drunk man."

"Oh, Aendi!" said Leah. "Ya mustn't go on so."

"We'll have to look after you better. Can't have my bride-to-be chasin' down stallions." Jonas grinned playfully.

She returned his smile, enjoying his company. "You're such a tease."

"You're just noticin'?"

Aunt Lizzie coughed slightly and looked their way. "You two best be takin' your lovey-dovey talk out to the barn."

"Jah, a gut idea" — Jonas eyed the serving dishes of piping hot food — "right after breakfast, maybe."

They discussed quietly between them what could be done to help his father. "I'm thinkin' Bishop Lapp isn't the *only* one who can befriend Dat," Jonas said. "In time your Dat might just be someone to come alongside him, too."

Leah agreed, listening as Jonas mentioned other men who might lead his father to lasting peace.

Just then Leah heard her father's voice, and then Peter's, too. "Well, what do ya know," she whispered. "Maybe their grudge *is* comin' to an end."

"I sure hope so," Jonas whispered.

Leah agreed. *What better thing to happen on Easter Monday?*

Jonas led the way in the pouring rain to Eli's, eager for his father to visit with Jake. Evidently Leah's risking her life for his had made a startling difference in his father. Jonas had seen it firsthand in the way his Dat had talked almost agreeably with Abram and Aunt Lizzie at the breakfast table not but an hour ago, even remaining at his place well after he'd finished eating.

Could it be he's softening toward the Ebersols?

When they arrived at the small farmhouse, Jonas rushed to the house for a raincoat for his father and then they hurried together through the puddles to the back door.

Inside the outer room, Jonas called into the kitchen, "Jake, you've got yourself a visitor."

Jake's eyes popped wide at the sight of

Dat, and before he could speak, their father was already saying, "Hullo, son."

"Come in," Jake said, eyes alight. He pulled up a chair for Dat and then went to pour coffee, his movements belying an undoubted sudden case of nerves. "We fellas have to fend for ourselves . . . cookin' and whatnot. A jolting experience, to say the least." Quickly he offered both Jonas and Dat biscuits and some apple butter. "Eli baked these up this mornin'."

Jonas reached for one and took a single bite, eating it plain, keenly reminded of Eli's mediocre baking skills.

Jake volunteered to pour more coffee for Dat the moment he finished his first cup and encouraged him to have another biscuit.

"Mighty gut seein' you, Jake," said Dat, looking at his son for the longest time. Jonas nearly dropped his coffee cup, and his father shifted his weight in the chair, sighing. "It was foolish and wrong of me to send you away. I knew it then . . . know it now, too."

After receiving no response from Jake, who was obviously at a loss for words, Dat turned to Jonas. "I was out of order, talkin' the way I did to you . . . that day Dr. Schwartz came to the house."

Jake spoke up at last. "It takes some getting used to, seein' you here. That's all."

Dat's eyes watered and his expression was somber. He gazed at both of them as if he had lost them for too long and was bound and determined to get them back. "You'll be seein' a lot more of me, if you're willin'."

Jake frowned and plunked down at the head of the table, where Eli always sat. "If you're sayin' I'm welcome at home, I don't mean to be rilpsich — rude — but I don't think I can agree to it, unless . . ." Jake hesitated, glancing at Jonas.

"What is it?" Dat asked.

"Well, are you and Mamma agreeable to attendin' Jonas's wedding?" Jake's tone was respectful, but his face was painfully sincere.

Jonas felt the urge to give in to a chuckle but quickly squelched it. He was touched by Jake's obvious loyalty and wanted to help his brother along, eager to hear what his father might say, as well. He addressed Dat himself. "*Will* ya come and witness my marriage to Abram's Leah?"

Dat's eyes locked with his. "An Ebersol, ya say?"

"A peach of a girl." Jonas did not breathe.

A shroud of silence hung over the room as his father appeared to consider Jonas's request. Then, shaking his head, he replied, "No . . . I'd have to say a young woman who risks her life for an old man like this is not a piece of fruit so much as she is an angel in disguise." He rose unexpectedly. "Just say when and where, and the whole family will be there with our blessing."

Jonas went to shake his father's extended hand and bumped into Jake, who was headed like an arrow to its mark. Dat wrapped his burly arms around both of them before standing to offer the sort of genuine smile Jonas hadn't seen on his face since before he'd returned for good from Ohio. He couldn't help wondering what Bishop Lapp might think if he were observing this small reunion.

"Tell Mamma and Mandie I'll be home in time for supper," said Jake, walking Dat to the door.

Jonas took up the rear, deciding not to say a word just now about his plans to stay on here with Eli till Leah and he were married. What mattered now was that his little brother had been welcomed home and, seemingly, all was well.

CHAPTER
THIRTY-FIVE

In the weeks that followed, Abram marveled at the loving care Jonas demonstrated toward Leah. Without fail he walked over from the blacksmith shop each day, carrying his brown lunch bag to sit next to her at the table, doting while he benefited from helpings of Lizzie's tasty fruit pies or chocolate cakes. Seeing Leah and Jonas cooing at each other like turtledoves made Abram's heart mighty glad.

Adah Peachey Ebersol stopped by to see Leah several times a week, as well, but it was Sadie who spent nearly every free moment with her sister, doing for her even when she protested. There were times when Abram saw them whispering like young girls, their heads close together, eyes bright with their newest secret.

Most surprising to Abram, though, were Peter Mast's visits. The man came over often, saying he was "on his way somewhere," but really — or so Abram thought — he was coming to see about Leah, concerned she was mending properly. Peter took each opportunity to apologize anew to Abram, declaring up and down he was *"es Schlimmscht vun Narre"* — the worst of fools.

Abram had insisted there was more than one *Glotzkopp* between them. He'd apologized more than once for having been deceitful enough nearly eighteen years ago to let Peter think Gid was courting Leah while she was engaged to Jonas. Both Abram and Peter agreed they had plenty of lost years to make up for, and it was Peter who said, " 'Tis a gut thing we didn't go to our graves shunnin' each other." Abram wholeheartedly agreed, mighty glad to have renewed the kinship.

Following Peter's overnight stay, Abram made the decision to help him get his drinking under control, hoping Peter might remain consistently sober for as long as it might take till he had the willpower on his own. Both Jonas and Jake were helping their father keep a good distance from strong drink, too — Jake especially, now that he was living at home again.

On this particular morning, however, when Peter dropped in to visit, both men got to talking. "What say you to having a reunion between our families, and right soon?" asked Peter.

Abram leaned on his shovel. "Sounds fine to me. Come to think of it, Lydiann and Abe have never met Fannie and most of your children."

"Likewise our Mandie and . . ." Peter paused for a second. "But would it be too uncomfortable for Jake and Lydiann, do ya think?"

"Oh, it's bound to be tickly, but it'll have to happen sometime. Anyway, Jake was over here for a short visit on Christmas Day . . . talked to Sadie for a while. Lydiann stayed put in the kitchen the whole time." Abram scratched his head, surprised at Peter's thoughtful consideration. "I'll have Leah see how Lyddie feels 'bout it." He didn't say he himself wished to spend some time getting acquainted with his only grandson. That day would come, he felt sure.

"All right, then." Peter headed for the barn door. "Talk to Lizzie, and I'll say something to Fannie."

"Well, I'll be seein' ya. Have a wunderbaar day!" he called, still getting used to *this* cousin's stopping by to chew the fat.

Lydiann caught up with Mamma Leah, who was walking very slowly back from the outhouse. "Sure's a nice day, ain't?"

"The weather's teasin' us, I think." Mamma smiled faintly. "Somethin' on your mind, dear?"

Lydiann looked warily at the sky. "Cousin Peter and Dat . . . they sure have been spendin' quite a lot of time together, visitin' and walking round the barn and such."

"Jah, the way it used to be."

She sighed. "It's right nice, them talkin' to each other again, but . . . to tell the truth, it's got me worried some."

"Why's that, Lyddie?"

"Well, with me havin' cared for Jake as my beau, it seems kind of awkward, them no longer being at odds." She felt she ought to come right out and say what she was thinking. "And since you're goin' to marry Jonas come fall, it just seems the families will be gettin' together more and more often."

Mamma stopped right there on the narrow path. "You don't have feelings for Jake yet, do ya?"

"Well, no, ain't that. . . ."

"I guess it's a gut thing we're havin' this chat, Lyddie, 'cause Dat tells me he and Peter want to have a get-together with both families on one of the no-church Sundays, comin' up fairly soon."

Lyddie nodded. "Makes sense. Abe and I

don't know the Mast cousins." *Except for Jake and Mandie,* she thought.

She looked at the tender young grass shoots pushing through the soil and the bright blue of the springtime sky. "Will it still be strange, uh . . . when Jake's married someday, and I'm married to someone else? Will he and I sit across the table, remembering our first singing and ride together under the moon? Will we always see that in each other's eyes?"

Mamma was quiet for a moment. "You wouldn't want to start seein' someone else as long as you have those thoughts of Jake."

Even now Lyddie didn't see how she could erase the past.

"I daresay it'll take some time, but you and a *new* beau — if he can make you forget you cared so deeply for Jake — will build your own lovely memories together. And when those most precious thoughts and hopes and recollections fill up all the spaces in your mind, there will be scarcely any room for the ones you made before."

"Oh, that's dear of you!" Lyddie replied as they turned to walk toward the house. "I can't wait for all those things to come true . . . one day."

They headed into the house, and right away Lydiann smelled how clean the kitchen was, the walls and floor having been scrubbed down by Sadie. And something delicious was baking in the oven — probably one of Aunt Lizzie's favorite desserts, apple crispett.

"God's ways are higher than ours," Mamma Leah whispered to her as they hung their shawls on the wooden pegs.

"That's for sure," she agreed.

Mamma kissed her on the forehead, and as she did, Lydiann noticed a tear. She was filled again with gratitude as she slipped off her shoes to help keep the floor shining clean.

Following the noon meal Leah was tickled to see her friend Adah arrive, and she welcomed her inside. "I'm all done in, so I have a gut excuse to sit and enjoy a cup of tea," Leah said.

Adah looked a bit tuckered out, as well, but her green eyes twinkled as she spoke. "Don't go to any trouble for me."

"Aw, tea's no bother." Leah carried two of her prettiest teacups and saucers to the table and sat down, waiting for the water to boil in the teakettle. "So nice of you to come by again."

They talked of how the weather had been cooperating with the farmers, and Adah said how busy her husband was sterilizing the tobacco beds and plowing the fields. "Sam and the boys will be plantin' potatoes here perty quick, ya know," Adah said. "They're actually a little behind."

Leah enjoyed the serene talk, listening as Adah spoke of the things to be done before she planted her vegetable garden.

When she had poured hot chamomile tea for both of them and offered honey to Adah, who preferred it to sugar, they settled down to visiting in earnest.

"So how *are* you doin'?" Adah asked with a mischievous look.

Leah assumed she wanted to talk about the prospects for a wedding. "You're askin' when I'm gonna be Jonas's bride, ain't?"

Adah's face reddened slightly at her admission. "Oh, I'm so happy for ya, Leah! Can it be that you two will be husband and wife after all?"

"Well, the Lord willin' and the creek don't rise," Leah joked, going on to say that she and Jonas had already decided they'd like theirs to be one of the first weddings of the season.

"When's the date?" Adah rose to look at the calendar on the back of the cellar steps.

"November third."

With her finger, Adah found the month

and day. Her eyes sparkled as she turned and came back to the table, wearing the biggest smile as she sat down. "What a wonderful-gut day that'll be." Adah frowned suddenly. "Seems there's a goings-on amongst Englishers that day, isn't there?"

Leah nodded. "When I told Mary Ruth the date, she said she and Robert would have to get out and vote for America's next president right quick after the weddin' feast."

"Jah, I heard there's a man from Arizona who's runnin' against President Johnson. My Mennonite cousin keeps sayin' we need this Goldwater for president, since he's very conservative, but I daresay we should let the English fret over all of that."

"Prob'ly so." Leah raised her teacup and thought back over all the happy years she'd had with her best friend, Adah, and here they were, talking at last of Leah and Jonas's wedding, months away though it was.

Adah stirred more honey into her tea and sighed. She eyed Leah. "You're still young enough to have babies."

Leah had contemplated that very notion, especially lately. Being she would turn thirty-four in October, she could still hope to birth several children before the change crept up on her. "If I'm anything like the

Brenneman women, surely I will, but who's to know, really."

"Your dearest dream, jah?"

Leah agreed. "Jonas and I will trust the Lord for our family."

Adah nodded, and Leah felt warmed by the sweet and knowing look on her dearest friend's face.

Abram was jubilant over his and Peter's plan for a family reunion on this, the third Sunday in April. Peter, Fannie, and as many of their family as could make it had come for dinner, which meant all but two of the married Mast daughters — Katie and Martha — had come from Grasshopper Level for the feast on this no-church day.

Abram supervised as Gid and Abe, and Jonas and his brother Eli set up two long extra tables in the kitchen, as well as a medium-sized one in the room next to the front room for the children. Lizzie, Sadie, Lydiann, and Mary Ruth had done most all of the cooking, with Leah pitching in as much as she could, even though she was still moving a bit cautiously.

Abram and Peter stood outside talking and watching the dogs romp back and forth over the yard while Peter puffed on his pipe. "Seems Fannie's taken right up with Lizzie, and vice versa," Peter was saying.

"Oh jah, the women folk have no trouble pickin' up where they left off." Abram could hear the chatter coming from the house; the happy sound of kinfolk was downright pleasing to his ears.

"And it looks like Jake and Lydiann hardly even notice each other. A gut sign." Abram had taken note of this the moment the Mast family arrived.

"Jah, I have a feelin' he might be lookin' for a new girl . . . heard he's goin' to singings again." Peter drew on his pipe for a moment, a faraway look in his eye, as if he had something else on his mind. "Say, I've been thinkin' . . . wouldn't ya like to meet Jake officially? I mean, as your grandson?"

"Why, sure. When's a gut time?"

Before Abram could stop him, Peter hurried to the house, returning in less than a minute with Jake following him.

"Hullo," Jake said warmly, extending his hand.

Abram nodded, firmly gripping the lad's hand. "*Willkumm,* Jake. Mighty nice to meet ya."

Jake ran his thumbs up and down his suspenders, glancing first at Peter and then at Abram. "Seems I've got me two families now. Not a bad spot to be in."

Peter grinned and placed his hand on Jake's shoulder. "That you have. Two of everything, I daresay."

"Best of all is us comin' back together on a day like this, ain't?" Jake said, smiling at both men.

Abram agreed, aware of a growing sense of satisfaction as he looked at his handsome and mannerly grandson. "Can't think of anything better!"

It was much later, in the midst of pie serving and coffee pouring, when Hannah leaned over and whispered to Lizzie at the table, the usual roses in Hannah's cheeks fading. As if he sensed something, Gid immediately got up from the table, helping Hannah do the same. "We best be heading home right quick."

Lizzie told Abe to ride to summon the midwife, and Gid agreed. "No hex doctor."

Sadie rose to assist Hannah out the back door, followed by Lizzie and Gid, who told his girls to "stay put with Dawdi Abram." The girls seemed glad for a chance to enjoy their newfound cousins and indulge in more dessert.

About the time Abe was getting ready to head out for afternoon milking, word came back from the log house that yet another baby girl Peachey had made her entrance into the world.

Abram was relieved to learn Hannah had not insisted on a hex doctor for this baby. It was becoming apparent Gid was having his way on that issue. *A mighty good thing for them all,* he felt.

"We named her Ada, without an *h,*" Gid told them.

Leah spoke up. "Named after your sister?"

Gid nodded and chuckled a bit. "I s'pose if we keep on havin' girls, *both* my sisters' names and all of Hannah's will end up in our family Bible."

Abram took the comment humorously, even though he caught the slightest hint of disappointment, which flickered . . . then faded, on Gid's face.

Jake certainly hadn't been staring, or at least he didn't think so. Still, he could not ignore the way Abram gestured as he spoke even now with a measure of tenderness about Gid and Hannah's newest baby girl up yonder. Jake had been fascinated to meet the ruddy-faced man his father had despised for Jake's entire lifetime — his own grandfather.

This day the blood association brought with it a tangible sense of happiness, especially because Jake wanted to believe that his existence — and the acknowledgment of his identity — was in some way responsible for bringing the two families together. And for this, he was glad to have borne the pain of rejection.

A peculiar way to mend fences, he thought as he helped his older brother Eli carry the extra tables from the kitchen to a storage shed behind the henhouse.

Returning to the yard, he saw Mandie and Lydiann walking on the mule road a short distance away, talking and laughing. His eye caught Lydiann's, but he felt only the slightest pull of discontent — more regret than anything. No getting around it, she was the prettiest girl he'd ever known, which was in her favor. Any young man would take a shine to her, and as long as she wore that winning smile, she need never worry about being a maidel. He hoped for her sake that she would find a beau who would treat her with the love and kindness he observed in Jonas's interactions with Leah.

Continuing on, he saw Sadie waving to him from the well, and he hurried to her to insist on pumping the water for her glass, moved again by her sweetness and obvious fondness for him.

"There's a volleyball game 'bout to start,"

she said, her blue eyes shining.

He could hear the voices drifting from the other side of the house and nodded, tipping his straw hat. "You gonna come play, too?" he asked.

"I'll catch up in a bit."

He found Jonas and Abe setting up a net amidst a group of eager players on the narrow stretch of yard along the lane. When asked to join in the game of boys against girls, Jake removed his straw hat and hung it on a low branch, aware of Dat and Abram leaning against the tree's trunk, still deep in conversation, Abram's expressive hands moving like slow waves in a wheat field as he talked.

Jake forced his attention back to the players, amazed afresh at the sight of his newly extended family enjoying one another's company here on Ebersol soil, as if the partition of years had fully collapsed.

CHAPTER
THIRTY-SIX

A full month had come and gone since the Ebersol and Mast family reunion, and Lizzie was anxious to plant the charity garden in the small plot of land offered by Abram. She, Sadie, Leah, and Lydiann all settled in for a long morning of work, laughing and talking as they planted lettuce, kohlrabi, Brussels sprouts, endive, eggplant, and carrots. Come July, they would be planting three hundred celery sets in another garden plot set aside for that vegetable, creamed celery being a traditional necessity for wedding feasts. At times Lizzie had to pinch herself to believe things were happening as they were for her darling girl. *Long time comin'. . . .*

Today, following noon dinner, she needed to run an errand over to Fishers' General Store for several bolts of fabric and sewing notions. She invited Leah to ride along, thinking it would be nice to have a mother-daughter chat.

When they were out on the road, a mile or so from the house, Lizzie said, "Whenever you want to sit down and talk 'bout who to assign to the work on your wedding day, we can start makin' our lists."

"I've begun doin' some of that already," Leah admitted.

"Knowin' you, I figured as much. There's goin' to be plenty to do, what with three hundred and fifty or more folk comin'."

"Uncle Jesse and Aunt Mary's children and grandchildren alone make for over sixty guests. And I want to invite all of Mamma's and your Brenneman side over in Hickory Hollow, too."

"Absolutely. Maybe we should plan for closer to four hundred guests. What do ya say?"

"Maybe so." Leah turned and looked at her. "Do ya think Uncle Noah and Aunt Becky will want to come?"

"Aw, I'm surprised you'd be askin', after all this time."

Leah nodded. "I'd like to invite them." She was silent for a while before adding, "And Jonas wants to send written invitations to several of his closest friends in Ohio, as well. Can you help me with that, too?"

Lizzie smiled, noticing the pure radiance on Leah's face. "Sadie might enjoy doin' some of the writing and addressing, too, since you both have a right nice hand."

"I 'spect she'll be thinkin' ahead to her own wedding here 'fore too long. She and Eli plan to wait till early December for that, though. Hannah says Gid thinks their waitin' till us first-timers are married is a very gut idea."

Lizzie laughed a little. "Well, then, it seems everyone knows everyone else's business, ain't so?" Of course, both girls' plans were quite different than those of the younger couples, who kept quiet about who they were even courting till the bishop published them two Sundays before the wedding day. Jonas and Leah, as well as Eli and Sadie, were certainly exceptions to the rule.

"Most of all, it's wonderful to know Peter and Fannie will be comin'. Jonas is 'specially glad."

"And havin' you as his bride-to-be makes him more than happy, I'd imagine." Lizzie leaned her shoulder against Leah, and they both laughed.

"My only challenge is choosing two single girls to be my wedding attendants," Leah said. "I truly wish Adah or Hannah or Sadie could be standin' up next to me, but, of course, that's impossible now." She was laughing again. "Everyone even close to my age has been long married."

"That's all right." Lizzie patted her hand. "You're havin' your special time just as our dear Lord planned it."

"Do you honestly believe God picks out husbands and matches them up with the right woman?"

"Well, now, I think I do, Leah."

Leah listened as Aunt Lizzie explained herself, saying she'd once read of a mother praying for the young man who would become her daughter's husband, even as the infant slept in her arms. "She asked the Lord to protect him and keep him till such time as the two would meet."

"That's the sweetest thing," Leah said.

At that Lizzie opened her heart in a most unexpected way. "You know, dear girl, since you're goin' to be a wife in the comin' months, I thought it might be the time to tell you . . . 'bout your natural father." She seemed hesitant, yet her words had a ring of determination. "I know there was a time when you felt it wasn't important to know, but how do you feel now?"

Watching her lovely hazel eyes, Leah knew

deep love for the woman who'd birthed her under such dreadful circumstances. "Honestly . . . I *have* been wonderin' again here lately."

Lizzie's eyes glistened. "You're sure?"

"Jah, I'd like to know."

Slowly, quietly, Lizzie began to tell her the last piece in the story of a rumschpringe gone reckless — thankfully for Leah, skipping over many of the details. "It may be difficult to believe, but it was Henry Schwartz who was the spruced-up young man drivin' his fast automobile that New Year's Eve . . . the day I was bound to hitchhike my way to town."

"What?" Leah could scarcely believe her ears. "Our doctor?"

Lizzie bowed her head. "Sad, but true."

"Never would I have thought this. . . . Oh, Aunt Lizzie."

They sat without speaking for the longest time before Lizzie continued, "I s'pose he doesn't suspect who *you* are, neither."

The truth slowly trickled into Leah's brain. "Then he doesn't know about me at all?"

Lizzie shook her head, tears threatening to spill. "He never knew I birthed you. Didn't even know who I was, or that I was Amish . . . I looked far different back then."

She reminded Leah of how she'd cut her hair and donned English clothes, turning her back on her Plain upbringing. "Rebellious as can be, I was."

Rebellious.

The word stung like a nettle, and Leah suddenly wondered about poor Lorraine. "What was Dr. Schwartz thinkin', for pity's sake? At the time he had to have been married with young sons, for sure!"

Lizzie put her hand over her heart. " 'Tis so. I'm awful sorry to say, but later that night, when he was beginning to sober up, he had the urge to confess to me that he'd been separated from his family for over a year. Lorraine and the boys had gone home to live with her parents while he finished his studies to become a doctor. He told me it was a trying time for them, but that was all I knew. Bein' from Hickory Hollow, I had no idea I'd ever see him again." Lizzie stopped to catch her breath. "When I found out I was in the family way, well, I was just stunned. And I wouldn't have known where to find him, even if I'd wanted to. I felt just awful, in every which way you can imagine." She added that it was then she'd felt compelled to make things right with God and the church.

Leah's heart broke anew for Lizzie — and

for the man who was her natural father. "Seems like Dr. Schwartz made things even worse for himself with his doings. But . . . as you say, he has no idea I'm his daughter." She couldn't help wondering if Lorraine had been aware of the extent of her husband's betrayal. *She seems like the kind of woman who might love a man in spite of himself.*

Leah wondered if the doctor's immoral tendencies had been passed along to Derry, the boy who'd gotten Sadie in trouble — the boy who had been, in fact, Leah's own half brother. The realization was startling.

Lizzie let the reins fall onto her lap. "What I've just shared should be for your ears only, Leah. Dr. Schwartz need never know."

Wholeheartedly Leah agreed. "Nothing gut can come of tellin', for sure and for certain. But I won't be keepin' any secrets from Jonas. I'll tell him once he becomes my husband."

"You're wise in that, I should say, provided he keeps it under his hat."

"No question 'bout it, Jonas can be trusted."

Moments later Leah realized she had another half brother in Robert. And, come to think of it, she was both cousin *and* aunt to Jake, and the same for baby Ruthie.

Strange as it seemed, she was even more closely related on the Schwartz side than the Ebersol!

Her mind in a whirl now as she pondered the many connections, she said more to herself than to Lizzie, "I s'pose it might be best for me not to think too hard 'bout all this."

Lizzie seemed to understand. "Why don't you give this to the Lord, just as I've had to."

"Oh, I'll be talkin' to God 'bout this, all right." She would also set her heart to pray even more often for Dr. Schwartz and Lorraine in the coming days. Recently the couple had actually talked of doing some volunteer work overseas, possibly getting involved with a mission organization — and this after the doctor had appeared to nearly give up on life. *God can work such miracles,* she thought.

Happy to be able to say it, she told Lizzie, "Mary Ruth says Dr. Schwartz has been attendin' church with his wife every Sunday since Easter."

"Well, that's glorious news." Lizzie clapped her hands. "Praise be!"

They rode along in the buggy, smiling into each other's faces, soaking up all the love their hearts could hold.

401

With admiration, Leah reached to pat Aunt Lizzie's hand, thinking of the many honorable and godly traits her natural mother daily demonstrated.

It was toward the latter part of August, and Hannah had tucked four-month-old baby Ada into her crib for a morning nap. The weeks since this wee one's birth had seemed nearly endless to Hannah, and she needed to get out of the house for a bit. Since the older girls were already back in school, she'd asked Gid if, on his way to the blacksmith's shop, he could see whether either Leah or Lizzie could watch Ada for a couple of hours this morning.

It wasn't long before Leah came with her needlework, wearing a bright smile. "Go out for a mornin' ride, Hannah, and don't worry 'bout a thing. I'll take care of Ada as if she were my own," she said, nearly shooing her out the door.

"I won't be long. It's lookin' to be another scorcher of a day without a speck of rain."

Leah waved good-bye, and Hannah thought again that it was too bad her sister was getting married so late in life. *Leah would've made a loving mother to quite a brood, given the chance.* Here lately Leah had told her that she believed the Lord had kept Jonas just for her, though Hannah didn't quite know what to think about that.

Eager to get going, she took her father's horse and carriage down east a ways, heading for the cemetery. Soon she found herself alone beneath the sleek blue sky and knobby trunks of trees, the breezes surrounding her like sultry whispers. The day would soon be blistering hot, and she wouldn't want to be outdoors once the sun rose high overhead. But she had needed to come here, to this hushed and tranquil place where so many of her dear ones lay in their graves, awaiting the Judgment Day.

Wandering along the rows of headstones, she was cautious not to step on the grassy plots. As a young girl, she'd felt nearly ill when she had accidentally tripped and planted one bare foot right in the middle of a newly laid grave, feeling as guilty as if she'd committed the worst possible of sins. It wouldn't do to make that mistake again.

Presently she spied the small white markers for Dawdi and Mammi Ebersol's graves and dear Mamma's, too. She blinked back tears as Dawdi John and Mammi Brenneman's gravestones also came into view. Overcome with an immense burden of sadness, she sat on an old tree stump cut nearly level with the ground. "Why must anybody die?" she spoke aloud.

She had long decided there were no sensible answers when it came to this final circumstance; all were helpless against the sting of death.

Numerous times over the years she had longed to rush to Dat's house and talk to Mamma about everything from how the baby blues seemed to catch some women unawares to why it seemed the Lord God heavenly Father listened intently to some folk's prayers and not at all to others. Such thoughts ofttimes made her feel as gloomy as she did this moment.

Aware of the heaviness in the air and the ache in her heart, Hannah sat there watching the birds, some in flight and others perched and calling back and forth in the many trees surrounding the cemetery. *Can it really be true that God cares for each of them, just as Gid says?*

When at last she rose to stroll down yet another row of tombstones, she heard someone sneeze. Turning to look, she saw Deacon Stoltzfus's wife, Sarah, painstakingly making her way through the wild ferns and up the slope toward the cemetery.

"Hullo," Hannah called so as not to alarm her.

The older woman was startled nonetheless, eyes wide at the sight of her. "Ach, I didn't expect to see Preacher Peachey's wife here on such a fine summer's day."

Hannah might've said the same of her. "Oh, I come here every so often," she admitted. "I miss my relatives terribly . . . 'specially Mamma."

Tears sprang up in the woman's eyes, and Hannah felt sorry for having said the wrong thing altogether.

"I've never told a soul, but I visit this place quite often." Sarah leaned against a tree trunk to steady herself, her lip quivering. After a time she moved onward without saying more, her gaze intent on a grave marker not far from Bishop Bontrager's own.

Her son Elias, Mary Ruth's first beau . . . dead fifteen years.

Hannah recognized the same sort of unresolved grief in Sarah as herself — the heartrending anguish she'd felt at the loss of each and every relative who'd passed away from her earliest teen years till now. Every passing had left her feeling more and more alone to struggle with her fear — even abhorrence — of death. "I think I know how you must feel," she suddenly called after Sarah.

The woman turned, her face wet with tears. "Oh, Hannah, you surely do, losin'

405

your mamma 'n' all."

"Jah, such wretched turmoil . . . feelin' trapped in one place, unable to forget the pain." She stopped to catch her breath, aware now of the sun's rays beating hard against her back. "Why is it the Lord God chooses to take some young and healthy ones and let others suffer long past their time of usefulness?" Hannah asked. "I don't understand ever so many things — the ins and outs of the Ordnung we're s'posed to take at face value, or the divine lot fallin' on an austere man, making *him* bishop, instead of a kinder, more compassionate man." She felt the words pour out of her, powerless to stop even though she was on dangerous ground, talking this way about the Lord's anointed.

Sarah made no answer and Hannah reached out, impulsively clasping her wrinkled hand. "You aren't alone, Sarah. I promise ya that."

They walked together through the thick grass, slowly moving toward Elias's grave. When they found it, they stood silently, two ministers' wives, both tormented by long-held grief.

Hannah considered the burial services she'd attended from her childhood on — the endless funeral sermons and processions of horses and carriages creeping down back roads to this burial place, the earthy smell of freshly dug graves, her fear as the first shovelful of dirt struck against a wooden coffin. She remembered having often felt guilty to be among the living, yet never wanting to experience death herself.

Sarah was crying now, her stooped shoulders heaving and her hand over her face as the two of them stood beneath the arching branches of an ancient oak tree.

In that instant Hannah pitied Sarah more than she pitied herself. This poor woman must never again be alone in her sorrow, not if Hannah had any say in it. "Come, I'll take you home," she said gently, thinking it was dangerous for her to be walking alone on the road. "No one needs to know you were here today . . . no one but me."

"Oh, denki . . . such a *liewe* — dear girl."

Hannah helped Elias's brokenhearted mamma creep down the grassy hill toward the waiting horse and buggy, tending to her as if she were her own mother.

Sunday morning Lydiann got herself settled on a bench on the side with the women folk, glad Dat had decided to have Preaching service here in the barn, where occasional breezes could be felt this late August morning. The sun hadn't been up but three hours, and already it was nearly unbearable out, the bugs thicker than ever. Grateful for the pretty flower hankie Hannah had made for her last Christmas, she waved it back and forth in front of her face, hoping for some relief, but anxious lest she breathe in a fly. *Best not to do any yawnin' during the second sermon,* Lydiann thought.

She'd chosen to sit with some of the girls her own age for these summer Preaching services, and Mamma hadn't minded at all. Deep into courting age now, Lydiann had discovered as many nice Mennonite boys — and good-looking ones, too — as Amish fellas. Cute boys aside, lately she'd been leaning in the direction of the Mennonites, mostly because the sermons made a whole lot of sense to her. Besides that, she liked to understand what was being talked about, something that wouldn't be the case with the sermons given today in High German, here in Dat's bank barn.

She looked over at her sisters and Aunt Lizzie and Mamma Leah, all of them sitting together, with Hannah's girls nearby and baby Ada snuggled in Aunt Lizzie's arms. Lydiann's heart was full with joy for Mamma Leah. She would never forget the way Mamma's pretty eyes had lit up at Jonas's return from Ohio. And now Mamma was in a perpetual state of anticipation, waiting to be united with her beloved — the boy Mamma had always loved, or so the story went.

Lydiann felt sure she'd be one of Mamma's bride attendants. And most likely, Jonas would ask one of his teenaged nephews, perhaps one of his sister Anna's sons and Leah's Uncle Jesse Ebersol's younger boys.

But she oughtn't be pondering such things as who she might be paired up with at Mamma and Jonas's wedding, not with the ministers making their entrance and the Preaching service about to begin. Yet it was next to impossible to sweep such exciting thoughts of love away. How could she, when she longed for the same kind of love Mamma and Jonas shared? That precious, narrow distance between two innocent hearts. . . .

They were well into the three-hour meeting and Deacon Stoltzfus's reading of a chapter from the Bible when a horsehair floated past Lydiann, soaring horizontally over the heads of the People.

Right away she knew what her brother and his friends were up to, all of them sitting in the back row of benches on the men's side, where they could conceal their assembly line and usual antics. One of the boys, probably Abe, mischief maker that he was, had put a long horsehair or two in his pocket this morning for this stunt. Several times now she'd witnessed her brother catch a fly between his thumb and forefinger, baiting it first with his own disgusting spit. Another boy would make a small, open loop in the end of the horsehair, and the captured insect, still alive, would have its head strung through the horsehair with the loop closing skillfully around its neck. Abe and his friends would repeat the process till four or five flies were tied to a single horsehair, finally releasing the clever creation to buzz and dip and dive over the entire assembly.

Abe never gets caught, she thought, assuming many of the flock were already dozing off due to the heat and the length of the meeting.

The airborne horsehair was about to soar past Jonas Mast, who was wide awake. He glanced up and saw the boys' prank, and the biggest grin appeared on his face.

She watched the flies drift farther toward the front, right over the deacon's head, but he never paid any mind and droned on as he read the Scripture in High German.

Lydiann sighed and fanned her handkerchief harder, wishing Abe's practical joke might flutter *her* way. If so, she'd catch it but good and show Dat what sort of things his only son was doing during Preaching these days. *Wouldn't that be a fine howdy do?*

CHAPTER
THIRTY-SEVEN

When Leah finished drying the last plate following the common meal of the first Preaching service in September, she was altogether willing to accept an afternoon ride with Jonas. She never tired of his company. Listening to his infectious laughter, or to whatever happened to be on his mind, was such a delight. They had truly become the best of friends again. The admiration she found in his eyes whenever she looked his way was even more profound than before he'd left Lancaster County.

"Dat says he wants to talk with us sometime fairly soon," Leah mentioned when they were well on their way.

Jonas glanced at her, his eyebrows raised in obvious curiosity.

"Neither he nor Aunt Lizzie said what's on his mind, so I won't be guessin'."

A smile stretched across his tan face. "Could it be your father wants to offer his blessing on our marriage?"

"Well, I doubt that's necessary anymore, knowin' how he's come to regard you, Jonas." For sure and for certain, her father had dropped plenty of hints this past year indicating how pleased he was with Jonas's return home . . . and into her life, too.

Jonas let the reins lay across his knees and reached for her hand. "Then we best be waitin'."

"Jah, we've become real gut at *that.*" She was unable to suppress a titter, and he joined in, their laughter blending with the melodies of birds and insects surrounding them.

Lizzie always did her best praying in the woods, speaking out loud into the air, saying what was on her heart and mind. She felt she needed to do exactly this today, as she and Leah had been hard at it for hours on end, deciding who of their many relatives and friends should be asked to help on the day of the wedding. With such a large celebration, there was need for a great many cooks, servers, men to set up benches, and teenage boys to tend to the numerous horses when guests arrived.

Presently she made her way up the long hill, past the stone wall surrounding the side

413

of the log house, the snug abode where she'd spent so many years living alone, growing in the nurture and admonition of the Lord while watching little Leah become a kind and thoughtful young woman.

She waved to Gid, who was up working on his roof, nailing down the shingles that had blown off in last night's fierce wind. Abe and Jonas were doing the same at the main house. Such a gale had come up in the wee hours. *Like to waken the dead,* she recalled, picking up her pace.

Deliberately she pushed her feet hard into the grassy path that led to the crest of the glimmering hillock a good ways from here. As she went, she took in all the various hues of dark green brushwood, reddening sumac, and hints of gold and orange from oak, maple, and locust, all soon to be ablaze with the brilliance of autumn. Deeply she breathed in the sweet smells.

The sky began to disappear as the woods closed in around her. Multitudes of black-birds soared above, fluttering from tree to tree — nature's resonance bringing peace to her mind.

The sun-drenched outcroppings signaled she was approaching the densest part of the forest, not so far from the hunters' shack where Leah had had her beginnings. The place had become more and more rundown over the years, though Lizzie had been keeping herself so busy she scarcely ever ventured into the woods this far. Still, something within her urged her onward.

At last she arrived at the summit, and, catching her breath, she turned to look at the ramshackle structure. There, strewn on the ground, lay so many rickety boards like cast-off lumber. "Well, I declare." She put her hands on her hips and began to laugh. "The effect of a single night's storm!" she said right out.

Lest by some miracle she be heard, she ceased her hilarity and went over and tugged on a sliver of the decaying wood. "A stark reminder of God's forgiveness and grace." She pushed it down into her pocket. "Help me never forget all your tender mercies, Lord."

Later, when she returned home, she told Abram about all the rotting firewood up yonder, and he said he'd ask Jonas, Gid, and Abe to go up and haul back the debris. Sadie must have overheard, because her face burst into a jubilant smile. Lizzie knew exactly how she felt.

Abram mentioned he'd never used the shanty, it having been built by Englishers years ago. "But that doesn't mean there oughtn't to be a place for shelter from the elements come huntin' season," he said, and Abe agreed.

Her husband had a point, and there was time between now and deer hunting season to get other hunters interested in pitching in money for lumber and whatnot. Just a few menfolk could easily construct a replacement in a single day.

Lizzie went about her cooking chores, well aware of Sadie's zipped lip — and, bless her heart, if she didn't wear a grin clean past supper and on into eventide, when Abram read from the old Bible to all of them.

Listening intently to the Word of Life, Lizzie pressed the stubby splinter of wood deep in her pocket — a somber reminder that only the dear Lord could see . . . and understand.

Mid-September brought a distinct coolness to the night air, and Abram much preferred such temperatures for sleeping. Since a boy, he had eagerly anticipated the coming of autumn, and with Leah's coming marriage, this year was no exception.

Lizzie cut a piece of carrot cake for both Jonas and Leah while Abram cheerfully told of his plan. "I'd like my new son and his bride to live here in this house, once you're wed," he told them.

Leah's smile widened and Jonas reached out a hand to shake Abram's. "You have no idea how grateful Leah and I are 'bout this. Denki, Abram . . . thank you!"

"Jah," Leah said, eyes bright with tears, "we appreciate this so much, Dat . . . and Lizzie."

Abram inhaled and felt good all over. "With Lizzie and me settled into the Dawdi Haus, Abe and Lydiann can come and go 'tween it and the main house as they please," he suggested.

Leah looked at Jonas, nodding her head. "This answers the question I've been ponderin' for some time now."

Jonas slipped his arm around her. "You'll be keepin' your word to your mamma and then some, jah?"

Abram went on to say there were a number of bedrooms to choose from, as far as Lydiann and Abe were concerned. By this he was letting Leah know she didn't have to fret about his children's welfare. Abe could continue to sleep in the first-floor bedroom in this house, and Lydiann could sleep upstairs next door in the second bedroom. "There's plenty of room for everyone . . . includin' any little ones to come, the Lord willin'."

Leah spoke up. "Sadie may want to stay in one of the Dawdi Haus bedrooms till she's married, which would mean Lyddie could have my old room upstairs for a while."

Abram didn't need to pretend surprise about Sadie and Eli Yoder, for the news was common knowledge among the family . . . and the grapevine. "Jah, my eldest daughters will both be happily hitched before year's end." He looked kindly at Lizzie, who'd just planted herself down next to him at the table.

"The Lord's been gut to us all," she said, eyes smiling.

"And for that we give Him all the glory and praise." Abram would have reached over and clasped Lizzie's hand but for the young lovebirds present.

Later, he thought, anxious to hold his Lizzie near.

CHAPTER
THIRTY-EIGHT

By the time late October rolled around, there were radiant hues of reds, oranges, and gold in every direction and things were shaping up nicely for Leah's wedding.

A week before, Lizzie, Sadie, Leah, and Lydiann, along with a half-dozen other women, washed down all the upstairs bedroom walls and the hallway, too, scrubbing woodwork and windows in preparation for painting, as each room in the house would be put to good use during the daylong festivities.

Meanwhile, the menfolk were building a temporary enclosure for the front porch, to provide additional space.

Toward the end of the hectic afternoon, Lizzie sought out Leah and found her in the kitchen of the Dawdi Haus, where she and Sadie were catching their breath, having some hot tea and strawberry jam on toast. "Oh, I hope I'm not interruptin'," she said, standing back from the table.

"Not at all, Aunt Lizzie . . . please, come join us." Leah rose to pull out a chair.

"Well, denki, but I came to show you some hope-chest items I've put aside." Not to exclude Sadie, she added quickly, "I have keepsakes for your sister, too . . . when the time comes."

To this Sadie smiled, waving Leah on. "I'll warm up your tea when you return."

Lizzie led the way back to the main house and up the steps to the bedroom she shared with Abram — for now. Opening the long chest at the foot of the bed, Lizzie removed several quilts. "I want you to have these," she said, presenting first a purple, red, and green diamond-in-the-square quilt and then two others, both the sixteen-patch pattern. "My mother and her mother — your great-grandmammi — made these when she was eighteen . . . for her own wedding."

"Oh, Lizzie, they're beautiful!" Leah ran her fingers down the wide binding that served to identify the quilt's Lancaster County origin.

"You won't see that width in other places round the state . . . nor in the Midwest," Lizzie reminded her.

Leah was obviously pleased and gave her a quick hug. "Mammi Brenneman was a new quilter when she made these?"

"No, she started much earlier . . . at fourteen, I believe."

"Well, I'll take good care of them." There was absolute delight on Leah's face.

"Maybe one day you'll hand them down to your own daughter."

Leah squeezed her hand. "Denki ever so much." Then she paused, studying her for a quiet moment. "You were always Aunt Lizzie to my sisters and me," she said, "and I've never called you Mamma . . . but I'd like to start. Today — from now on."

Her joy spilling from her lips, Lizzie whispered, "Oh, Leah . . . my dear, dear girl."

On the day before Leah's wedding a whole string of helpers, like so many sparrows, worked steadily to remove the wall partitions between the front room, downstairs bedroom, and kitchen, before unloading the bench wagon and setting up the seating.

By midmorning Jonas had already wrung the necks of a good three-dozen chickens, aided by Abe in the chopping off of heads. Aunt Lizzie, Sadie, and Lydiann plucked and cleaned the fowl and baked them for the roast, which was similar to stuffing but with finely chopped pieces of chicken mixed in. It would be served as the main dish at tomorrow's wedding feast.

The creaking of the windmill had long since replaced the pleasant song of birds and raspy crickets, and the ladybugs and other insects were nestled deep in their underground hideaways. The recent snow flurries had resulted in no accumulation, making travel to the Ebersol Cottage tomorrow easier for the People. And for this Leah was thankful.

Immediately following the noon meal, at Aunt Lizzie's urging, Leah and Sadie set out for a walk to the high meadow behind the barn, in the grassland, away from the buzz of wedding preparations. One last sisterly walk before Leah became Jonas's bride.

Arm in arm, Leah matched Sadie's lengthy strides. "I can't tell ya how glad I am that Eli's stayin' put in Gobbler's Knob," she said.

"And to think his Ohio bishop sent permission some weeks ago to transfer his membership here."

Leah nodded. "This means we'll be seein' each other quite a lot, even after you're married."

"Livin' close enough to borrow a cup of sugar now and then." Sadie's smile was warm, even playful. "Remember the way you and I always talked when we were little girls?"

"Jah . . . and I still can hardly believe Dat gave the main house to Jonas and me."

Sadie let go of Leah and leaned down to pull up a slender piece of dry, wild grass. She twirled it around between her fingers, surely lost in thought. "Makes sense, really — the way it ought to be — 'specially after Dat was so opposed to Jonas back when."

"Seems like nearly a lifetime ago." Leah couldn't help but smile. "I have to say, the Lord has blessed Jonas and me. Not just because of Dat's present generosity . . . it goes so much further than that."

Sadie reached over and tickled Leah's face with the grassy shoot. "You deserve every happiness, sister. And don't forget, I'm askin' the Lord God to give you a houseful of children."

Leah laughed softly. "Speakin' of that, you'll be seein' Jake again today, jah?"

"I'm excited the entire Mast clan is comin' for the weddin' . . . and staying all day, too, is what Dat says."

" 'Tis true," Leah replied. "Jonas is nearly jumpin' up and down 'bout it."

"Well, no wonder."

They walked all the way to the edge of the property and turned to look back at the gray stone farmhouse built by Dat's bishop-grandfather. "Just think, Dat and Mamma weren't even born yet when the foundation was laid for the Ebersol Cottage," Leah said thoughtfully.

"And such a large, comfortable place it is." Sadie let the blade of grass fall from her fingers, a gentle breeze stirring the loose hairs at her temple. "I've never understood why you called our house a cottage."

"Well, it's a cozy abode, ain't? It just seemed right somehow to call it that." Leah sighed. "So many happy days . . . and years spent here."

"And many more to come, the Lord willin'." Sadie offered her prettiest smile. "I've learned so much about God's love in Dat's big house. Beginning with Mamma and then from you, Leah — the way you give and give, expecting nothin' in return."

"Well, now, we've both been through a-plenty."

Sadie looked at the sky, squinting up. "Watching you live your life has been better for me than a sermon, sister."

Leah felt her face blush at that. "Oh, now."

"No . . . I'm serious. I wish I might've walked the narrow way earlier in my life."

"Well, you are now and that's what matters."

They reminisced about their childhood days, including their fondest memories of dear Mamma. "I hope there's a way she knows how happy we are."

"Oh, surely there is," Sadie said quickly. "Mamma would be the first person to wish you well . . . I just know it. She always liked Jonas, don't forget."

Leah knew that to be true. A bittersweet feeling came and went like a feather fluttering past her in the breeze, and she and Sadie made their way back toward the house, keenly aware of the many changes ahead.

CHAPTER
THIRTY-NINE

November third.

Leah awakened hours before daybreak, lying in bed still as can be, needing to return to sleep, but thoughts of Jonas and their wedding keeping her much too alert to rest.

She pushed back the blankets and quilt coverlet and rose to greet the day, getting herself dressed, not yet in her newly sewn blue cape dress and full white apron, but in a green everyday dress and black apron.

As she brushed through her long hair, preparing to wind it up into the customary bun, she thought again of Mamma, remembering a summer's day when she and Sadie had taken themselves off on a hiking adventure through the woods after having been repeatedly warned to stay away. The two of them had gotten lost, though not for long, and both had fallen, badly banging up their elbows and ripping their dresses. Leah recalled Mamma bursting into tears at the sight of them all *lumbich,* and she smiled now at the recollection, recalling how very loving Mamma had been, taking them in her arms to soothe away the hurts.

She was glad for the memory, though she cringed now at what a dreadful wait Mamma had endured. Breathing a prayer of thanksgiving for the lessons of obedience she'd learned along the way, Leah was wholly grateful for her loving family, and for God's hand on her life . . . and on Jonas's.

Abram headed for the milk house to deposit the morning's fresh milk, whispering to himself, "Leah's gettin' herself a husband today." The realization had been long coming, yet it was not until this moment that he had fully embraced it.

Jonas will care for her, just as I have all these years, he thought, lifting the heavy door to the cooler.

Once he'd put in the milk cans, he went and stood at the window, peering out. Had he ever really forgiven himself for the part he'd played in keeping the adoring couple apart?

He removed his black hat and shook his head, astounded that Leah regarded him at all as her father. True, he was not her natural parent, and Lizzie had shared with him some time back that Leah now knew the truth on that matter. Abram had asked Lizzie not to reveal it to him, to which Lizzie had screwed up her face into a hard frown and asked if he wasn't dealing with "the green-eyed monster." Well, sure, he was, or had been. But life went on, and one's time allotted to living on earth was entirely too brief to be harboring enmity.

Abram's Leah, he thought, thinking over all the years Lizzie's only child had been described that way. No longer. Jonas had somehow managed to wait for what he did not know would ever come to him. *A bit like faith in the Lord Jesus — not seeing, yet believing.*

Heading toward the barn, Abram breathed in the crisp air, glad for the glistening, snowy coating of powdery white that covered fields, barnyard, and the yards. All was still, and the sky was nearly as white as the ground, the clouds seemingly suspended motionless there. "Such a fine day. . . ."

Jonas sat tall and handsome directly across from Leah, wearing his new black suit and a little black bow tie that stood out nicely against his pressed white shirt. Nathaniel King Jr., Jonas's nephew, and Zeke Ebersol,

428

Uncle Jesse's eldest grandson, sat on either side of Leah's groom, wearing similar suits and bow ties, faces shiny from scrubbing.

Leah wondered what Lydiann was thinking, knowing she would be paired up with blond, good-looking Nathaniel for the blessed day of celebration. Lydiann and Mandie Mast were her two beaming attendants.

The house was filled with not only every Ebersol family member age sixteen and up, but also the Mast family adults. And members from both the Gobbler's Knob and Grasshopper Level church districts, and even a handful of Jonas's friends from Ohio — Preacher Sol Raber and Emma Graber — were present. Henry and Lorraine Schwartz came and sat in the back with all the other invited Englishers, including the Nolts and a host of other neighbors who had frequented the Ebersol roadside stand through the years.

Leah caught Jonas's loving gaze and his unexpected wink, and her heart thrilled to his playful expression. She sat still, her eyes never wavering from her darling, hoping he might see the affection in her own heart written on her face.

She pondered all she'd come to know and understand through the years about relationships, especially between a man and a woman. In her mind, the sort of trust she and Jonas had tested over time went far beyond what anyone around them might notice. The tender care they'd had for each other even as youngsters had made the many years of their separation all the more bitter for them.

Yet here they were. She could hardly wait to stand before the bishop and the nearly four hundred guests, ever so ready to say she believed Jonas's and her marriage was definitely from God, that she accepted her brother in the fellowship as her husband.

When the ministers began to file slowly into the room, Leah lowered her head as was customary. *Thank you, Lord, for keeping Jonas only for me . . . and me for him.*

The song leader — *der Vorsinger* — began the third verse of the Lob Lied from the Ausbund. Sitting between his attendants, Jonas lifted his voice in song as he looked across to his bride and her half of the wedding party.

Preacher Gid presented the opening sermon, recounting the stories of creation, Adam and Eve in the garden, the birth of the first children, the sacrifice of burnt offerings, all the way to the great flood and

Noah's praiseworthiness for having descendants who did not marry unbelievers. Jonas was again impressed at his detailed telling; Gid had certainly grown in his knowledge of Scripture since becoming a Preacher.

Levi King, the newly ordained Gobbler's Knob bishop, gave the main sermon. It would be he who put forth the important questions when the time came for them to be pronounced as husband and wife.

At this moment, however, Jonas looked fondly at his bride. Would he lose all sense of time, not to mention his own good sense, while Bishop King continued the chronicling of Bible stories from the love of Isaac and Rebekah to the marriage of Jacob and Rachel?

Leah is beautiful, he thought, observing her face and radiant expression. He could no longer resist staring at her loveliness — her pretty lips, the color of her hazel-gold eyes, and the rich brunette hue of her hair. He contemplated Leah's waist-length tresses, now tucked devoutly beneath her Kapp.

Tonight . . . he chided himself.

"Husbands, love your wives, even as Christ also loved the church, and gave himself for it," the bishop was saying.

Sadie caught a glimpse of Eli sitting with the other men on this most holy day. *Can it be that I, too, will soon stand where Leah is, beside my husband-to-be?*

She could scarcely believe how richly God had answered her prayers, giving her the chance to get to know and be known by her son and the opportunity to wed again in a mere month.

For whither thou goest, I will go; and where thou lodgest, I will lodge: thy people shall be my people, and thy God my God. . . .

Eli had quoted that same Scripture not so many nights ago as they were discussing where they should live — whether to continue renting the present farmhouse, where Eli had been living with Jonas, or to purchase a house of their own. "Or we could build one," he'd said, seemingly eager to do the latter.

But just now the bishop was asking Jonas if he would be loyal and tend to Leah's needs. "Will you care for her as a God-fearing husband?"

"Jah," Jonas answered in a clear, strong voice.

When the bishop looked at Leah and asked the same question, Sadie saw there were tears welling up in her sister's eyes.

May God bless their happy union.

Sadie was almost overwhelmed by the tenderness and love between Leah and Jonas. Composing herself, she wondered when she'd ever seen Leah's face glow with such happiness. Perhaps once, on the Sunday afternoon following Leah's and Jonas's baptisms. They'd gone off riding together and Leah had confided in her later that she'd never been happier in her whole life. At the time Sadie had secretly guessed Jonas might've stolen a kiss or two — no doubt Leah's first ever.

The bishop further addressed the couple, particularly Jonas. "Do you stand in the assurance that this sister is intended of the Lord God to be your wedded wife?"

"Jah," Jonas answered with confidence.

"Do you promise before God and His church gathered here today that you will nevermore depart from her, but will look after her, care for her needs, and cherish her until our dear God and Father will separate you one from the other?"

Jonas paused ever so briefly, and Sadie wondered if the mention of separation through death was the reason, but as his resounding "jah" came forth, Leah broke into another smile.

The same questions were asked of Leah, and soon the bishop was offering the final words, so familiar to Sadie and to all of the People. Jonas reached for Leah's hands, their locked gaze evident to all.

Sadie held her breath lest she sob with joy, reaching under her sleeve to find the butterfly hankie she always kept tucked away there. For sure and for certain, this incredibly hopeful day encompassed all that dear Leah had ever dreamed of, both for Jonas . . . and for herself.

Do you promise before God and His church . . .

Lydiann stood tall as can be next to Mamma Leah, her precious mother. Truly, her sister was that to her. Attending the woman who'd loved and nurtured her all these years, Lydiann felt as warm and good as ever she could remember. She hoped if or when the day came for her to marry, she, too, might look as lovely and *in love* as Mamma did this very instant.

Indeed, she could dream, and she surely did, that *her* dearest beau would come along and find her soon — or, as Mamma often said, when it was God's time.

The bishop went on. "The God of Abraham, of Isaac, and of Jacob be ever with you. And may He grant you His divine and abundant blessing and grant you mercy through Jesus Christ. Amen."

Together with her handsome partner, Lydiann followed Jonas and Mamma out of the front room to the upstairs, where they were to wait privately — she and Mandie in one bedroom, the young men in another — till the wedding feast was ready to be served. All Lydiann could think of was the wonder of love, hardly able to wait for such a day to dawn for her.

"Jonas, your eyes are shining," Leah whispered when they were alone in the room where they would spend their wedding night.

Her husband seemed to be saying many things with his eyes today. His strong, warm fingers curled around hers, and he pulled her into his arms. "You're right where you belong, love."

She leaned her head against his heart, and after a time, she looked up at him. Slowly he cupped her face in his hands and his lips found hers.

I could fly, she thought, eager for more of his tender kisses.

He held her close and she never wanted to let go. "I know why I was born . . . it was for you, Leah. Always for you."

She gave him her best smile and then let

out a little giggle. They both laughed, though trying their best not to be heard by the bridal attendants down the hall. Certainly, their laughter would not reach the ears of the People, already busy with work below. The men assigned to setting up tables were placing three benches side by side to create one table, elevating it with a special trestle beneath. White tablecloths would be distributed and placed on the many tables soon to be laden with the wedding feast: roast chicken with bread stuffing, mashed potatoes and gravy, coleslaw, celery sticks, creamed celery, peaches, prunes, pickles, freshly made bread, jams and jellies, cherry pies, and cream-filled doughnuts galore.

Leah could scarcely wait to sit at the Eck, the extra-special corner table reserved for Jonas and her and their wedding attendants, where the bride was expected to sit to the left of the groom, just as they would sit in their family buggy from now on as husband and wife.

Jonas took her hand and led her to the window. There he kissed her again, his lips lingering longer this time.

"I'm Leah Mast," she whispered, coming up for air. She turned to look out at the forest and the sky with her darling. A sudden multitude of birds soared up into the spacious blue sky, and she lifted her face once again to Jonas's. "Together for always."

EPILOGUE

Although it has been nearly two years since Jonas and I said our vows to God and each other, I feel as dearly cherished by him as I did on our wedding day. We talk over everything at the end of each day, never allowing a single thing to come between us.

We were both delighted when our new bishop gave permission for Jonas to make and sell fine furniture. So far it's only a part-time job, and in the rest of his working hours he continues to assist Gid in the blacksmith shop, but Jonas does seem to have a near-constant grin on his handsome face. Someday I wouldn't be surprised if he is able to be full-time in his woodworking shop as word about his gift gets out not only amongst the People but also with English-ers.

As is our custom, I quit working for Dr. Schwartz and his wife several weeks before I got married, and it is Lydiann who now earns a bit of pin money by checking on the house when the Schwartzes are overseas helping with their church-related mission projects. Especially because of the change in the doctor's heart, I was relieved to hear from Lorraine that Peter Mast vowed never to press charges against him for what he did so long ago, which was awful good of Peter to go and say, seeing how Dr. Schwartz lived in fear of that very thing.

A few weeks following Jonas's and my wedding, Eli and Sadie were married. About a hundred family members were on hand for the half-day affair, and Sadie was the prettiest bride I've ever seen. Now she's the happy mother of blue-eyed, fair-haired Leah — my sweet little namesake. Goodness knows Sadie has longed for this baby! To think I'll be hearing my own name for many years to come when they visit or on Sunday-go-to-meeting days.

Jake still lives in Grasshopper Level, working at home, having taken over many of the duties of the orchard and farm from Peter. He happily takes Mandie to singings, as brothers do. And he's seeing a serious "sweetheart," too, I hear. Sadie says he spends much of his leisure time visiting her and Eli, often playing blocks with his wee half sister, who reportedly has learned to stick out her tiny tongue on command when he is near.

A few months ago Hannah surprised Gid with his firstborn son — named Gideon, of course. So tiny Ada has a close-in-age playmate, and their big sisters keep out a watchful eye, acting as live-in baby-sitters, Hannah says. Thankfully my sister is more settled than she's been in years, regularly enjoying quilting bees and other work frolics, even though she has more children than ever before.

Mary Ruth is expecting her second baby late spring of next year, and she and Robert are as busy as ever in the work of their church. When she and Hannah and their families get together, it's most enjoyable for all of us to watch their children frolic, Ruthie and Ada in particular playing much as the twins themselves once did.

As for dear Lydiann, she has decided to follow in Mary Ruth's footsteps and join the Mennonite church, and I gather from her recent confidences in me that she plans to become Mrs. Carl Nolt not long after her church baptism. There is that certain bounce to her step, giving us all cause to smile — even Dat, I daresay.

Well, it's nearly time for Jonas to come

home for the noon meal, and I look forward to his company. What with cooing twin boys to make over, I sometimes forget how to talk like a grown-up.

Jonas is as gentle a father as ever was with our little ones. Having *two* babies instead of one was quite a big surprise, but Jonas believes it's the Lord's way of making up for lost time. That just may be, and I'd have to say tiny Abraham and Peter are the joy of our lives. They look ever so much like both Jonas *and* me, our families say, but truly I think both boys bear a strong likeness to Jonas and his father. I had wondered, even worried a bit while carrying them close to my heart, how I'd feel if either of them bore a resemblance to Dr. Schwartz, just as Jake has always looked so much like Derek — as if the secret was determined to be known, stamped as it is upon his face — but that fretting was needless in the end.

And then there is our Abe, who unnerves all of us when he says he's "livin' in his rumschpringe," and this with a mischievous grin. At present he is thrilled to have two *boys* in the Ebersol Cottage, and both he and Jonas like to get right down close and jabber in Dutch to our babies.

As for me, I like to whisper to my sons while holding them near, one in each arm.

Always I begin with that day of days — Second Christmas on Grasshopper Level — when I first caught the blue-eyed gaze of the dearest boy ever. "I'm talking 'bout your father," I say, leaning down and kissing each downy head.

Just today Dat came into the kitchen while I was relating to my babies how I'd fallen for Jonas back before I was old enough to know better. "Well," he said right out, "just listen to you go on so." He was smiling to beat the band, and when I waited to hear what was on his mind, he said, "I can only hope I live long enough to tell these young'uns how wonderful-gut it is that their mamma ended up married to their Dat."

"Oh, now . . . for goodness' sakes," I said.

"No . . . no, 'tis quite a love story." His gray head bobbed up and down, as if to emphasize the words.

I couldn't help but thank God anew for the enduring love strands, divine and otherwise, that brought Jonas and me together, strands that bind us together even now.

Dat stood near where I sat in the rocking chair, gazing down at the matching bundles in my arms. "Bless the Lord and Father of us all," he said, a catch in his voice.

"You're not becomin' *weechhatzich,* are ya?" I looked up at him.

"Softhearted?" To this he waved casually. "Well, ain't such a terrible thing, I don't think."

I rose from the rocker with his help and went and tucked my babies into the double-wide wooden cradle crafted by their father. Then I followed Dat into the front room, walking past the spot where Jonas and I had stood and promised to love each other all the days of our lives.

Dat bade farewell as he walked through the doorway connecting the Dawdi Haus to this one, and I stood at the window and stared out at the multicolored patchwork squares of fertile fields stretching out in all directions. After a while I turned and walked the length of the room, recalling the several times Jonas and I had hosted Preaching service here as husband and wife, thankful for the way Jonas's heart was turned toward the Lord and His Word.

The familiar creak of the kitchen door signaled my darling's arrival, and I hurried to greet him, always eager for his strong embrace and fervent kisses.

"How's my perty wife?" he asked, holding me ever so tight.

"Busy as a honeybee, I s'pose."

"Must be why you're so sweet."

I laughed softly, not wanting to wake the

babies. That brought another smile to his handsome face . . . and a kiss for me. Then, hand in hand, we tiptoed over to the wide cradle to gaze at our most precious gifts, ever grateful to God.

ACKNOWLEDGMENTS

My first debt of gratitude is to my husband, Dave, for making it possible for me to skip meals and work late in order to create a saga-style series like this from idea to publication. There would be no ABRAM'S DAUGHTERS without the encouragement, love, and constant support of our family, as well. Thanks to Julie for reading the first draft with such enthusiasm . . . and for making all those healthy snacks. I also always appreciate Janie's and Jonathan's earnest prayers. And my gratefulness goes to my son-in-law, Kenny, for his research assistance.

This final book could never have come together in the amazing way it did without the fine attention to detail from my editors: Carol Johnson, Rochelle Glöege, and David Horton. I also wish to thank Julie Klassen and Cheri Hansen for their editorial input; Jerad Milgrim for his military research assistance; Fay Landis, Priscilla Stoltzfus, and Hank Hershberger for their answers to Amish-related questions; and Carol Johnson for her description of the café in Florence, Italy.

My heartfelt appreciation goes to Monk and Marijane Troyer for their contribution of the "flying horsehair escapade," and for permitting me to include it. To the anonymous Lancaster County research assistants who wish to remain so, I offer my ongoing debt of gratitude and love.

For readers interested in making the Amish roast referred to in this book, the recipe is found on page 82 of *The Beverly Lewis Amish Heritage Cookbook*.

As always, I offer earnest thanks to my loyal readers for the thoughtful e-mail (and snail mail) notes and comments — so encouraging to me. To my faithful partners in prayer, may the Lord Jesus bless each one.

"And I pray that you, being rooted and established in love, may have power, together with all the saints, to grasp how wide and long and high and deep is the love of Christ, and to know this love that surpasses knowledge — that you may be filled to the measure of all the fullness of God." — Ephesians 3:17b–19, NIV

ABOUT THE AUTHOR

Beverly Lewis, born in the heart of Pennsylvania Dutch country, fondly recalls her growing-up years. A keen interest in her mother's Plain family heritage has led Beverly to set many of her popular stories in Lancaster County.

A former schoolteacher and accomplished pianist, Beverly is a member of the National League of American Pen Women (the Pikes Peak branch). She is the 2003 recipient of the Distinguished Alumnus Award at Evangel University, Springfield, Missouri, and her blockbuster novel, *The Shunning,* recently won the Gold Book Award. Her bestselling novel *October Song* won the Silver Seal in the Benjamin Franklin Awards, and *The Postcard* and *Sanctuary* (a collaboration with her husband, David) received Silver Angel Awards, as did her delightful picture book for all ages, *Annika's*

Secret Wish. Beverly and her husband make their home in the Colorado foothills.

The employees of Thorndike Press hope you have enjoyed this Large Print book. All our Thorndike and Wheeler Large Print titles are designed for easy reading, and all our books are made to last. Other Thorndike Press Large Print books are available at your library, through selected bookstores, or directly from us.

For information about titles, please call:

(800) 223-1244

or visit our Web site at:

www.gale.com/thorndike
www.gale.com/wheeler

To share your comments, please write:

Publisher
Thorndike Press
295 Kennedy Memorial Drive
Waterville, ME 04901

The Time the World Drowned

Bible Stories in Rhythm and Rhyme

Written by Sheri Dunham Haan
Illustrated by Daniel J. Hochstatter

vw SG

Contents

Preface

Although rhythm and stories both date back almost farther in history than we can trace, very few such stories are based on the Bible. And even fewer have been written down for young children to enjoy.

Nursery age children will probably enjoy the stories most by hearing them read. Soon children begin clapping hands or tapping feet while they listen to the strong cadence. Older children will want to do more complicated clapping rhythms. A family with young children can use these stories effectively as devotions.

Read these stories at a pace that is comfortable for you. As you become more familiar with them, you and your child will enjoy a quick, lively pace. Read a line and have your child chant it back to you. Use the stories as a happy, natural way to reinforce Bible truths.

The Time the World Drowned
—Genesis 6–9

Most all the people God had made
Began to be so bad,
That God planned to destroy them
Though it made him very sad.

God spoke to his friend Noah,
Telling him to build a boat,
To build it very carefully
So it would surely float.

Noah worked for months and years.
And when the boat was done,
He put two of every creature in
And didn't miss a one!

Then Noah and his folks went in
And God sealed up the door.
Then God started floods and rain.
Oh! How it did pour!

For forty days and nights it rained.
The wicked were all drowned.
But on the inside of the boat
All was safe and sound!

When God had dried his soggy world,
He opened up the door;
He promised Noah and his folks
To bless them evermore!
          And
He'd drown the world no more.
Yes, he'd drown the world no more!

David and the Giant
—1 Samuel 17:1-50

Young David left his father's house
With lots of cheese and bread;
He was off to see his brothers,
To do as father said.

When David reached their campground,
He found the soldiers scared;
Not one would fight the giant
There wasn't one who dared!

This giant was Goliath,

He was a monstrous man;

Each time he screamed and shouted,

All the soldiers ran!

One day as great Goliath roared,
"Send over your best man,"
David picked up five small stones
And tucked them in his hand.

Young David took his slingshot
And loaded it with care.
And as he swung it 'round and 'round,
One stone sailed through the air.

932494

Right between Goliath's eyes
It sunk into his head.
Just like that, Goliath fell,
The giant crashed down dead!
     Yes!
Goliath crashed down dead!

Saved By the Queen
—*Esther 3–7*

Haman was a scheming man
Who got the king's okay
To do away with all the Jews
And do it his own way.

Queen Esther thought and worried,
"I wish my husband knew
That even though I am the queen,
I also am a Jew!"

She soon decided on a plan
To try to save the Jews.
She asked the king to visit her—
There was no time to lose!

That night she held a banquet;
The king and Haman came.
But all she said to them that night
Was, "Won't you come again?"

They came again to eat with her
And then she broke the news,
"Dear king, I am about to die
When Haman kills the Jews!"

The king screamed into Haman's face,
"What? You would kill my wife?
Well, I will hang you high and dry
And give the Jews their life!
Yes!
The Jews will keep their life!"

The Christmas Story

—*Luke 2:8-20*

Just outside of Bethlehem,
Some shepherds watched their sheep;
These shepherds looked for danger
While their lambs were fast asleep.

Suddenly the dark night sky
Was filled with dazzling light,
An angel of the Lord appeared
To calm the shepherds' fright.

"Don't be afraid," the angel said,
"I bring you news of joy.
In Bethlehem this very night
Was born a baby boy!"

"He is the baby Jesus
Who is Christ the Lord to all,
You'll find him in a manger
In a little cattle stall."

All at once the sky was filled

With angels shouting praise.

Their words of peace and glory

Left the shepherds so amazed.

Just like that—they disappeared,
The angels left the sky;
The shepherds hurried off to find
That manger stall nearby.

Finally the shepherds found
The Christ, their newborn King!
They hurried off to tell the news
Of this amazing thing!

The shepherds spoke of angels
About their songs of glory
The shepherds spoke of Jesus
And this special Christmas story.

The Faith that Healed a Friend
—Luke 5:17-26

There was a man whose legs were weak

His arms were useless too;

He laid upon his bed each day

Without a thing to do.

One day his friends heard super news,
That Jesus was in town;
They heard he made the lame to walk—
To run and jump around.

They put their friend upon a cot
And brought him down the street;
They knew for sure that Jesus
Could fix his hands and feet.

They found the house where Jesus stayed
But many folks were there;
Somehow they had to get inside—
There was no time to spare.

They brought their friend up to the roof

'Cause it was nice and flat.

Then they made a great big hole

And let him down through that!

The people in the house that day
Were shocked by this surprise;
A man was coming through the roof—
Right before their eyes!

Jesus saw the friends' great faith;
He said,"Young man—Today
Not only will you walk and run,
I'll wash your sins away!"

The Power of Pentecost
—Acts 2:1-16

Some people who loved Jesus

Met in a home one day,

It was time to celebrate

To praise and sing and pray.

While they met together

They heard a roaring sound

Like a mighty windstorm

Blowing all around.

On the top of each one's head

There sat a fire-like tongue;

God had sent his Spirit,

His work had now begun!

Crowds came hurrying to see
What this was all about,
Unusual things were happening
Of that there was no doubt!

Each believer spoke in tongues
That he had never learned;
The listening crowd was quite amazed,
Though some were more concerned.

"I think these folks are drunk," called one.

But Peter cried, "Not true!

We are full of God's great power,

And he will fill you too!

    Yes!

God can fill you too."